LORDS OF THE UNDERWORLD BOOK THREE

Patron of Mercy

Sam Burns
W.M. Fawkes

Copyright © 2019 by FlickerFox Books.

All rights reserved. No part of this publication may be reproduced, distributed, or transmitted in any form or by any means, including photocopying, recording, or other electronic or mechanical methods, without the prior written permission of the author, except in the case of brief quotations embodied in critical reviews and certain other noncommercial uses permitted by copyright law.

Content Warning: this book is intended for adult audiences only, and contains graphic violence, swearing, and graphic sex scenes.

Trigger Warnings: gun violence, stabbing, blood, loss of a loved one

Cover art © 2019 by Natasha Snow Designs; www.natashasnowdesigns.com
Editing by Clause & Effect

CAST & GLOSSARY

Thanatos: God of merciful death.
Lach: Formerly Glaucus/Glaukos. An ancient, immortal human. Occasionally confused for a sea god. In actuality, just a trash pirate.

Gods

Charon: Ferryman to the underworld. Thanatos's brother.
Cronus: Titan god of time.
Dionysus: God of wine and theater.
Eris: Goddess of discord. Thanatos's sister.
Gaia: Titan goddess of the earth.
Hades: God of the underworld
Hebe: Goddess of youth. Daughter of Zeus and Hera.
Hephaestus: God of fire & craftsmen. Son of Zeus and Hera.
Hera: Goddess of marriage. Queen of Olympus.
Hermes: God of travelers. Messenger. Son of Zeus.
Hypnos: God of sleep. Thanatos's brother.
Keres: Goddesses of death.
Nerites: Only male Nereid. Consort of Poseidon.
Persephone: Goddess of springtime. Queen of the Underworld.
Poseidon: God of the sea.

Zeus: God of the sky. King of Olympus.

Others

Alexia: Lach's mother. *Deceased.*
Fidelis Filii: The Faithful Sons. Cult.
Julian Bell: Vampire and huntsman of the New York City Hunt.
Markos: Lach's father. *Deceased.*
Martina Paget: Archaeologist. Friend of Lach.
Philon: Lach's younger brother. *Deceased.*

GOD CALL

"There are secrets the gods don't want you to know." Lach was sitting in Hysteria at eleven in the morning talking to a woman behind the bar who'd hardly glanced up at him. She had yet to say a word.

He pulled his flintlock pistol out of the holster under his jacket and set it down flat on the glossy wood in front of him. "Can I have one of those?" he asked, waving at the clean bar rags. The linen guys had just dropped off a fresh batch at the back door.

She shrugged and tossed him one. From his pocket, he dug out a small tool kit and set to cleaning it. A pistol like his would last a lifetime if properly cared for, and Lach was long lived.

"Thanks. Anyway, like I was saying, there are immortal creatures all over the world. But what the gods won't tell you is that if you kill one of them—"

Dionysus sidled up to him from somewhere in the back, leaning his forearms on the bar. "Cleo's not listening to you," he said, looking sidelong at Lach, a smirk on his full lips. Dionysus had a broad, frank face. The angle of his brow always held a hint of challenge, and the flicker of his black eyes promised a great deal of fun—or madness, depending on the day.

"Listen, Dio, I know you're one of those pod-god sons of Zeus who want to keep us little folk down, but you're telling me you don't want Cleo here to achieve immortality? You don't want her by your side, dusting your shot glasses forever?"

"I don't want Cleo getting the wrong idea, go off and try to kill a Kere, and have her head ripped off her shoulders. Put the gun away, Lach. It's not legal."

"I have all my permits, Dionysus. Anyway, this is an antique."

"There's no open carry in DC, Lach. And I don't give a damn if it is an antique. My bar, my rules."

With a sigh, Lach wiped off the pistol's barrel and tucked it away again. He'd won it off a man in a duel, after he'd shot the original owner square in the chest and walked away like the true badass he was.

"Not every immortal creature is Kere-level horrifying, you know," Lach said. He had won his immortality in a foolish gambit to feed his family. After slaughtering one of Helios's prized cattle back before paved roads were a thing, he'd stopped aging. Frankly, it'd taken him a while to notice, even with the weird looks he'd gotten from other villagers. "I think you're hoarding resources. You know, that's *just* like you one-percenters."

Dionysus laughed aloud. "Too right." He waved to Cleo. "What do you want?" he asked Lach.

"Double whiskey."

"It's eleven a.m."

"Can I get a triple then? Long day ahead of me."

"Not a chance." Dionysus signed something to her, and Lach's stomach sank as he watched the god's fingers move.

"She really wasn't listening."

"She really wasn't." Dionysus barely contained his laughter. "I mean, she can read lips, but Cleo, like pretty much everyone else with sense, knows you are completely full of shit. Not worth the effort, really."

Cleo smiled at him and shrugged. With a firm hand, Dionysus clapped his shoulder as she poured a whiskey for him and a water for Dionysus.

"How'd you even get in here?" Dionysus asked him once he'd taken a sip. "We're closed. You do know how business hours work, right?"

Lach smirked. He had a habit of getting in places he wasn't allowed—old temples, dragon hoards, closed nightclubs. "I came in the back door with the laundry guy."

Dionysus stared at him. "Well, you haven't changed a bit in the last decade." It'd been that long since they'd seen each other. There was a lot of world to cover, and Lach preferred the open ocean to cities that grew too fast for him to keep up with. "What do you want?"

"Can you do that thing?" Lach asked. Dionysus cocked a brow. "You know, that thing you do. I need to get in touch with Hermes, and he's not picking up his phone."

"Ah, the *thing*. Yes, of course."

Dionysus stood, gave his chest a soft pound with his fist, and cleared his throat. "Hermes," he said in a low, booming voice.

Ariadne, Dionysus's wife, stuck her head out the office door. She had light brown skin and coal-dark eyes that swam with desire as she stared at her husband. "You sound like Morgan Freeman," she said.

"Wouldn't Morgan Freeman sound like him?" Lach asked. "Dio's way older."

"No," Ariadne said.

"Definitely not. Respect to the master," Dionysus agreed, kissing his fingers and holding them up.

A few seconds, they waited, but Hermes didn't come. All Olympians could call him—what kind of messenger god would he be if they couldn't contact him? It was a modulation in their throats, a power in their blood. Lach had to rely on his cell phone and the often-spotty radio when he was out at sea.

"I haven't seen him around lately. He's avoiding Dad. I'll try again," Dionysus said. "Hermes," he called.

By the time the second syllable left his lips, Ariadne slid up to him and wrapped her arms around Dionysus's neck. She pulled him down into a kiss—the kind of kiss that was like a crash—a *sexy* crash—you couldn't help but stare at. Lach saw way more of their tongues than he ever wanted to.

Suddenly, Hermes was there. He groaned, throwing his hand over his eyes. "Please tell me you did not call me here because you're feeling voyeuristic."

Dionysus and Ariadne didn't disengage from their searing kiss, so Lach leaned around them and held up his hand. "Nope. Actually, you're here for me. I needed you."

"Did you, Lach?" Hermes's bright blue eyes turned appraising. He was cut from the same cloth as Zeus—with golden hair and eyes like the sky. Most of his children were similar, like gingerbread men who'd all been shaped the same but had small variations from baking.

"I need to talk to Thanatos." At once, the wind went out of the god. Hermes had a certain reputation. If someone said they needed him, they usually got him—not that Lach was judging. There had definitely been some kind of appeal in living like that. Right up until the moment he'd realized he was three thousand years old and completely alone.

Ariadne pushed Dionysus into the bar. Raising her eyebrows, Cleo stared at the pair of them.

"Why don't you two lovebirds take it into the office?" Lach suggested.

All he got in return was a grunt, but they shuffled their feet, hips bumping into barstools as they made their way toward the back room.

Cleo looked at Hermes and cocked a brow. She signed to him. Without a beat, he signed back. Some gods, those most connected with humanity, picked up languages fast. For Lach, it'd always been the hardest part of being immortal. He'd gone from ancient Greek to Norse. There'd been a time when, sailing the Atlantic, it'd been in his interest to learn French. But languages came slower to him—just another way he wasn't as good as the gods around him.

Lach wasn't a god at all, but something else. He had the immortality—and the considerable prowess—of a cow, bought on accident. Poseidon had shown the world people like him could die. Men from Odysseus's boat had slaughtered Helios's cattle too, and when their ship had capsized in a storm, Poseidon had torn them apart. Lach had done the god of the sea a solid, so he'd made his way back to shore when Helios had meant to kill him. That was it—chance and the mercy of amused gods kept Lach alive.

It didn't make them like him—he'd broken the rules without bending over for Zeus or some other lusty god—and there weren't many immortal humans to keep him company. Most mortal ones were more trouble than they were worth.

Cleo set a Sprite in front of Hermes and turned away from them to restock shelves with liquor enough to get them through the weekend. Left to their own devices, Hermes propped his elbow on the counter and turned to look at Lach.

"Okay, you know I like you, Lach, but uh, Thanatos isn't going to want to talk to you."

No surprises there. Frankly, if their positions were switched, Lach would've sailed to the other side of the globe to get away from Thanatos. Hell, he practically had, though that was only because he was a piece of shit who hadn't known what he had until he lost it. Okay, and then he'd aged a couple thousand years. Even the biggest asshole in the world got a little perspective over the course of millennia—Lach would know.

"I know. But it's life and death."

Hermes stared at him like he'd gone crazy.

"I'm serious," Lach insisted. "I need Thanatos's help, or a lot of people are going to die."

"You've completely lost it," Hermes said. "Honestly, you're sitting here at a night club, day drinking, and you think I'm going to buy that the fate of the world hangs on me playing telephone with your ex? He's busy, Glaucus."

The last, Hermes said gently. Almost no one called him that anymore. That Hermes was now meant he was speaking to the man Lach had been, the one who'd made more mistakes than a hecatoncherie could count on all his hands. A man who didn't deserve to call on Thanatos.

"He'll be a lot busier if everyone dies."

"Did the math on that one, pal. Only for a little while. You'd be amazed how many spirits Charon can fit on his train at a time."

Lach stared at him. "Seriously? Gods, you're a dick."

It wasn't especially godlike to give a shit when mortals were in peril, but Lach was out on a limb here, and he'd made promises.

"Give me your damn fancy phone," Lach said, holding out his hand.

Hermes rolled his eyes as he dug it out of his pocket. "You have got to get your own smartphone, Lach. This isn't nineteen-ninety."

"My phone works fine."

Grudgingly, Hermes passed it over. It didn't take more than a cursory search of NPR to find the problem—it was spring, and plants weren't growing. The trees were blooming feebly, but the plants that returned every year, the ones farmers had to sow in loamy soil, that fed people and animals, weren't.

"Okay, there's a drought. That's hardly—" Hermes broke off when Lach snatched his phone back. He searched the BBC next. The problem wasn't only in the United States. It was global. Nothing was growing anywhere it should be. He shoved the phone back at Hermes.

"It's a pattern. And it's divine. I've got a way to fix it, but I need to talk to Thanatos. Can you tell him that?"

Hermes was staring at the face of a little girl in the middle of an article.

Thin and hollow cheeked, her luminous eyes looked huge. He lasted less than ten seconds before he flinched and shoved his phone back in his pocket.

"Fine. Fine." Hermes finished his drink. "I'm going to go tell the god of death that humanity is doomed if he doesn't talk to his ex. That's going to go fucking great. Really nice to see you, Lach. Truly."

For once, Hermes didn't rush out but dragged his feet toward the exit.

"You're the best, Hermes," Lach called after him. Hermes waved his hand and slipped through the back.

Alone with Cleo, Lach was the only one who could hear the muffled sounds coming from the club's office, but there was nothing to do but sit and wait.

When he lifted his hand, Cleo turned to look at him. "Can I get another?"

She stared at him like, despite the fact that they didn't know each other, she could see the fuckery rolling off him in waves. But she poured him another shot. If Thanatos showed up, he might need a bit of liquid courage anyway.

"Thanks," he said, his fingertips at his lips. He tipped his hand out. Even Lach knew that much ASL.

Cleo gave him a thumbs up, and he settled in to wait.

BROTHERLY LOVE

"So the guy keeps yelling, 'Do you know who I am?' and trying to get in my face." Charon rolled his eyes as he took a bite of his sandwich and didn't even swallow before he continued talking. "Until this tiny girl who died in a shooting, maybe twelve years old, walks up and goes 'I know who you are,' and slugs him right in the face."

Thanatos was grateful every single day that he was the god of merciful death. So many souls he retrieved were peaceful. Some were pleased to go with him. Angry old men and children with gunshot wounds weren't his kind of charge. As the ferryman who took souls to Hades, his brother Charon had to deal with all the dead, not only those peaceful souls Thanatos delivered to him.

"You okay?" Charon asked through another mouthful of meatballs and cheese. "You're quieter than usual today."

Thanatos shrugged. "It's looking like a bad year, is all."

Charon flinched and nodded, his gaze drifting to the floor of his train. People came and went as they ate together, and Charon directed them with the practiced ease of a man who dealt with over a hundred thousand passengers a day. Thanatos didn't know how he managed it.

Drinking seemed to figure heavily into the equation.

They ate in silence for a few minutes, and Charon seemed to be working up the nerve to say something. He was interrupted when a stronger presence than one of the spirits of the departed boarded the train. They looked up at the same time to find an apprehensive Hermes.

"Heeey, guys. Fancy finding you together like this." He squirmed under their attention, one foot tapping. He looked like he was considering running off.

Charon took a drink and cleared his throat. "What do you need, Hermes? Back in Daddy's good graces and here to demand an accounting?"

Hermes's eyes went wide, and he shook his head emphatically. "No! Nothing like that. Me and the old man, totally still on the outs. He's holed up on Olympus brooding like they cancelled his favorite TV show."

Thanatos ignored Hermes in favor of watching his brother. "An accounting of what?"

Charon's eyes darted away from meeting his, so he looked at Hermes and raised an eyebrow.

"Hey, don't shoot the messenger, right?" Hermes asked, hands up in supplication. He was always a little slippery, but he was acting more skittish than normal.

Thanatos waited him out, watching, that single eyebrow raised.

After a moment, the younger god sighed, put upon and frustrated. "Charon absolutely did not help me break Prometheus out of lockup. He would never piss Zeus off like that. It's all on me." He sighed and muttered under his breath, "Just like everything else lately."

Thanatos turned, eyes wide, to demand more information from his brother, but Hermes interrupted.

"Look, I'm sure you guys have lots of things to discuss, but I actually need to relay a message," he said as he came to stand in front of Thanatos. Just out of reach, he noted absently, should he get irritated and grab for Hermes.

He frowned at that. How bad could the message be, that he expected Thanatos of all people to attack him? Among his fellow gods, Thanatos liked to think he had the least violent reputation. When the silence had dragged on for more than a minute, he sighed and rolled his hand in a circular motion. "Well? What message?"

Hermes took a deep breath. "Lach wants to see you and he's got a pretty good reason so I think you should go even though I'm sure you won't want to and that's totally understandable of you but—"

Thanatos put up his hand in the universal sign to stop Hermes. "Who's Lach?"

Next to him, Charon let out an angry sound that was almost a growl. "Abso-fucking-lutely not."

Thanatos looked at his brother. "Lach?"

Again, his brother wouldn't meet his gaze.

"Glaucus," Hermes interrupted. "It's what Glaucus goes by now."

It seemed impossible that after so many years, that name would still have the ability to make Thanatos feel like he'd been struck in the solar plexus. The air left him, and the ichor in his veins rushed in his ears, loud enough to drown out the noise of the train around them.

The memory of last time he'd seen the owner of that name rushed back in bright, angry images, worn and faded at the edges, but no less painful for that fact.

"I'm immortal, Thanatos. Why would I tie myself to Death?"

That sweet voice spewing those poisonous words; it was all of Thanatos's insecurities boiled down into a single question. Why, in fact, would anyone want to bind themselves to the embodiment of death?

Hermes guided souls, but he was a messenger.

Charon ferried the dead, but it was nothing more than a job to him.

Thanatos was, unquestionably and incontrovertibly, death itself. No one would ever want to tie themselves to him for long. They would always remember what he was, and like Glaucus, leave him alone. His sweet, beautiful, golden Glaucus. But not his. Not anymore. Maybe never had been.

In the thousands of years since he'd last seen Glaucus, he'd tried a few more times to forge a bond with someone else, but everyone left eventually. None had destroyed him quite so thoroughly as Glaucus. He didn't think he'd ever managed to piece his heart back together enough to be broken again.

"—you hear me, Hermes?" Charon was saying, almost shouting—an exceptionally strange behavior from his brother. "After what that jackass did last time, he has no right to be asking for anything."

Hermes didn't look surprised, just resigned to the abuse, and that was what snapped Thanatos's attention back to the situation at hand. Hermes was a manipulative little bastard, but it was nothing more than Zeus had made him. The downtrodden way he accepted Charon's anger hurt Thanatos almost physically. Like he thought he deserved it.

"Charon," Thanatos interrupted.

His brother spun to look at him, eyes wide and bright. "No. Absolutely not. You remember what that ass did to you last time you let him in?"

"I do."

"I was picking up the pieces for a century, Thanatos. I'm not going to let him—"

"Charon."

"No!"

Thanatos stood and put his hands on his brother's shoulders. "I understand. I'm sorry I leaned on you so heavily—"

"That's not the problem—"

He took his right hand from Charon's shoulder and put a finger on his lips to stop the flow of words. "I know. You're a good brother. I appreciate you trying to help me. You can't possibly know how much I appreciate you. But Hermes wouldn't come here and ask this of me if it weren't important."

"That's true," Hermes said, his voice hopeful. Thanatos didn't know if the hope was for affirmation or no more yelling, but either made sense. With a father and stepmother like his, Hermes had surely dealt with more than his share of yelling. When Charon turned to him, he flinched. But then he took a deep breath, steeled himself, and when he spoke, his voice was stronger. "He says he has a way to fix what's happening. With the plants. And how, um, people are going . . . to starve?"

Hermes looked confused, as though he wasn't sure that was what he'd meant, or if it had been, he wasn't sure why. The messenger god wasn't well known as charitable, so Thanatos understood his confusion.

After a long pause, Hermes sighed. "Look, he showed me these pictures, and there was this little girl with big brown eyes, and who the hell can say no to kids? She was hungry, and I figured if you can help him feed her or something . . ." He threw up his hands and turned around. "That's it. I said I'd tell you he wants to see you. He's at Dionysus's club in DC. It's your call if you let the little kid starve. It's not up to me."

He stormed off the train the second the doors opened, then back on a moment later, huffing. "Funny, Charon, letting me wander off into Hades. I need to get back upworld. I have work to do."

Charon gave a nonchalant shrug, but he said nothing. He was still pouting. Hermes threw himself into a seat facing away from them, also pouting.

As always, somehow, it fell to Thanatos to act like the only adult in a group of ancient immortals. He nudged the forgotten sandwich in his brother's direction. "Eat your lunch."

It was still light out when he arrived at Hysteria. Hermes hadn't said anything about going at a certain time. Glaucus—Lach—was probably right inside, acting ridiculous and looking beautiful and impossible and like the most frustrating thing Thanatos had ever known.

He stood there and watched the sun go down.

People came and went, and a long line formed around the club. People stared at him, and one or two tried to talk to him, but he didn't pay much attention.

Every time the door opened, he tensed, as though Lach were going to come out and immediately tear his heart out again. Could he do that? Was Thanatos so weak?

He couldn't leave. Masses of lives were at stake. Maybe they wouldn't die right away, but the short-lived weren't especially forward thinking. If the crops didn't grow anywhere for a whole season, they'd start to starve. It'd hit the poor first, the people least able to take care of themselves. They might have a handful of months, but it would move fast. If they did nothing, by the time they began to notice, it would be too late. He wasn't the kind of god who could ignore that kind of suffering.

Still—

"I knew you'd come," a voice said out of nowhere. That voice. Filled with so much self-confidence and snark, like everything out of his mouth was a joke at someone else's expense. Thanatos had always found it charming, until he'd been the joke. "How about a drink?"

He spun to look at Glaucus—at Lach—and narrowed his eyes, refusing to acknowledge how kind the millennia had been to his erstwhile lover. He'd put on pounds of muscle, making him less whip thin and more wiry. He was a little broader, but nothing close to bulky. Those sharp cheekbones were the same though. The wide mouth, set in a constant arrogant grin. Those perfect lips that had taken his own, always so demanding, like no other mortal Thanatos had ever known.

He shook his head, trying to clear the haze that always descended when he got caught up in memories of this man, who had made his life incredible for a few short years, and then miserable for so much longer. Remembering that Lach was watching him, he straightened his spine and tried to act unaffected. "If this is just about what you can manipulate me into doing, I'm leaving."

Moving faster than Thanatos would have thought possible, Lach got in front of him. "No drink then? How about, ah, pizza? I know a place."

"I'm not here for food."

Lach sighed and leaned forward, the dark circles under his eyes suddenly much more prominent. "Just come eat the pizza. I swear, I'll tell you everything."

PIZZA PARLEY

Lach sat under stark lighting on a plastic bench at a grungy pizza joint a few blocks away from Hysteria. It hadn't occurred to him until they got there that, while he had no real idea what Thanatos liked anymore, he was pretty fucking sure it wasn't this.

Somehow, he'd always imagined his reunion with Thanatos would be something more. He'd fantasized about a crash of lips and tangled limbs—about shouting and glaring and an airing of grievances that would've put the Costanzas' Festivus to shame. He'd expected passion or anger or *something*.

Instead, they sat down with paper plates on a table that clearly hadn't been wiped off since the last diners, and neither of them said anything. Thanatos reached for the napkin dispenser, pulling out brown paper napkins and dabbing the grease from his single slice of veggie.

"Oh, come on now," Lach said, shifting in his seat. "That's the best part."

Thanatos shot him a dry look. Wilting under it, Lach thought about stuffing his own face for the distraction. He went so far as to pick up his pizza before he set it down again. He wasn't there to hide from Thanatos, and he only had so long before the god's patience with him disappeared.

"So, how've you been?" he asked. "You good? You look good."

"Glaucus—"

"Um, Lach. It's Lach now. If you want to call me Glaucus though—" It'd have been fine. It wasn't his preference. His given name reminded him of his family, of the world that was lost to him forever. And only the Greeks pronounced it right anyway. But Thanatos was Greek, and hearing it reminded Lach of the way he used to say it—back when he'd liked him.

Lach fell silent as he watched Thanatos's tongue press against the inside of his cheek. Thanatos had never been cruel outright, even when he'd deserved it; he could only imagine the things Thanatos was thinking now.

"I can see why you'd want to shed Glaucus." There was no bite in his words but a deep chill settled in Lach's chest at Thanatos's flat delivery.

"Uh, well, yeah." His finger pressed into the edge of his paper plate, smoothing out the scalloped edges. "After I left Greece, I traveled north. Spent some time with the Norsemen. Sailed to Britain. Lach just worked better there, not an uncommon name, and I—"

"Lach."

"Yeah?"

"I don't care."

Lach's nose flared as he took a deep breath. Under the table, he pinched his hands together between his knees. "Okay. Fair enough."

He wasn't surprised. The last time they'd seen each other had been so long ago, and while the weight of guilt and loss had never lifted off of him, there was no reason for Thanatos to still think about him. Lach hadn't burned that bridge; he'd bombed it and left a smoking crater in his wake. And he'd known exactly what he was doing as he'd done it. Thanatos shouldn't have wasted any time thinking about an arrogant immortal human who'd wounded him on purpose.

It still hurt to hear it though. His tongue was dry in his mouth. Unsure how to follow that up, he stayed quiet until Thanatos threw him a bone. He was still that generous, at least.

"Hermes said you had something important to tell me—something that might help people."

"Yeah." Lach stared down at his pizza, greasy glory and all, and realized he didn't want to eat it. He pushed his plate toward the middle of the table and leaned forward on his elbows. "Nothing's growing."

"Persephone comes back in springtime, and Demeter makes sure the plants grow so humans don't starve. That's the deal."

Lach cocked a brow. Humans starved all the time, all over the place. But he supposed that wasn't Demeter's fault. Humans were perfectly capable of hurting themselves. There was plenty of food to go around, but some places had too much and wasted it, and others didn't have near enough.

"I don't know what to tell you. Maybe she's not as happy to see her daughter as she used to be. But she's throwing some kind of fit, and if nothing starts growing, in a few months, people are going to start dying."

"And you've got some way to make crops grow?" Thanatos asked.

Admittedly, Lach wasn't known for his agricultural prowess.

Lach ran his tongue along the edge of his teeth, leaned back, and shrugged. "Not exactly. Gaia said we need Cronus's scythe. With his power, Demeter's mood swings wouldn't matter."

"Still working for Gaia, huh?" Thanatos asked. He leaned away from his untouched pizza too. "Nice to know there are some relationships you can stand to keep forever."

Lach flinched. Frankly, maintaining a relationship with Gaia was easy; she didn't care about him. She'd speak to him, sometimes every few months, sometimes with decades between meetings, and request something. After that, it was a simple exchange. She'd give him riches, and Lach would run her errands. It was always weird to have a goddess suddenly speaking into his head, but he'd adapted. There was something freeing about it, like she wasn't *really* there so he couldn't *really* let her down. Not once in three thousand years had she asked him how his day was going.

"Well, yeah. There's the one," Lach said, forcing a grin like it was a joke. Thanatos didn't smile.

"I still don't see what this has to do with me. Why didn't you ask Hermes?"

"He's on the lam."

Thanatos cocked his brow. "Didn't stop you from sending him to me."

"And he doesn't know the underworld as well as you. Trust me"—fat chance—"I asked. He said he didn't know where Hades kept Cronus. You weren't my first choice."

Well, Lach had always been a liar; why stop now? When Gaia had tapped him for this, his first thought was that he could twist it into an excuse to see Thanatos. It was an absurd notion, sure to end in nothing but heartache, but it was the first time in millennia that Lach had a reason to reach out to the underworld.

Thanatos scoffed. "You always were a flatterer."

"You wanted me to call you first?" Lach asked. The hardness in Thanatos's gaze made him straighten in his seat.

"No."

Lach smirked. "Didn't think so."

In centuries past, he'd stood in the middle of graveyards when he docked in port towns. As the years ticked by, the gods' powers lessened. Once, they could travel anywhere with a thought. In time, they were relegated to their own domains. But Lach had called to Thanatos in a graveyard before, and he'd come at once. Every time Lach had lingered in one since, he'd thought about uttering his name, wondering if he would come or not—if he already knew Lach was there, thinking about him. But he'd never summoned the courage to call. Now, he had an excuse. He doubted Thanatos would come for him, but for the good of humanity, Lach had hoped he would show up.

Hell, even that day, even with a ready excuse, he'd thought Thanatos might not come. Lach had sat at the counter in Hysteria for hours, until he was drunk. Cleo brought him water and enough time passed that, by the time that he left, dejected, he was sober again.

The thrill he'd felt when he'd stepped outside and seen Thanatos had gotten the better of him. Sitting in that pizza booth, it was clear he'd messed this up from the start.

"So, will you help me get to Cronus and back out again?" Lach asked.

At that, Thanatos laughed out loud. It was booming, filling the small parlor until most eyes turned toward them. "Not a chance."

Lach blinked. "Sorry?"

"Demeter's throwing a shit fit, and your first option is to go see a murderous titan who ate his own kids? No. That's crazy. He'd kill you sooner than help you. Gaia's out of touch."

Thanatos slid out of his seat. Self-composed, he straightened his jacket and buttoned the front. The suit he wore looked like it cost more than Lach's whole wardrobe; grunge chic wasn't a thing. The last time Lach had seen him, his clothes had hung in loose folds. They'd always been nicer than Lach's, but now, they were staunch and fashionable. Lach missed the tunics he could slip his hands inside and that easy smile Thanatos had saved just for him.

Flustered, it took Lach a moment to realize Thanatos was leaving.

"Wait!" he called as Thanatos moved toward the door. "Where are we going?"

"We?"

"Yeah, Thanatos. I made promises."

Thanatos scoffed. Lach tried to shrug it off. No matter what he'd planned, this wasn't all about reconnecting with his ex. There were people to save.

"Just give me one second," he said, holding up his hands like that could stall Thanatos. "I need a to-go box."

The guy at the counter took way too long to notice him, but Thanatos lingered, tapping his foot. Lach dropped their three slices—Thanatos's veggie, and Lach's Hawaiian—all in the same box. When Lach rejoined him at the door, Thanatos was staring.

"So good you couldn't leave it behind?" Bitterness pursed Thanatos's full lips.

Lach licked his own nervously. "Um, yeah. I'll—I'll eat it later."

Thanatos rolled his eyes and turned to go. But hey, at least he'd waited?

GROWING A PLAN

It didn't make any sense. Thousands of years had passed. There was no reason that looking at the man should make Thanatos feel like there were a knife twisting in his gut. But Lach had to go and be everything he'd ever loved in Glaucus. Clever and roguish, with a quick smile and the most ridiculous, inane plans.

Going to see Cronus in Hades was possibly the worst idea Thanatos had ever heard, and Lach had been known for some awful ones back in the day. Cronus hadn't been pleasant to deal with, even at his pinnacle, when he'd been convinced that he was going to stay in power forever. Thousands of years deposed, all of them spent imprisoned in Tartarus, were unlikely to have made him nicer.

On his best day, he'd have eaten Lach whole. Possibly literally.

Thanatos doubted Cronus had good days anymore. He thought it might have been a kindness if Zeus had simply destroyed his father and dispersed his component atoms to the winds.

He sighed and tapped his foot as Lach joined him at the door to the pizza place. Despite the less than ideal level of cleanliness and excessive grease, the pizza had smelled good. Thanatos liked a good pizza. Unfortunately, his stomach was determined to eat itself, so the last thing he wanted was food. He needed to get Lach the information he wanted and get away.

"Okay, so if we can't visit Cronus—"

Thanatos snorted. "Visit? Do you think he's going to invite you for a nice cup of tea? He's in Tartarus, not a palace in exile somewhere."

"So who *can* help us? Someone must be able to." Lach looked positively desperate, and it made something in Thanatos soften. Maybe he was the same old Lach, but he was trying to do something good. At least, he said he was. Lach had also always been one to play fast and loose with the truth.

It was a good thing Thanatos knew someone who might have insight into the problem, and she was easy to find.

Persephone's apartment in DC was on the small side, since she spent relatively little time there. As little as possible, in fact. She saw it as a stop-gap, a place to sleep during those months when she wasn't allowed to go home to her husband and children.

Thanatos sent a quiet apology into the universe for leading Lach to it, but hopefully he'd forget he knew about it. Or more likely, Persephone would simply never be there if he came calling for more favors.

He knocked softly, hoping it wasn't so late that she was already in bed. During her months aboveground, Persephone tended to sleep when the sun did, and he wasn't sure how long it had been down.

She answered the door, and he sighed in relief. She was wearing soft green pajamas, hair pulled back, and her face bore signs of exhaustion. There were dark rings under her eyes, and a tightness around her mouth that he wasn't familiar with, but she smiled at him. "Thanatos. To what do I owe the pleasure?"

He frowned and looked over at Lach, then back to her. "I'm not sure pleasure is the right word, but thank you. It's always lovely to see you." He decided to get straight to the point instead of wasting her time. "Is the growing season really proving a failure?"

She flinched. "It's early yet."

It was a close-run thing, but he didn't start banging his head against the doorjamb. He softened his voice further, knowing Demeter was a touchy subject for her, and asked, "Your mother?"

She pursed her lips, and the corner of one eye seemed to twitch with a mind of its own. "Not answering her calls."

Dammit. Lach had been telling the truth, and there was a clear problem. A problem Cronus's scythe might be able to fix, exactly as he'd claimed. However, that did not mean that going to see Cronus was the best option left to them.

"Has anyone managed to talk to Cronus since his imprisonment?"

She cocked her head and drew her brows together. "I don't think so. Why?"

Thanatos let his gaze slide to Lach. "He thinks he has a way to fix this and needs Cronus's scythe."

"That . . . could work," she said, her voice distant and thoughtful. "But no, no one has ever managed to have a civil conversation with him that I know of." She stepped out of the doorway. "Come in, sit down. Tea? I'm going to make myself some."

"That would be lovely, thank you," he agreed.

"Got any coffee?" Lach asked. Of course.

She didn't seem bothered, just waved an absent hand at the single-serving coffee maker on her counter. "The kids got me that last year, if you can figure out how to work it."

He jumped up and started toying with the machine, plugging it in and looking through the controls. Thanatos could see the precise moment he turned on his old charm, when he looked at Persephone with a wide smile and sparkling eyes. "You don't have any idea where the scythe would be, do you?"

She laughed, bright and bubbly, and the sound filled the room. "I'd be the last person Cronus would give information to. And I've never tried to have a chat with him."

Lach tilted his head to one side and then the other, and sighed melodramatically. "I guess, if you want to be all logical about it. But it's a magical item, right? Like, really, really magical. And related to your personal specialty: growing things."

"Clever," she agreed. She had no idea. The man was always full of clever ideas, alongside the ridiculous ones. It was why people always listened to him. You never knew whether his next suggestion was going to be genius or suicide.

"Why does Gaia care?" Thanatos asked, and his voice came out waspish. He wasn't entirely sure why, but he wasn't going to second-guess himself. He'd given himself permission to react to Lach with his instincts, and he was allowed to be angry. "She'll be fine if all the people starve to death. Their continued existence has actually proven detrimental to her."

Lach turned that bright grin on him and nodded. "You know, I asked her the same thing. What she said amounted to . . . I guess she thinks of us like fried food. Sure, we're super unhealthy and make her miserable sometimes, but she likes us? As a whole, not individually. She thinks we're interesting."

Persephone leaned against the counter as she let the electric kettle heat up, and looked at Lach. "So you're saying she thinks of you as a resident in an ant farm, basically, and you're fine with that?"

"She wants the ant farm to survive, so yeah," he agreed.

She leaned over and looked at the takeout box Lach had left on the counter next to the coffee machine. "Smells good. That place near Hysteria?"

Lach nodded enthusiastically. "Best pizza in the city."

She drifted forward a step and looked at the box speculatively. "Would you mind? I mean, I don't need—"

"No, it's all good." He picked up the box and whipped it open for her.

Persephone took out the slice of veggie pizza and took a dainty bite. She hummed. "It's even good cold," she mumbled after chewing and swallowing.

Lach looked at Thanatos from the corner of his eye, and Thanatos struggled not to react. He'd left it, after all. He didn't have the right to complain that Lach had given someone else his food. He told himself he didn't care, but it didn't fool him for a minute.

Something about that damned pirate made him care about pointless things every time. He looked away.

Eventually, Persephone made her way back over, munching on one of Lach's slices of pizza as he ate the other. She handed Thanatos a mug of tea and sat down in an overstuffed chair across from the sofa where Thanatos had planted himself.

Lach looked at the sofa, and Thanatos, for a long while before gingerly setting himself on the opposite corner, huddled against the arm. Persephone noticed, of course, but thankfully she didn't say anything. Never let it be said that the queen of the underworld couldn't be the soul of discretion when necessary.

When she finished her second slice of pizza and curled up with her tea, she sighed with a strange combination of sated pleasure and frustration. "She's breaking the deal, of course. We're all trying to pretend she's not, but it's not subtle."

"And not answering your calls," Thanatos added.

She nodded and sighed. For a second, she looked very much like the ancient goddess she was, instead of the eternally youthful harbinger of spring. "And not answering my calls, Hermes or telephone. My first thought was that if she's not going to follow through, it means I can go home." Her eyes went haunted, expression bleak and near to tears. "How selfish can I be?"

"It's hardly your fault that your first thought was about how her actions affect you," Thanatos pointed out. He'd known a lot of people during his years. Humans were just like gods, and almost without deviation, they thought of how every situation affected them, first and foremost. It wasn't a failing; it was their nature. The good ones were the ones who immediately followed up by considering everyone else. Like staying on the surface and continuing to fulfill her half of the promise. Like trying desperately to get something to grow to mitigate the disaster.

"How bad is it going to be?" he asked, finally.

She stared at her mug and didn't answer, which he supposed was an answer in and of itself.

Finally, she looked up at them. "What about Prometheus?"

ALONE WITH FRIENDS

L ive long enough, and Lach's circle of acquaintances was bound to include some gods. He and Hermes shared a certain predisposition for sticky fingers, and hell, Lach pretty much only had a cell phone because Hermes had insisted. He'd bonded with Poseidon since he'd become immortal—first for getting on Helios's bad side, then for going on a covert mission, admittedly on accident, with Poseidon's nymph lover, Nerites.

Nevertheless, gods weren't concerned with day-to-day trifles, and Lach wasn't part of any juicy gossip circles. Maybe if he were following Hebe on social media, but that seemed like an awful lot of work, and his flip phone didn't run apps. In any case, at sea, he had missed out on all the current events. He hadn't known Prometheus had escaped Tartarus.

The titan god of foresight had been locked away long before Lach had been born, but he'd heard stories of him. Prometheus had given humans power when they'd had none. He'd allowed them a measure of independence from the gods. By all accounts, he was a goddamn hero. Thanatos had certainly liked him.

"So we're going to New York?" Lach asked, shifting a reusable grocery bag on his shoulder. Persephone had given him some fresh fruit before they left—she and Dionysus weren't content to sit on their laurels while Demeter let the world burn, at least.

Thanatos cocked a brow at him—there was still some question if there was a "we" involved at all, but Lach had started this. He was going to see it through.

"I suppose," Thanatos said evenly. It lacked the enthusiasm he'd hoped for, but Lach would take it.

They were standing on the sidewalk outside Persephone's apartment. That had been a trip. It didn't seem like a place someone lived, unless you counted all the potted flowers blooming on every shelf as if they were expertly cared for. It was still weird to think that gods lived like people and Persephone had cozy green pajamas.

What kind of pajamas did Thanatos have? Gods above, he imagined they were silk. When they'd been together before, Lach had run his hands over Thanatos's tunic and marveled that anything could be woven so finely.

His expression must've hinted at his wandering thoughts. Thanatos was staring at him, his lips pursed. Under that look, Lach wilted, turned, and started walking.

At first, he didn't notice that Thanatos wasn't following him. But there was no stoic presence at his side, no smooth footsteps.

He turned around when he reached the corner. Thanatos continued to stand there watching him.

"You coming?" Lach called.

A frown carved a line between Thanatos's brows, but in a moment, he moved to catch up.

"Where are you going?" Thanatos asked. "We can just . . . go."

Thanatos offered his hand. He'd always had deceptively broad hands—always gentle, but the kind of hands you could trust not to fail. Lach didn't take it.

He'd momentarily forgotten that particular benefit of godhood—they could travel pretty much anywhere with a thought. Thanatos could jump to a graveyard half a world away. Last he checked, there were a fair few graveyards and funeral homes in New York City.

If he took Thanatos's hand now, they'd disappear, be there in an instant, and this whole adventure could be over in a single night.

"Absolutely not," Lach said, leaning back.

"What?" Thanatos looked at him like he'd gone crazy. Clearly, this was the most pragmatic option. In Thanatos land, that made it the best.

"That shit makes me nauseous."

Thanatos scowled. "No, it doesn't."

"It totally does. You don't remember all the times I asked you to walk me home?"

"I thought you just liked to walk with me."

In fact, Lach had. Sure, disappearing and reappearing somewhere else in the same instant wasn't a particularly enjoyable experience, but it was tolerable. He simply hadn't wanted those nights with Thanatos to end and had dragged them out as long as he could.

"Yeah, I was being *nice*." Lach sniffed and rubbed his nose with the back of his wrist. "I didn't want to make you feel bad."

"Not a concern any more, is it?" Thanatos challenged.

Stubborn as ever, Lach stuck out his chin. "Guess not."

He wondered at what point Thanatos would lose patience with him and disappear on his own. Not yet.

"Okay," Thanatos said, "so what's your plan?"

"We should take my boat, Mis. She's great"

"Your boat?" Thanatos echoed. "That would take days, Lach."

"Only, like, *a* day. She's a *magic* boat."

She was, in fact, the best boat in the entire world. Misericordia became whatever he needed her to be—a skiff, a yacht, his preferred sail boat. Built by Hephaestus for Poseidon, she was everything anyone could want in a ship, and fast as hell to boot.

"Uh huh. Where did you get your magic boat?"

"Poseidon gave her to me."

"He *gave* her to you?" Thanatos sounded skeptical. With his arms crossed, he somehow managed to stare down his nose at Lach even though he was the shorter of the two—by only a hair.

"Yes, he gave her to me. I helped Nerites get away from some whalers."

"Right."

Lach's nose flared. He wanted to be angry at Thanatos for doubting him, but he couldn't afford to. Thanatos had every reason in the world to question him, and Lach was in a precarious position already. With his teeth clenched and his jaw aching, he huffed through his nose.

"Maybe you can't take me to New York, but I can take you," Lach offered. "On the boat. That Poseidon gave me. For saving Nerites."

Thanatos laughed aloud. "Not a chance."

The blood rushed out of Lach's head. He'd said no to Thanatos's offer because it meant this would be over too fast; instead, he'd inadvertently ended it sooner. "Sorry?"

"I'm not getting on a boat with you, Lach."

"Why not?"

"I'm a god. I'm busy. I don't have time for drawn out sailing trips."

"Oh." He had something of a point. There were plenty of mortals. Lach didn't even know how many died in a day.

"Yeah."

"But don't you think we should, you know, travel together and come up with some kind of game plan? Aren't there things I should know about Prometheus before I meet him?" Lach was stretching. They both knew it.

"Oh, Lach, you've got your charm." While the words weren't cruel, there was underlying snideness that coiled in Lach's gut, turning his greasy pizza to a block of dirt. "You'll be fine."

Thanatos was the first to uncross his arms and relax—probably because this meant less to him. "I'll see you in New York, Lach. The Hunt Building."

Lach had heard Persephone too, but what business Prometheus had with vampires was completely beyond him.

Before he had the chance to come up with a better excuse to stick together, Thanatos was gone.

"That could've gone better," he mumbled.

It was dark out, and the tourists had retreated from DC's streets. He dragged his feet down blocks to the metro. He'd left his boat docked at a marina at the fork of the Potomac and Anacostia rivers. Without any super special god powers, it took Lach the better part of an hour to get back.

Misericordia was the closest thing to a home he'd had in centuries. He slept wherever they docked and spent most of his time far out at sea. She held everything he owned, including his embarrassingly large collection of nineties sitcoms on DVD.

Before he stepped onto the deck, he undid the ropes so they could sail out. The best thing about a sentient boat: she could sail for him while he slept. Okay, maybe that was the second-best thing. She was also sort of like family, though he'd probably get locked away for saying something like that.

"Just you and me tonight, pretty miss." He slid his hand over the tiller.

If only she could talk back to him, he'd be set.

Not wanting to be rude, he took the time to guide her out to sea. No one, not even a boat, liked to start an adventure alone. But soon, the river fell away in a swath of navy water under a dark sky. The stars weren't visible with all the light pollution, but if he sailed far enough out, they'd be magnificent. "We're headed to New York. You think you can manage?"

No response. But like always, she'd do magnificently.

Yawning, he went below deck, shedding his clothes in crumpled heaps on the floor until he stood there in nothing but plaid boxers, raking his eyes over his collection of box-set DVDs.

"What should I watch tonight?" he asked her.

There was a soft rattle. A second later, a box fell off the shelf onto the floor. He turned it over. It was a show called *Alone*—not his favorite.

"Oh, haha. You're very funny."

He stuck it back on the shelf and picked out another. "You know what I'm going to do? I'm going to watch *Friends*, because I don't have any."

He grinned. He liked to think Mis enjoyed his humor, even if she didn't have a voice to laugh. She hadn't thrown him overboard yet.

Once he queued up an episode, he crawled into bed. The master bedroom—which was basically a bed with enough space for one person to walk around it and a tiny attached bathroom—was clean and comfortable when Mis had her way, but without fail, Lach messed it up with abandoned clothes, beer bottles, and protein bar wrappers. On the wall opposite the bed, it sported a flat-screen television. Lach might not be up to date on all modern conveniences, but he liked TV. It was nice to be able to hear voices, even prerecorded ones.

"You know, Mis, I still think Rachel could've done better. I mean, Ross can talk a big game, but she's clearly the superior mage." If she'd been more confident, she might've caught someone who appreciated her. Or at least she'd have been able to say what she wanted.

He sighed, sinking back into the pillows. "You're right. She definitely could've had it worse." Rachel could've been sleeping alone with a sour stomach, talking to a boat who'd never talk back.

THE GIFT OF DEATH

He watched Lach walk away, and it made his gut twist the same way it had all those years ago. This time he'd been the one acting like an ass. Somehow, it hurt just the same.

He shook his head and looked around. Lach was obviously heading for the closest metro station, and Thanatos needed some time alone, so he turned in the opposite direction.

The pull of a soul in need of his guidance drew his attention. Not all of those who died needed him. Not even all of those who died peacefully. Hermes helped some, and many had an innate sense of where to go when they died. Sometimes, though, they needed a helping hand.

He allowed the tug to pull him in and the universe sped around him, too fast to see anything but a blur. It was a little disconcerting, even after having done it billions of times during his existence.

That, like everything right now, made him think of Lach. Had he been so thoughtless, that he had never noticed Glaucus's discomfort traveling on his arm? Being drawn from one place to another with no understanding of the place you were going was a strain, and he'd never considered how it made Lach feel to travel with him, only of the convenience and speed.

He had always tried not to become so detached from the world that he didn't empathize with the feelings of others, but sometimes he felt like the world had turned into an incomprehensible mass of new information. It was too much, too fast, and always changing.

It made him feel as ancient as he was. He wondered if someday, the universe would move beyond him, no longer require death. Strangely, the thought brought him nothing but peace.

The pulling stopped, and he found himself in a hospital room. In much of the world they looked similar, so he was never sure where he was until he heard the language.

English. American. The room was in a panic, nurses chattering, a doctor with a defibrillator, and a sobbing woman who was refusing to leave, despite one of the nurses trying to usher her out. It was an odd scene for someone Thanatos had been called to guide.

The child was sitting in a chair at her own bedside, still and quiet, and he understood. She was only eight or nine, and the condition of her body in the bed said it had been a long illness. The living were loath to let someone so young go, even when there was no other possibility. The children were often the most accepting.

She turned to look at him. "Are you here to take me away?"

He nodded.

"Are you sure?" She bit her lip and looked at the sobbing woman. "I should stay, shouldn't I? For Mom?"

"Do you think that would help her?" he asked. He couldn't let people stay, but it was always best to let them come to that conclusion on their own.

"She'll be lonely if I go."

"She won't be able to see you if you stay."

She frowned and looked over at her body, where the doctor had finally given in to the inevitable, hanging her head and clenching her fists in frustration. "I made everyone sad."

"No. This isn't because of you. It happened to you as much as to them. You couldn't control it." He walked over to crouch beside where she sat, hands folded primly on her lap, watching the events unfolding almost impassively.

She turned to look at him. "Are you God?"

"Not in the sense you mean, no. I'm just Thanatos. I came to take you where you're going."

"Can Mom come?"

"Someday," he agreed. He looked over at the woman and felt nothing like a pull. He wasn't one of those gods cursed to see the future, but he didn't think she was slated to see him anytime soon. "But not today."

"I don't want to be alone."

He smiled at her. "Then you won't be."

She smiled back and took his hand.

He watched the girl play with half a dozen other children in Elysium, all of them waiting for their parents. It would be like a very long day in the sun, playing tag and exploring and eating sweets, and then their parents would come and call for them, one by one.

People always wanted to put off going to Elysium for as long as possible, but Thanatos thought that if they knew it like he did, they would be less hesitant.

When he had realized Lach had been made immortal, he had been sorry for him. Living forever, toiling eternally with pain and frustration, seemed like more of a punishment than a gift. He didn't know why gods were always sharing immortality with their favored humans. It felt like a selfish gift—one more for themselves than the mortals. A small part of him wanted to give everyone the gift of Elysium.

He supposed that was what made him Death, and what made him incomprehensible and awful to humanity.

What made Lach run from him.

What would always make him turn away eventually, even if he needed Thanatos's help today.

He lost himself in work, seeing to one soul after another, even many who didn't need him, to try to forget that he was meeting Lach the next evening. Seeing him was always going to be little more than a reminder that Lach wasn't, couldn't ever be, in love with him.

He tried to harden his heart. He couldn't let himself be broken again. He didn't want to put that on Charon, and Charon was the most sympathetic of all his brothers and sisters. Goodness knew Eris wasn't going to offer a shoulder to cry on, unless she was amused by his pain.

The Hunt Building was not a place Thanatos could transport himself to. It was the central location for vampires in New York, and they were an opposing force to his own: creatures who were already dead and would never go to Elysium peacefully. Lach would probably love them.

He chose the closest cemetery in Manhattan and walked the distance, taking the time to stop and get a drink, sauntering rather than walking with purpose. He was putting off getting there, of course, and he knew it.

Prometheus was his friend. Had always been his friend. He had agreed to aid Prometheus's creations, humanity, to their peaceful rest. Prometheus was bright and clever and one of the best, most loyal companions anyone could have.

And Thanatos had allowed him to languish, imprisoned, for millennia. Not for a good reason, like mad Cronus. Because Zeus was petty and angry that humanity had the ability to defend themselves from his whims.

Prometheus had gone willingly. He'd committed the crime he was accused of, if it could truly be considered a crime, and he had gone in knowing that it wouldn't be pleasant. Thanatos had visited him whenever he could find the time without catching Zeus's attention. Hades had always seemed to hold the same opinion as Thanatos about the punishment, and looked the other way when he had slipped in.

Never once had Prometheus asked Thanatos to free him.

He wasn't unintelligent. He had known, every time, that his friend wanted to be free. He liked to believe that if Prometheus had ever asked, he would have broken him out without hesitation, Zeus be damned. But Prometheus had never asked, and Thanatos would never know.

For millennia, he had been conflicted and guilty about his friend's incarceration, but never more than now that Prometheus was free. Would he even be willing to talk to Thanatos, the supposed friend who had allowed him to suffer?

He stopped in front of the building and stared at it. Its energy was strange, almost like Olympus itself, but despite being filled with immortal creatures, it didn't feel as stagnant as the home of the gods. There was something vital about it. A young woman—vampire—on her way in turned and held the door open for him with a questioning smile.

He inclined his head to her. "Thank you."

She nodded to him and headed toward a bank of elevators on the right. To the left was a desk with a bright, smiling employee sitting behind it. They gave him the same expression of polite interest that the young woman had. "Can I help you?"

Practically dragging his feet like a toddler, he walked to the counter, head down and eyes trained on the floor. He felt like a puppy who had failed to learn what the newspapers on the floor were for.

There was no time to act like a child though. If Persephone and Lach were right, millions, possibly billions of lives were at stake. Even with his opinion on Elysium, such a mass death could have catastrophic consequences for the planet itself. His guilt over leaving Prometheus to suffer for millennia couldn't come before that. If those years hadn't changed Prometheus completely—and Thanatos had seen no indication that they had—he would agree, and he would help them without a second thought.

"I'm here to see Prometheus if he's in," he told the smiling, young attendant, glancing at their name tag. "Please, Jordan."

Jordan's smile didn't falter. "I believe he's here. Whom shall I say is calling?"

He sighed. Maybe the whole thing would be moot because Prometheus would refuse to see him entirely. "Thanatos."

Jordan bit their lip, looking intrigued. "You're, um, an old friend?"

"I suppose I am," he agreed.

Without any more questions, they grabbed the phone on the desk and punched in a code. With the hand that wasn't on the phone, they fingered a worn copy of a textbook about . . . the Greek pantheon. Huh. Had Prometheus told the vampires who he was?

Thanatos snorted. Of course he had. Prometheus was so like Lach in many ways, but in simple honesty, they couldn't be more dissimilar. Lach would lie about the color of the sky because he could. Prometheus would tell a building full of vampires that he was an immortal titan because it was true.

Jordan, who had been talking, stopped and looked at the phone, confused.

"Something wrong?" Thanatos asked. Maybe while he'd been lost in thought, Prometheus had been telling the front desk personnel to eject him.

"Um, I'm not sure." They looked at the phone, then put it back to their ear. "Hello?"

"Did he hang up?"

"No, he just seems to be go—"

"Thanatos!" came the shout from behind them. Prometheus rushed out of one of the elevators, looking hale and fit. He had a wide grin on his face that Thanatos hadn't seen in so long he'd almost forgotten it existed. His hair was sun-bleached for the first time in thousands of years, and his arms were spread wide in welcome.

Of course.

Because, like Prometheus wouldn't lie about his nature to a hunt of vampires, neither would he hold a grudge against a friend who had failed him. He crossed the lobby in scant seconds and wrapped Thanatos in a tight hug.

No one had hugged Thanatos in an age. There were familiar touches by his brother, the occasional spirit who took his hand, or accidental grazes by people who pulled away instantly because no one truly wanted to touch Death. But only Prometheus would so unthinkingly wrap his arms around Thanatos.

He returned the gesture, twining his arms around his old friend and holding him tight, burying his face in Prometheus's neck. His dearest friend was free and happy, and suddenly the world seemed more like a place worth saving.

BIG APPLE, BIG PROBLEMS

The Hunt Building cut like a shard through the hazy red sky. It was night, but Lach couldn't see the stars in New York. Even if he'd been able to stand the sheer number of people in large cities, pressing in on each other with no room to breathe, he couldn't stay anywhere he couldn't see the stars. On land, there were fewer and fewer places without light pollution.

People didn't know what they were missing. When he got out to sea and could see the silken twist of the Milky Way, all the other bullshit fell into perspective.

He felt small in the face of all that splendor. But Thanatos had been born to it. Starlight and chaos, he was too big and important for Lach. Yet he'd gotten to hold Thanatos in his arms once. Just like the man on the other side of the glass door who was wrapping Thanatos up in his embrace.

They were there by the welcome desk. From outside, Lach watched Thanatos hesitate a second. The spark of hope in Lach's chest flickered out when he twined his arms around the man and squeezed him close. Sour and dry, he ran his tongue across the roof of his mouth.

He'd always known that Thanatos had counted Prometheus a friend, but he'd never thought there was anything more between them. Why should he have worried? In more than a decade, he'd never met the man.

It occurred to Lach now that that was only because they'd been held apart by the vengeance of Olympus. Thanatos and Prometheus could have been anything to each other. They could be again now.

"Going in?" someone asked.

Lach startled. An amused young man stood behind him, balancing a pastry box in one hand and a tray of coffee on the other. There was a badge gleaming on his belt.

"Oh, um, yeah." Stepping out of the way, Lach held the door open for the man. In a flash—too fast for human steps—he'd crossed the lobby to a bank of elevators.

Though there were people, humans and vampires, all around, Lach's footsteps echoed across the granite floors. No matter how loud every step was to his own ears, when he approached Thanatos and Prometheus, he had to clear his throat before Thanatos lifted his head from Prometheus's shoulder.

He blinked at Lach. Whatever openness he'd felt a moment before locked down under a hard scowl. But even as Thanatos stepped away, Prometheus shifted naturally, keeping a hand on the small of Thanatos's back.

"Hi," Lach said with a tight smile.

Thanatos didn't reply.

"Can we help you?" Prometheus asked earnestly.

"Oh, I'm with him." Lach looked pointedly at Thanatos. For half a second, he thought Thanatos would deny it.

"I'm sorry. I didn't see you there," Prometheus said.

"We came separately," Lach replied.

"Oh . . ." Frowning, Prometheus looked between them.

"This is Lach. Lach, Prometheus," Thanatos offered. He still hadn't pulled away from the hand on his back. Lach had an itch to shoot Prometheus's arm off and see how fast he could repair it. Assumedly, he'd gotten pretty good at healing himself.

"We actually came to talk to you about Cronus," Lach began. "I'm sure you're busy. We won't take up much of your time."

Prometheus smiled handsomely with his fucking handsome face and his well trimmed beard and his ridiculous kind eyes and seriously, fuck that guy.

"Don't be silly," he said. And damn if he didn't have a low, godly rumble of a voice that made Lach want to hang on every word and cozy up in front of a fire on a bear pelt. "You have to come upstairs. Jordan, can you get my guests checked in?"

Prometheus led them over to the front desk. Thanatos went first, filling out his information and signing his name on a clipboard.

"No I.D.?" Jordan asked.

Thanatos shrugged. "Afraid not."

"No big deal. We've gotten pretty used to dealing with gods." Admiration shone from Jordan's eyes.

"Thank you, Jordan," Thanatos said. He stepped away, and while Lach wrote his information down on the sheet under Thanatos's, he heard his laugh. He glanced back to see Thanatos grinning and Prometheus squeezing his arm.

"Are you . . . like them?" Jordan asked. Their green gaze flicked toward Prometheus and Thanatos.

Lach sucked in his cheeks and blew out a breath. "Not even a little."

With his inferiority established, Jordan hardly glanced at him when they asked for Lach's identification. He had that, at least. Lach was a card-carrying member of the twenty-first century, even if the name on his ID was false.

"All set?" Prometheus asked.

He led them to the elevators. After scanning his ID on a security panel, he pushed the button for the top floor.

"What, so you're in charge of the vampires now?" Lach asked.

Over the years, more than one person had confused Lach with a vampire. When he'd first become immortal, he'd kept to himself, hung out in graveyards, hadn't aged. But he didn't need to suck blood out of bilge rats to survive long voyages, so there were some advantages to being an anomaly.

Thanatos sent him a narrow-eyed, unimpressed look. Prometheus only smiled softly as he led the way out into a reception area.

"I am not. That would be Julian Bell, Master of New York. Matthew—" A harried man stood behind a desk opposite the elevator, shuffling papers around.

"Adrian left cronuts in the kitchen," Matthew said without looking up.

"Did you get one?" Prometheus asked.

Matthew shot him a look that said he clearly didn't have time for donuts, croissants, or anything in between.

"I'll bring you one," Prometheus offered.

Past the public parts of the floor, there was a more comfortable suite. All modern, it opened up to a kitchen with dark granite countertops. Prometheus made a beeline for the box on the counter. He flipped the lid open and, with a thin paper napkin, picked one out and put it on a plate.

"Help yourselves," he said. "I'll be right back."

For a second, that left him alone with Thanatos. Crossing his arms, Lach leaned back against the counter.

"So, Prometheus, huh?"

Thanatos stuck out his chin. "What about him?"

"You two are close." Was there as much envy sharpening his words as Lach imagined?

"Yup."

Neither one of them moved toward the cronuts. Seconds ticked by without any other explanation. Clearly, Thanatos didn't think he was owed one. Hell, he wasn't wrong.

Prometheus returned then. Somehow, the titan's energy seemed to fill the room, working into the chasm Lach felt between himself and Thanatos.

"You don't want one?" Prometheus asked. "Adrian assured me they're very good."

"I'd love one," Thanatos replied smoothly, sending Prometheus a genuine smile. Lach had bought him a slice of the best pizza in DC, and he hadn't gotten even a hint of a smile like that. "Thank you."

Daintily, Prometheus put one on a plate for him and passed him a napkin. "Lach?"

"Sure," Lach grunted, way too surly to manage good manners. Thanatos narrowed his eyes at him, so he huffed out a low "thanks."

Prometheus, despite this less-than-pleasant exchange, remained delighted as he leaned against the counter and ate his cronut. He hummed his pleasure, glancing between the two of them for confirmation.

Thanatos took a bite and nodded. "It's very good."

Loath to be left behind, Lach took a bite of his. Gods damn it all, it was delicious. Defeated, he sighed, but Prometheus seemed to think it was in satisfaction.

"I'm determined to try every pastry on the eastern seaboard," Prometheus informed them. "Breads are *much* better now."

Thanatos laughed. "Don't I know it? Breads, cheeses, wine—all so much better."

"I didn't know," Prometheus replied. A shadow passed between the two of them, and Thanatos reached out to touch his arm.

"I'm sorry."

Thanatos met his eyes frankly, no hardness there, none of the defensiveness he'd shown Lach. Once upon a time, Thanatos had looked at him like that. After so long, it shouldn't have hurt that things had changed, but leaning against that counter, Lach was lost. These two beings before him were immeasurably powerful and kind. They made each other smile and laugh, and exchanged comforting touches like that meant nothing. All Lach wanted to do right then was stuff his face with another cronut. Or four.

Lach brushed his wavy hair back from his face, more to fidget than because it bothered him. He'd gotten used to the light brown curls falling in his eyes.

"There is absolutely nothing to be sorry for," Prometheus said gently, reaching out to squeeze Thanatos's hand.

Chewing on the edges of his tongue, Lach reminded himself that he wasn't there to win over Thanatos. He was there because he'd watched his little brother waste away when the fish had swum from his father's nets and Helios's glow kept things from growing on the island where he'd been born. Because there weren't many worse ways to die, and people were in trouble.

"Should I be jealous?" a man asked in a pleasant rumble of a voice. He had broad, sharp features and the kind of scruff on his cheeks that Lach wanted tickling his thighs.

Prometheus laughed. With his own heart all twisted up, it was like Lach had missed the punchline.

"Julian, this is Thanatos, and his friend Lach."

Julian smiled charmingly and stepped in to shake each of their hands. "Nice to meet you," he said.

"How'd your meeting with the huntsman go?" Prometheus asked.

"All quiet. Did you get a cronut?" Julian asked when he returned to Prometheus's side, slipping his arm around the titan's waist. Prometheus looked at him like he was deep fried and covered in sugar, and for the first time, Lach considered that whatever had been between Thanatos and Prometheus, it might not be what he thought.

"I did. But I'm planning on another," Prometheus said.

Elated, Lach grinned at Thanatos. Only Thanatos didn't look half as thrilled as Lach felt when he stared back at him.

"So," Thanatos said, turning to the pair of them, "we actually came to talk about Cronus."

DONUT BONES

He didn't know what was going on in Lach's head, going from stunned to surly to thrilled in the space of a few minutes, but Thanatos was almost worried about him. And annoyed, because Prometheus had been through enough without Lach being weird to him.

"Cronus another of Zeus's bizarre family?" Julian asked, leaning over to look at the box of pastries. He was a beautiful man, and the smile he gave Prometheus was almost blinding.

Thanatos hadn't known going into the situation that Prometheus was already romantically involved with someone, but he couldn't say it surprised him. His friend had always been singularly magnetic among titans and gods alike. Just another thing that had made it stranger he'd chosen to associate himself with a loner like Thanatos.

Prometheus nodded at Julian's question, but his gaze didn't leave Thanatos. "Zeus's father. But I have no idea why anyone would want anything to do with him."

Julian, who'd been in the middle of picking up a cronut, stopped and stared at Prometheus, then Thanatos. "Big, blonde, and sneering has a father? That doesn't sound like a guy I want to meet."

Lach snorted. "They're all dicks when it comes to you and me, vampy. But he might listen to Prometheus—"

"I told you we're not going to see Cronus," Thanatos told him with a quelling glare. "Much less asking Prometheus to—" He broke off, realizing how insensitive it would be to mention Tartarus to a man who had recently escaped it after millennia. "To have anything to do with Cronus. No one is talking to him. It's not an option."

"That's for the best," Prometheus agreed. "There was a reason I sided against Cronus during the war. I don't know what you could possibly need with him, but he was never helpful to anyone if he could avoid it. Better by far to deal with Zeus."

Julian almost choked on his pastry, so Thanatos assumed he was more familiar than he'd have liked with the king of Olympus. At the same time, Lach held a bottle of water out to Julian and Prometheus patted him on the back soothingly.

"Watch out for those donut bones, friend," Lach said with a twinkle in his eye.

Thanatos glared at Lach. He couldn't be respectful to Prometheus, but he could flirt with his lover? Of course he could. Lach had always appreciated a handsome man, and Julian was that. But the last thing Thanatos needed to add to the scenario was misplaced jealousy.

"We need his scythe," Thanatos announced, cutting to the chase. He couldn't imagine that Julian was interested in Lach, but he wasn't going to stand there and watch the man flirt with someone who was spoken for. Damn Lach and his flirting.

"Planning to travel in time?" Prometheus asked, eyes narrowed in a confused squint. "That's never a good idea. And not like you."

"No," Lach interrupted, waving away the specter of time travel. Once, Lach had dragged him directly into a dragon's nest—Thanatos didn't want to see the "adventure" dangerous enough to give Lach pause. "That's a terrible idea. Gaia says we can use it to make the plants grow again."

Julian perked up. "Do you think it'll work? It's looking bad. We're already trying to build up stores. We have people working in greenhouses, but the plants aren't doing much better than plants in fields."

"Vampires are worried about humans starving?" Lach asked.

With one stark look, Julian questioned Lach's wisdom, and maybe his parentage. "If the humans starve, we die too. It takes a certain population of humans to support one vampire. Hunt history says that more than one vampire to a thousand humans is downright dangerous to us."

Lach blinked, shocked. "Huh."

"Right," Thanatos agreed. "We're trying to stave off a worldwide famine, which would hurt everyone."

Prometheus gave Thanatos a look that said he knew there was one person present who wouldn't be too badly hurt, but he decided to let it pass without explanation. There were reasons he was helping. Sure, he thought Elysium was a better existence than life, but humans didn't.

Damn him, Glaucus didn't.

Thanatos would never forget the fire in his eyes when he'd demanded that Thanatos not take his baby brother away when the sickly boy was taken with fever.

It had been one of the first times Thanatos had truly been able to empathize with why humans feared him. Maybe he didn't take their loved ones away forever, since all good people were reunited in Elysium, but to humans, whose lives were so short, even a few decades of separation seemed exceedingly long. And that was assuming the humans were aware of Elysium, and believed they were going there.

Humans clung to their mortal lives, found value and comfort in them, and Thanatos wasn't going to ignore what they wanted. He didn't know what was best for everyone, and he wasn't arrogant or selfish enough to force his will on them.

For a moment, Prometheus watched him. Then his eyes darted to Lach, with his salt-curled hair and sun-brown skin, and he seemed to come to a realization. Thanatos scowled at that, ready to open his mouth and explain that his inclination to help had nothing to do with the damned human pirate. Something stilled his tongue. Maybe it was the strange way Lach had been acting, or maybe it was Prometheus's ready acceptance that Thanatos was doing something good, but he simply waited for Prometheus to go on.

"I can't tell you for sure where the scythe is." He glanced at Thanatos, and then away, focusing on Lach. "It's been a long time, so it's possible it's been moved. I'd be inclined to say not, though, since if someone had it, the whole world would probably know."

Thanatos shuddered. He'd mostly stayed out of the war, but he remembered what Cronus had been capable of doing with the scythe. He hadn't considered its power over harvests, since he had mostly seen it used for violence. Or the manipulation of time. He didn't want to imagine what the wrong people would do with such a powerful artifact. He almost didn't want to find it, humanity be damned.

Julian was looking back and forth between the two titans, expression pensive. "Is it that bad? Should we be looking for a different way to fix this?"

"No." Lach had always been decisive, but Thanatos had rarely heard him quite so certain. "Gaia says it needs to be the scythe. In thousands of years, she's never steered me wrong. Whenever I think I'm being smart and I can do it a better way, it always turns out she's right."

While Thanatos couldn't question Gaia's bigger-picture perspective, it irked him that Lach trusted her without question. Also, she didn't know everything. Thanatos had a twin brother people thought the same of. Like Gaia, he slept most of his life away. But Hypnos always had a skewed view of the world when he woke, having only experienced the passage of time through people's dreams, and Thanatos didn't imagine Gaia was any different.

Unlike Thanatos, Prometheus seemed to trust Lach and Gaia. He bit his lip and nodded. "There's an island. I don't know what it might be called now, but it's shaped like the scythe. That's where Cronus left it, and Zeus declared it off limits to the gods. At the time, they were all loyal enough to him to follow the order. Maybe they've since forgotten where it is?"

As unruly as the gods were, they occasionally had short memories. Or more loyalty than anyone, including they, would admit. "I would ask Athena if she's hoarded it away somewhere, but Zeus made her account for all the magical artifacts in her possession last year. It's possible that it's still where Zeus left it."

Lach took a deep breath, seeming to inflate, sagging shoulders straightening and chest expanding. "Then I guess we're off to the islands."

"Any islands in particular?" Julian asked, bemused.

"Sure," Lach agreed. "There's only one island I know of that fits that description and was populated by gods."

Thanatos nodded. "Santorini."

Julian cocked his head to one side. "In the south Aegean?"

"You know it?" Prometheus asked, considering.

Julian started to respond but Lach jumped into action, crowding up to Thanatos, smiling at Julian and Prometheus as he nudged Thanatos in the direction of the elevator. "Thanks so much for the help. We can handle it from here, thanks!"

"I know vampires in Greece, if—"

"We're good," Lach cut him off. "I know an archaeologist who's worked in Greece a lot. She can totally cover us. Thanks for the help!"

Thanatos was so surprised that it didn't occur to him to stop and demand that they wait and speak to Julian about his allies. The last thing he saw as he let Lach herd him out of the room was Prometheus's amused grin, damn the man.

"That was nice," Lach said lightly when he got Thanatos into the elevator. "Nice guys. Prometheus and his boyfriend."

Thanatos nodded, but he couldn't think of anything to say. What was going on in Lach's head?

When they got to the lobby, Jordan from the front desk waved at them. "Thanatos? Prometheus called down and asked me to give you his number, in case you needed more information. Or just, um, wanted to talk."

Lach let out a huffy sigh, but he didn't try to stop Thanatos from going to the desk and retrieving the number. He shifted from one foot to the other impatiently, as Thanatos took his time to put the number into his phone.

"So," he said brightly when Thanatos finally put his phone back into his pocket. "Off to Greece, huh? I can't wait to introduce you to Mis. You're going to love her."

Surely he didn't expect Thanatos to spend days aboard his boat after the last discussion they'd had on the matter. That was—

Lach threw up his hands defensively. "I know, I know, but . . . hear me out."

ROBIN HOOD RETURNS

Time to shine. Lach had one chance to convince Thanatos to travel with him, or he was going to end up sailing his ass across the Atlantic all by his lonesome.

So this was the absolute perfect time to forget how to speak English. And Greek. Basically every word in every tongue he'd ever known slipped out of his head at the exact same moment, and he stood there like a gods damned fool while Thanatos waited, arms crossed.

It reminded Lach of the last time he'd seen Thanatos on Thrinacia. Only back then, Thanatos had been willing to listen to any explanation, do anything for him, forgive him despite the fact that Lach had left for months without a word. And Lach had shoved that boundless consideration right back in his face.

On those docks, Lach had looked him straight in the eyes and said the worst thing he could've said—just because he knew it would hurt Thanatos. What right did he have to ask him for anything now?

"Can we talk about this outside?" Lach suggested. It was hard enough to have this conversation without an audience, and Jordan had yet to take their eyes off of Thanatos.

Thanatos gestured toward the door. "After you."

This was a critical moment; Lach knew better than to march ahead. He rushed forward to open the door but stepped out of the way to hold it for

Thanatos. Everything about the set of Thanatos's lips said it was too little and way too late.

On the sidewalk out front, Thanatos rounded on him. "So?"

Lach bit the tip of his tongue and smiled—hell, that smile had gotten him out of harder situations than this. Failed him now though.

"So," he started, when all Thanatos did was cock his brow at him, "I think we should travel together."

"I gathered. Because?"

"Because we need to make some kind of plan." Thanatos looked skeptical, so Lach pressed on. "There's no way that Zeus left Cronus's scythe out in the open on Santorini for anyone to take. It's probably hidden in some crypt, *Lost Ark* style."

"What's the lost ark?"

"*Raiders of the Lost Ark*? Classic action movie? Indiana Jones? Harrison Ford?"

Thanatos blinked at him.

Lach sighed. "I'm saying it's probably protected. Like with booby traps. Or magic. It won't be my first rodeo, but you never want to go into these things without, you know, considering the dangers ahead. I mean, I'll totally be fine. But you're not much of an adventurer, so we should run through the basics before we get there." Lach grinned.

The teasing clearly went over less well than he'd intended. Thanatos was scowling, the corners of his lips slipping farther down every second.

He tried again. "And, you know, there are mortals who think sailing is like a vacation."

"You're talking about cruises."

"I am. But I'll be doing all the hard work."

Okay, Thanatos had never been the vacation sort. He didn't look all that inclined to sit back and let Lach sweep him off to Greece.

"But I could really use your help?" Lach suggested. "She's a pretty big boat. A lot for one guy to handle on his own."

"You seem to have managed fine."

Lach sucked in his cheeks. It didn't feel right to complain about Misericordia or imply she was anything but the best boat to ever sail, even if it would get Thanatos on board.

"I guess, but . . . what if something happens? I mean, if I'm at sea, that's not your domain. We won't be able to talk."

"We can radio."

Lach sighed. "Satellite's glitchy."

Right then, a man swept by them on the sidewalk, close enough that his gray silk suit jacket brushed Lach's arm. They weren't alone on the sidewalk, despite the late hour. One fringe benefit of cities—there were always people around. With hardly a thought and a minute flick of his fingers, Lach unclasped the man's watch. It fell heavily into his hand. Slipping two fingers through the links, he dangled it up in the air for Thanatos to see.

"Plus traveling with me comes with perks," Lach said. He felt the same thrill of victory that made his blood rush every time he won a prize.

"Did you just steal that man's watch?" Thanatos demanded incredulously.

Lach frowned. It'd been second nature. A watch was within his grasp—why shouldn't he take it? "I didn't *not* steal that man's watch."

Thanatos shifted, his arms crossing tighter over his chest until they wrinkled his dark button-up.

"Oh, come on," Lach said, laughing. "It's a nice watch. And he doesn't need it. I got it for you. I'm basically Robin Hood."

"I'm not poor," Thanatos snapped.

Lach straightened. "Well, no—"

"And you don't know that man's rich."

Lach turned around. The man was almost at the end of the block, none the wiser to his missing watch. His suit was well pressed, his shoes had no scuffs, and he walked with the urgency of a man who was worried about things that did not matter—problems it was well within his means to fix.

"He's rich," Lach said definitively. Turning back to Thanatos, he smiled. "Come on. It looks like it's solid gold. You seriously don't want it?"

"I seriously do not," Thanatos said. Once upon a time in Thrinacia, when Lach hadn't had any money to give Thanatos a gift, he'd picked an orange off a cart in the market and given it to him. Apparently, it'd been more charming then. Of course, the vendor had laughed it off. Already thinking Lach some kind of witch, they hadn't wanted to cross him.

"Well, fine. I'll keep it." He slipped his own hand through it and scowled. Nothing about Lach's own style was suave enough for a gold watch. Most days, he wore T-shirts and clothes he could move around in easily while sailing. His hair, which fell in waves to his shoulders, was usually pulled back with an elastic band, unbrushed.

But it would've been nice on Thanatos, as put together as he always was. He was the sort of man—god—who could carry off nice things. Someone who knew how to move through a crowd. The gold would look fantastic against his brown skin—catch the glint in his bright honeyed eyes. Lach imagined that kind of luxury on his own wrist made him look even dingier by comparison.

"Give it back," Thanatos ordered.

"Excuse me?"

"That man might've worked hard for that watch. Or maybe his partner gave it to him. It could mean a lot."

"Or nothing."

"And if it means nothing, it's still his. His decision whether to value it or not."

Lach licked his lips, tipped his chin up, and thought about arguing. Loads of people took what they could from others without apology. People in silk suits with gold watches who were perfectly happy to let others go without food and water and shelter. They were happy to say that people who struggled to find the same success simply didn't work as hard, ignoring all their own advantages.

But this was Thanatos. All Lach wanted was a chance to spend some time with him, and the best way to ensure that was to stop being a dick now.

"Fine. I'll return it."

If he was expecting praise for that, he didn't get it. Deadpan, Thanatos stared at him and nodded after the man, so Lach took off jogging.

"Sir," he called. "Sir!"

The man stopped, pulling his phone away from his ear. It was one of those shiny new ones Hermes kept trying to talk him into. A full-screened sliver of glass, more accessory than tool. His eyes roamed over Lach, head to toe. He stiffened, though only long enough to notice that the glint in his hand wasn't from a switchblade. "What?" he demanded.

"You dropped this," Lach said, holding out the watch.

The man narrowed his eyes. "I hope it's not scuffed." He snatched it out of Lach's hand and continued on his way.

His arms spread, Lach turned around. "You're welcome," he said.

Thanatos was nowhere to be seen. The spot he'd occupied outside the Hunt Building was empty. "Thanatos?" Lach called. "Oh, come on!"

He walked back to where they'd been, but there was no sign of him. Lach had barely started to make his case, and Thanatos wasn't around to hear the rest of it.

"Please, come back," he said. Nothing.

Lach's face fell, his shoulders sagged, and the sigh that escaped him was completely defeated. He'd lost his chance.

Maybe it would've been better if he'd taken Thanatos's hand to start. Maybe this quest would've been over too fast, but at least he would've had a shot to prove he was different. Anyone could grow if they had enough time. He needed to show Thanatos that he'd changed.

He probably hadn't changed enough to earn forgiveness.

"Listen," he said, dragging his feet along the sidewalk. He tipped his head back to look up at the night sky. He was never sure why people did that. Olympus was, in theory, high up. Still, he didn't think he could talk to the sky and Thanatos would hear him. It would've been better to talk to the ground and hope his voice carried to the underworld. "I'm sorry. I was trying to be funny. Or maybe charmingly contrarian? I obviously missed the mark."

There he was, talking to the sky like a gods damned loon. Shit on a stick. He dragged his hand down his face, shut his eyes, and pinched the bridge of his nose.

"Thanatos—" He didn't know what to say that would convince Thanatos to come back, much less to get on a boat with him for weeks. He dropped his arms by his sides, empty. "I really don't want to do this alone. Please?"

Lach waited one beat, then two. No response came.

MORE'S THE PITY

Damn it all, why did he have to say please? Thanatos had only been watching to make sure that Lach followed through and returned what he'd stolen as promised. He hadn't intended to stay and talk to him; he thought he'd meet Lach on Santorini in a few weeks. Months. Gods, he didn't know how long a boat took to go that far, even if it was a magic boat.

Thanatos had been right, and he clung to it like a dying man to a sinking ship. The watch had belonged to that rich man, and it wasn't right to take someone's belongings. Even if the man had been rude to Lach without knowing the rogue had stolen his watch to begin with.

Returning it had been the right thing to do.

Thanatos sighed.

He shouldn't have watched at all. He might have spent the evening wondering if Lach had bothered to give it back if he hadn't, but at least he wouldn't have seen those pitiful eyes, and heard those soft words spoken into the night sky.

Thanatos had never been on a boat for longer than it took to retrieve a soul, and then only rarely. Boats left him with a feeling of vertigo, like the world was trying to remake itself beneath his feet.

Still, those damned eyes of Lach's had always been his greatest weakness. Thanatos wanted to obliterate any negative emotion he saw in them.

Lach's sadness, his rage, his fear—no matter how much he tried to hide them, Thanatos always saw them there and was taken with the urge to hold him until they went away. He didn't think it had ever worked, not really, but he had always tried before.

He watched Lach stumble down the sidewalk, shoulders slumped and hands in his pockets, his steps shuffling.

For reasons he couldn't explain, Thanatos followed.

Part of him expected the posture to change once Lach was out of sight of the Hunt Building, the spring to return to his step, and his usual devil-may-care attitude to resurface. Instead, he shuffled along one sidewalk after another, head down, dejection written on every line of his body.

Did he know that Thanatos was watching? Was that why he was being so dramatic?

On the other hand, Lach had always been prone to the dramatics. When he'd decided to leave Thanatos, he hadn't just left, he'd run away. And stayed away. And when Thanatos hadn't taken the clue and left for good during all that time, Lach had told him in no uncertain terms why he wanted nothing to do with Thanatos.

Block after block, Thanatos followed him, and Lach continued to shuffle along, hardly paying attention to where he was going, even as he made a short phone call. Still, he seemed to arrive at his destination, because after what felt like forever, he was standing in front of a sailboat.

At least, Thanatos thought it was a sailboat. What he knew about boats could fill a very small pamphlet, and it would mostly be made up of pictures. It had a sail—did that make it a sailboat?

Lach hopped aboard with the precision of an expert sailor and stood there, staring out at the river. He shook his head and disappeared below deck as Thanatos watched from the dock.

He should go. Lach would be fine. He'd been fine for thousands of years, and he'd made it very clear that his version of fine didn't have a damn thing to do with Thanatos. He didn't want or need him there, not really.

So why had he been so damn determined to get Thanatos on his boat? It seemed like a nice enough boat and all, but they mostly looked the same to him. Lach didn't want to spend time with him. Planning, he'd said, but it didn't seem like there was much to plan.

They couldn't plan for booby traps they didn't know about or crypts they hadn't located. They had no idea what, if anything, protected the scythe.

So the purpose of spending days, or weeks, or however long the trip took, on a boat with Lach seemed like a particularly virulent form of self-inflicted harm on both their parts.

Thanatos was no great admirer of himself, but he'd never been one to deliberately hurt himself either.

After a long while, Lach came back to the—deck? topside?—with a bottle of beer in one hand, and sat down on the edge of the boat, legs dangling over the side, staring into the dark water.

The image that painted was beyond disturbing. Lach, contemplating the deep. Lach had never been one to contemplate anything.

Thanatos sighed the sigh of the deeply put-upon.

"Fine," he announced, allowing himself to become visible once again. "I'll travel with you on your boat. But I still think this is a mistake and a waste of time."

Lach turned around so fast that he knocked his beer over, then snatched it back up, mopping up the spill with his sleeve and muttering apologies to the boat under his breath. A mere second later, though, he was hopping up and striding across the distance between them.

There was the spring in his step, the almost annoying confidence, and the fey grin that had the dual effect of giving Thanatos butterflies in his stomach and rebreaking his heart at the same time.

"Definitely not a mistake!" Lach told him, eyes sparkling with excitement. He started to hold a hand out to Thanatos to help him aboard, realized there was a beer in his hand, and quickly turned to set it down. "Sorry, sorry, wasn't expecting you—um, to be so early. I thought you'd change your mind in the morning."

Thanatos rolled his eyes and didn't dignify that nonsense with a response. He tried not to focus on the warmth of Lach's hand in his as he pulled him aboard. That led nowhere healthy, and Thanatos wasn't going to further complicate the messy situation they found themselves in.

He would finish this trip, help Lach save the harvest, and then they would part ways. Thanatos couldn't afford to get attached again; it would only end in tears.

FAITHFUL SONS

The Brazilian air was warm and sticky, even in May, and Martina Paget was ready to be done with it. She was sure it was a lovely place when on vacation, but she wasn't on vacation.

"They must have been sacrifices," the irritating, nasal voice of her Midwestern counterpart said. He was rubbing against her last nerve. Of course the human remains found in the pit near Parque Arqueológico do Solstício had to be human sacrifices, because Jim desperately wanted them to be. That was the kind of story that garnered attention and drew in money. Not to mention confirming his opinion of his culture's superiority in his own mind. As though his ancestors hadn't sacrificed humans in their own ways.

"There's no indication of them being killed," she told him for the second time—in that conversation. "Let alone sacrificed. Much more likely it was an honored burial place."

He sniffed derisively and opened his mouth to start explaining her own profession to her, again, when her phone rang. Without a word or so much as a by-your-leave, she pulled the phone from her pocket, stood from the table, and walked away from him.

There was a mild breeze outside the building, and it felt amazing against her warm cheeks.

"Paget," she answered, her voice surprisingly calm.

The line was a little hollow-toned, so she assumed it was an international call, but that was no surprise. She knew precious few people in Brazil. "Hey, Martina." With that, the caller had her full attention.

Lach.

She'd known there was something special about him since she'd met him on one of her first dig sites, right out of college. Her mentor had introduced him as an authority on Greek artifacts without giving any indication of his credentials. Also, without a last name.

"Lach." She leaned against the side of the building and let her shoulders slump. Knowing Lach, if she waited a few seconds, he'd cut to the chase.

"I've got a weird request," he said after a moment, voice hesitant.

"Weirder than the time in Jakarta when you asked if I could get my hands on a live cobra and fourteen human-sized baskets?"

There was a long pause. "It was thirteen. And there was a rational explanation for that."

She laughed. "There always is with you. So what do you need?"

"I need some help finding a site on Santorini," he said. It was almost a whisper, like he wanted to keep it a secret from even himself. Her heart skipped a beat.

Santorini.

"Any site in particular?"

"Ha ha, funny lady." He sighed. "Yeah. I've got a friend who'll be able to help find what we're looking for when we get there, but you're familiar with the area, and I thought maybe you could help us narrow it down."

"This a paying job?" she asked, checking her nails—broken to the quick as usual—in an exaggerated manner that wouldn't even work in face-to-face negotiations. Not that she was expecting a negotiation. Lach never haggled. "I'm in Brazil right now. I'd need a plane ticket. Plus money for my time, of course."

"Of course," he agreed smoothly. "You're done there?"

So very done. She sighed. "Technically not, but if I don't get out of here, I'm going to end up on trial for murder. Jim Jackson is in charge of the dig."

"Ouch. I know he's always your favorite 'splainer."

"I like Greece better anyway. First love and all that. I could get there in a couple weeks." In truth she could be there in a few days, but she didn't want to seem too enthusiastic. He had to think she was doing him a favor.

Plus it would give her time to wriggle her way out of this dig without burning too many bridges.

"Perfect," Lach said. "That's perfect. I'll wire you money in . . . Brazil, you said? And meet you in Greece in a few weeks."

She gave him her information and they hung up, then she stood there leaning against the building for a long while. She wished she weren't trying to quit smoking. A cigarette sounded amazing.

Finally, she took a deep breath and looked back at her phone, dialing the one number she would always know by heart.

"Paget," was the answer, more clipped than she'd managed at her most angry.

"Lach called me, and he's looking for something on Santorini."

Her father's laughter was dry and crackled over the line. "I knew your little degree would be useful eventually."

He hadn't known. He'd fought tooth and nail against her doing something as frivolous as going to college when she should be following in his footsteps like her younger brother, Roger. The family business was more important than a bunch of old bones, he'd told her again and again. It was the only time she'd ever questioned him, and she wasn't going to change that by disagreeing with him now. "I'm meeting him there. Should I wait and call you if I find anything?"

He hesitated for a long time, and she knew he was running the options. Almost certainly, he didn't want her to go, but Lach was a wild card. Most people could be counted on to act a certain way, but with Lach, you had to have dozens of backup plans, just in case.

A live cobra and thirteen baskets, for fuck's sake.

"Assume you'll meet him there," her father said. He was abrupt as ever, but she was used to it. "If nothing else, I suppose you should be there with everyone else. With luck, the sons will be able to handle your little friend before you have to deal with him."

She didn't know how he meant and wasn't sure she wanted to know. Instead, she agreed with him, hung up, and booked her plane tickets to Greece. A week was plenty of time to extricate herself from the dig and get out of Brazil, she decided.

Her father had all faith in the Fidelis Filii, led by her brother in all but name since father's stroke the year before. After all, he'd founded the organization himself.

Marty had never been one for faith, but she knew Lach well enough to know that if anyone were going to surprise Roger, it would be him. She had to get to Greece, and she fully expected to find Lach alive and well when she got there. She wondered if she could say the same of her brother.

She squared her shoulders to head back in, to where Jim was no doubt still blustering about human sacrifice. First things first, she had to tell him she was going.

To Greece.

To Santorini.

Santorini, where the king of the titans had been defeated by his traitorous children.

Santorini, where he was to rise again.

A BOAT WITH ONLY ONE BED

A mistake and a waste of time—Lach had been called worse. As long as Thanatos was traveling with him, he could improve on that. The bar was so low there was nowhere to go but up.

"I should give you the grand tour," Lach said once Thanatos was on board. His hand in Lach's was warm and soft as ever. He would never call Thanatos lazy, but labor hardened, he was not. Lach had always appreciated the smoothness of those hands. Now, he hesitated to let it go, offering his own as a steady place to hold onto until Thanatos got his footing. Too soon, Thanatos pulled away.

"This"—Lach swept out his arm over the ship—"is Misericordia."

Lach expected awe. Thanatos might be a god, but magic ships weren't common. Instead, Thanatos stared at him flatly.

"Seriously? Misericordia?"

For a second, Lach had forgotten what her name meant: an act of mercy. Heat swept up the back of his neck and turned his ears red. He'd never been gladder for his longish hair.

"Well, yeah. That's how I got her—a merciful act. I helped Nerites save some whales off the coast of Norway a couple decades back. Got him out of a bit of a pinch. Poseidon was grateful."

Thanatos raised his eyebrows and wrinkled his forehead. He crossed his arms, but the boat rocked under them, and a second later he held them out to catch his balance. Lach offered his own; Thanatos didn't take it. When he recovered, he still looked unconvinced.

"Oh," Lach said. "You think it's for you, 'cause you're the god of merciful death?" His laugh was high and tight. He wanted to lie about it—save face—but the whole reason Thanatos was there was so Lach could convince him that he wasn't a lying piece of shit. Lach dropped his hand and shrugged, trying for nonchalance. "Oh, um, well . . . yeah, I guess. I guess you might've crossed my mind."

Okay, Thanatos was definitely not swooning over the idea. Lach rubbed the back of his neck. "Or something," he added. "I don't know. Let me show you around."

He showed him around the deck, but other than some benches and a place off the back where Lach fished, there wasn't much to show. He pointed out things that moved, places to avoid that might prove dangerous. Then he took him down below.

"It's tight quarters down here, but there are two bedrooms," Lach said as he made his way down the narrow, steep stairs. He'd have let Thanatos go first, but he thought it was the more gracious thing to do to be there to catch him, even if he didn't need it.

Before he'd gone to DC, he'd prepared for a trip with Thanatos. That meant stocking up on better food than Lach usually ate and asking Mis to arrange a second room. She wasn't just magic; she was impossible. Changing from one bedroom to two, or even from sailboat to megayacht was nothing to her.

"This is the mess. There's where we eat," he said when they were both downstairs and able to stand up straight. "Up here's the—"

Lach led the way to the front cabin. It was a small guest bedroom and would have suited him fine if Thanatos didn't want to stay in his room surrounded by his stuff. It wasn't like Lach was a hoarder or anything, but those DVDs, the side-table bottle of rum, all his clothes—Thanatos might want his own space.

But when he pulled open the door to the new bedroom, it opened on a closet. He shut it, laughed breathily.

"Just a second," he said to Thanatos. Then he leaned in toward the door and lowered his voice. "Come on, Mis. Don't play me like this."

He opened the doors again. Still no bedroom. "Uh . . . this is the closet." It was piled full of board games, knickknacks, things Lach had forgotten he had that'd been stored away wherever Misericordia put things Lach didn't need anymore.

"It's a very nice closet," Thanatos said dryly.

"Yup! Sure is. Why don't we go back that way?" He indicated the narrow hallway that cut around the engine room toward the back. Thanatos led the way, but at the door, Lach sneaked around him. It was a tight squeeze, and he couldn't help brushing against him.

"Sorry," he mumbled.

"It's fine," Thanatos said, looking up at the ceiling while Lach opened the door.

"This is the master bedroom," Lach said. Thanatos stepped in and looked around. "The restroom's through there if you need to freshen up."

It was cleaner than he'd left it—thank the gods for Mis—but it was still clearly lived in. Obviously his space.

"I thought you said there were two bedrooms," Thanatos said.

Lach laughed. "You didn't see it? It's off the mess?"

Thanatos scowled.

"The dining-room bench?" Lach suggested.

"Ah. Obviously. Coziest bedroom I've ever seen."

"But you'll be sleeping in here," Lach hastened to add. "If you want. I'll stay out there. That's what I was thinking, anyway."

Damn, he wished Thanatos would say something. Lach watched as he walked around the room, brushed his finger over a side table.

"Can I get you anything? I've got beer, water, orange juice—" Lach asked.

"No, thank you."

"Okay."

Thanatos had moved on to look over his movie collection, lined up on the shelf under the flat-screen television on the wall. Lach didn't know what to do, so he stood there and watched, his tongue thick and awkward in his mouth.

"Okay, so . . . I guess I'll go ship us out. Do you want to come watch?"

"I think I'll stay here," Thanatos said mildly, never turning around to look at him.

"Sure. Okay. No problem. You get settled in, and we'll be on our way." It was the coward's way out, but Lach had to escape. Thanatos had caught him off guard; he'd retreat, regroup, and land the approach next time.

Up on deck, Lach grabbed his beer on the way to untying the ropes. It'd gone a little warm, but it was better than no beer at all.

When he got to the tiller, he sat down and took another swig. "You did me dirty, Mis."

There was no response but the gentle movement of water under them. He sighed. Maybe the night hadn't been a resounding success, but Thanatos was there. Assuming he didn't scare Thanatos off—even if he couldn't travel to the boat in a godly fashion, he could disappear from it in an instant—he'd have until they got to Santorini to make a connection. By the time they got the scythe, Lach would prove he wasn't the same man who'd broken Thanatos's heart.

That night, Lach didn't sleep well on the bench, but that meant he was up early enough to make breakfast. He had a folding hot plate. He set it up on the dining table—kitchen space was virtually nonexistent—and turned it on while he prepped the pancake batter and chopped up fruit.

Once he'd gotten everything on a plate, he looked over his handiwork. It wasn't great. The pancakes were uneven in size, and he'd cut the fruit in bite-size chunks.

Chunks! Thanatos regularly ate ambrosia. He wasn't going to appreciate lopsided melon chunks.

"Mis, do we have a melon baller?"

A drawer of utensils flew open, but he didn't see anything inside that might work. He stuck his hand in to rifle through it, and the drawer snapped shut, narrowly missing his fingers.

Lach hissed. "It's a reasonable thing to have," he protested, but when he pulled on the drawer handle again, it stayed stuck shut. Apparently Mis disagreed. After all, when in his life had Lach used a melon baller?

The battle lost, Lach looked over his handiwork. He had done his best and come out the other side with lopsided pancakes and melon chunks.

With a sigh, he picked up the plate and went to knock on the door to the master bedroom.

"Thanatos, you up?" A few quiet seconds slipped past. "I made breakfast."

TOPSY TURVY

Thanatos stared at the wall, horrified, incredulous, and . . . queasy.

There was only one possible explanation: this wasn't happening. Maybe he was hallucinating, or it was a nightmare, or maybe he was dead and Zeus had imprisoned him in Tartarus for some infraction he hadn't realized he'd committed.

He was one of the oldest beings on the planet. He had lived through wars, plagues, mass extinctions, meteor strikes, the fall of the Roman Empire, and the cancellation of Sense8. So there was no possibility whatsoever that he was seasick. None.

Sleep was a choice for gods, usually. He rested, and needed rest on occasion, but he didn't require eight hours a night like a human. But he had thought spending time on the deck of the boat by himself would prove boring, so he'd decided that sleep was a good way to avoid it.

Somehow, he hadn't gotten so much as a wink. The moment he'd closed his eyes, a general sense of unease had overcome him. Then had come the rolling in his stomach that matched the rolling of the boat on one wave after the next. His head pounded, his stomach twisted, and he stared at the wall. And it went on all night.

After all, his other choices were to leave, or to wake Lach up and admit that he felt ill. He'd said he would make the journey, and he wasn't a liar, so the first wasn't really an option. The second was worse. Showing weakness to Lach was like bleeding in shark-infested water.

Thanatos had always been good at keeping his silence. He kept so many people's secrets. Who better to tell your most closely held information than Death himself?

For the thousandth time, he told himself that it didn't make sense. He was a millennia-old immortal being who rarely needed to sleep or eat. He absorbed what he needed from the world around him, and the ichor in his veins provided a near-limitless source of energy.

And yet, his stomach rolled and kept threatening to expel anything that might be in it.

When Lach started whistling in the morning, it was both endearing and annoying at once. Thanatos decided, he thought rather charitably, to call it cute. When the whistling was followed up by frustrated muttering, it felt like he'd been hurtled back in time: Lach's unbreakable optimism, occasionally tempered by conversations with himself about things that annoyed him.

There was a soft knock on the door. "Thanatos?"

He wanted to insist that Lach go away. Lying there, sweating and breathing heavily was possibly the most undignified thing he'd ever done. He didn't want anyone to see him that way, let alone Lach.

After a moment, the knock came again, but this time instead of the quiet call of his name, it was followed by the door opening.

As much as he wanted to say something, anything, to deny Lach entry, he was worried that what came out would be a moan.

The smell of food invaded the cabin, and Thanatos tried to hold his breath. It wasn't as horrible as he'd expected it to be, though; no heavy eggs and salty meat.

"Thana—" Lach set the tray he was carrying on the end of the bed and climbed up next to Thanatos, mouth hanging open and eyes wide. "Holy crap, what's wrong?"

He tried to shake his head, but it made his stomach even angrier, so instead he curled in on himself.

Lach had never been one to give up easily, so he leaned in and ran a hand over Thanatos's forehead. His fingers were ice cold, which was wrong. He'd always had warm hands.

It was silent in the room for a moment before Lach sighed. "Seriously? This isn't fair. You can't be seasick."

"M'not," Thanatos muttered.

"Okay," Lach said, voice calm and agreeable, despite the thread of panic he was covering. "Let's get you topside, then. Okay?"

Thanatos tried to curl into a tighter ball instead. Getting up was definitely not going to happen.

Not to be deterred, Lach hopped up, came around the bed, put an arm around Thanatos's shoulders, and pulled him upright. The motion made the throbbing in his head worse, and like there was a direct line between his head and his belly, his stomach churned.

Weakly, he tried to push Lach off. For possibly the first time in their relationship, the human was stronger than him. Against all odds, against the nausea turning his stomach and the uneasiness in his heart, Lach's strength was comforting. The fact that someone was still competent and he wasn't alone with his misery was the most comforting thing he'd felt in a long, long time.

Practically bearing the entirety of his weight, Lach pushed him up the stairs and into the morning air. It made him dizzy, the rush of cool breeze against his face and sudden feeling of openness, but at the same time, it was good. That didn't stop him from stumbling over his own feet and almost falling on his face, but nimble and quick as ever, Lach circled and held him up.

Lach helped him over to a bench on the deck and settled him onto it, then pointed off into the distance. "Can you do me a huge favor and just . . . look over there? Keep an eye out, you know? Focus on the horizon?"

Thanatos tried to nod, but it made his body rebel, so he rasped out a barely there "yeah," and did as asked. He wasn't sure why Lach was giving him an assignment when he was feeling, and probably looking, as miserable as he'd ever been in his life, but it was good to have something to focus on. In fact, the longer he looked at the horizon, the more his whole body seemed to settle. The nausea receded, and the headache dulled to a slow throb.

He realized he was looking off the side of the boat, not where they were going or where they had come from. What was the purpose of staring at nothing?

Lach poked his head up from below deck and stared at Thanatos for a moment before disappearing again. When he returned, he was carrying the tray from before, and the previously inoffensive food suddenly smelled incredible. Pancakes? And some kind of fruit?

Lach set the tray next to him and gestured toward it dramatically. "Ta-da! Breakfast!"

Thanatos almost said something snarky. Something about the lopsided pancakes or the oddity of Lach being able to cook at all, but there was something on the man's face that stopped him. A thread of uncharacteristic uncertainty lurked in his eyes, and the way he nibbled on his lower lip as he glanced between Thanatos and the food.

So instead, Thanatos smiled at him. "Thank you. It smells wonderful." He picked the tray up, set it in his lap, and hesitantly picked up the fork. The first chunk of melon was better than ambrosia, and he hummed his approval around it.

Lach's answering smile was as bright as the sun.

"Aren't you eating?"

"I thought I'd test it out on you," Lach said, cocking a hip and leaning against the bench. "You know, make sure it wasn't poisonous first."

Thanatos rolled his eyes. "You've been providing your own food for thousands of years. I think you're well aware that you're capable of cooking."

"I don't do it much, actually," Lach mumbled. Then his voice went bright, and the cocky smile returned. "But it's great, right? Because I'm awesome."

He couldn't help it; he laughed. Lach hadn't changed at all. There was all the careless bravado that had sucked Thanatos in the first time.

And for some reason, for this one morning, he decided he was going to let himself enjoy that. It was probably a slippery slope, and he'd be sorry for it eventually, but he was so tired of the same bleak days of work and more work, with only the occasional bright spot of a meal with his brother or a horrible party in Hades.

Thanatos deserved this moment, warm and familiar and comforting. For once, he was going to let himself have it, tomorrow's inevitable heartbreak be damned. He cut a piece of lumpy pancake, and it was the finest pancake he'd eaten in his entire existence.

FILMS & FISH GUTS

It was some kind of epic karmic bullshit that Lach lied about getting queasy when Thanatos god-ported them to the other side of the planet, and now Thanatos was miserable and sick. Lach had been made immortal by mistake—he didn't believe that the Fates were all powerful and all knowing—but damn if it didn't seem like they were out to get him sometimes.

They spent the day on deck, Lach sailing and Thanatos staring out at the horizon. After a while, he started to look less peaked.

"I didn't realize gods could get sick," Lach said. In the late afternoon, when their course was set and there was less to do, he'd fished off the back of the boat. Now he sat over the water on a tiny stool, cleaning his catch on a small table in front of him.

"I'm not sick," Thanatos said. "It's disorienting, putting your feet somewhere unstable."

"Ah, so you're saying you have control issues," Lach teased. "I buy that."

Thanatos shot him a narrow eyed look, but Lach didn't feel any anger behind it as he sliced the fish open from tail to head.

"But if you don't stop that, I might get actually sick," Thanatos griped, grimacing as Lach dumped the fish guts into the water.

Chuckling, Lach shook his head. "I'd have thought you'd be a little more comfortable with this kind of thing, you know, considering." He waved his knife in Thanatos's general direction.

"I might be acquainted with death, but that does not mean I want to witness the particulars of it here."

"Fair enough." Lach slapped the fish down on the table. "I might suggest you turn around."

With a heavy sigh, Thanatos sank down on his bench and turned his face toward the purpling sky.

Lach finished scaling the fish. "I'm going to go cook this. You gonna be hungry for dinner?"

Thanatos had never had to eat, but just because he didn't have to to survive didn't mean he couldn't enjoy it. Common wisdom held that the way to a man's heart was through his stomach; Lach wanted to see if it worked for gods.

The god in question didn't lift his head so much as tuck his chin down so that he could look directly at Lach. "I guess. That seemed like quite the ordeal for the poor fish. Shame to let it go to waste."

Lach smirked. "Would be. I'll be back."

He seared the fish in lemon and olive oil—not the most ambitious, maybe, but it tasted like home. With a side of sautéed spinach, it looked like the kind of meal Thanatos wouldn't chuck directly into the open ocean. Lach couldn't cook pretty, but he hoped substance would win out.

When he got back on deck, the stars were scattered across the sky. Thanatos was still staring up.

"Bon appétit," Lach said.

When Thanatos looked at him, he smiled. It was the first one that Lach had seen since Thanatos had looked at Prometheus. His heart flopped anxiously in his chest.

"You want to eat up here?" Lach asked.

"Yeah. It's a nice night."

Thanatos straightened in his seat and reached out for his plate. Lach took a spot at the end of the bench. With his back to the cabin's wall, he could watch Thanatos while Thanatos watched the stars.

For a few minutes, they ate in silence. Taking smaller bites, he watched for any indication that Thanatos liked it. Or that he didn't.

"What?" Thanatos asked, turning his way. He smiled around a mouthful in his cheek.

Lach blinked. He could stare creepily with the best of them, but when it came time to talk, he floundered.

"Are things hard now?" Lach asked. He blanched. That kind of question ought to come with more specificity, dammit. "I mean with so many people in the world. Like, you probably deal with a lot every day."

"It's not as bad as you'd think," Thanatos said. Of course, Lach didn't think there was any circumstance that'd get Thanatos to complain. "Charon and Hermes have to deal with the worst of it."

"Yeah? I guess that makes sense . . ." Anyone who got greeted on the other side of life by Thanatos was lucky. Or nice. Probably both.

"Still, the world's changed a lot."

"You're telling me." Lach laughed. "I just bought a gods damned cell phone, and now Hermes is insisting I get a smart one? What the fuck is a smartphone, Thanatos?"

Thanatos blinked at him. "You don't have a smartphone."

Groaning, Lach threw his head back. "You're all helpless. If people are relying on their phones to be smarter than they are, we're already fucked. This is the bad timeline."

Thanatos's soft laugh warmed Lach's chest. "There's no such thing, Lach. It's a fine timeline."

"You'd say that no matter what," Lach complained. "You always see the best in everything."

Once upon a time, he'd seen the best in Lach too.

A small line appeared between Thanatos's eyebrows. Silence blanketed them, and Lach knew he'd made a misstep.

"Do you want to watch a movie?" he blurted out before Thanatos could think too hard about the time he'd wasted on people who weren't worth it.

Thanatos blinked. At this rate, Lach was going to give him whiplash on top of making him seasick.

"I just mean," Lach continued, "it might help to give yourself something to focus on when we go back below. Something other than, you know, the rocking."

Thanatos grimaced. "Don't remind me."

"Hey, you've been fine most of the day. You're doing great. You'll get used to it." He had to, or Lach was officially the worst ex-boyfriend to ever trick his potential paramour onto a sailboat.

Okay, he was already the worst ex-boyfriend to ever do that.

"So, you up for it?" Lach asked.

With a sigh, Thanatos shrugged. He finished the last bite of his food and stood up.

"Why not?"

Lach grinned. It might be a small victory, but it was a victory nonetheless.

"Great! I'll take your plate." He shoveled the last of his own food into his mouth, then stacked one on top of the other. "After you."

He let Thanatos lead the way down and stopped in the kitchen on his way to the back.

"I'll clean the dishes," he said. "Why don't you go pick out a movie? There's a whole shelf in the bedroom."

"I saw." There was something tempered in Thanatos's voice that made Lach uneasy.

"Well, whatever you want. I'll be there in a minute."

Cleaning two dishes, even with the pan he'd cooked in, went fast.

"You want anything to drink?" he called down the short hallway.

"A water'd be great. Thank you."

Lach grabbed a bottle and a beer for himself, then knocked on the open bedroom door. Thanatos's head popped up.

"Any luck?" Lach asked. He passed Thanatos the bottle of water.

"I don't know. You have a lot of movies . . . And a lot of seasons of *Frasier*."

"Best sitcom on television."

"Uh huh."

Lach glanced over the shelves. "What about this one?"

He picked out *The Holiday*, which was undoubtedly a top-five romantic comedy of all time. Thanatos stared at the cardboard sleeve of the DVD box. The corners of his lips tightened, and he shrugged.

"I was actually thinking about this one," he said, pulling out *Dead Poets Society*. Lach's stomach dropped. That was decidedly unromantic. In fact, the only thing less romantic he could think of was *Transformers*. Okay, or maybe *Alien*, but that was still a solid film.

But he'd said Thanatos could choose. "Sounds great. I love Robin Williams."

While Lach got the movie cued up, Thanatos crawled onto the bed. A condition of being on a sailboat—or maybe a condition this particular boat had manufactured—was that there wasn't much sitting space. Either Thanatos would let him sit beside him on the bed, or Lach would be standing through the whole thing.

"Do you mind?" Lach asked, nodding toward the empty side of the bed. The last time they'd shared a bed, Lach had crept out of it and disappeared for months.

Thanatos frowned. "Sure."

He seemed less than pleased but allowed Lach to scoot up next to him and lean back against the cushioned headboard.

The movie was as good as ever—moving and devastating and hopeful and sad. Lach drank his beer and thought about putting his arm around Thanatos, but their legs weren't close to touching. More than once, Lach shifted, angling his knee into Thanatos's space. Invariably, the god pulled away, so Lach thought better of pressing.

But when Thanatos caught his breath watching Neil Perry find his father's gun, Lach reached out and set his hand on top of Thanatos's. Loosely, he curled his fingers around the edge of Thanatos's palm. When Mr. Perry found his son, Thanatos squeezed hard.

The movie ended, and Lach sat still through the end of the credits and for minutes afterward, afraid that if he moved, Thanatos would retract his hand. In the end, he did anyway.

Thanatos twisted away, reaching for his water bottle on the side table. He needed both hands to unscrew the cap—Lach understood that, but he didn't understand why Thanatos didn't reach for him again afterward.

It was an awkward moment. Heaviness in Lach's chest kept him from cracking any jokes.

"So, you know, the guy who played Neil is in another movie, *Much Ado About Nothing*. It's all about mistakes and forgiveness and—"

"Lach."

"Yeah?"

"I know the plot of *Much Ado About Nothing*."

"Right." Lach laughed, rubbing the back of his warm neck. "Well, we could watch it tomorrow night if you want."

Thanatos stared at him long enough that Lach was sure he'd say no. Then he shrugged. "Sure."

"Great! It's a date."

Thanatos's eyes widened.

"A plan," Lach clarified. "It's a plan."

With a single slow nod, Thanatos confirmed it. A slow smile crept across Lach's face.

"Can I get you anything? Saltines? How are you feeling?" Lach asked.

"I'm fine."

"Right. Well, holler if you need anything. Good night, Thanatos."

"Good night, Lach."

Though Lach slipped out into the main area to sleep again on the uncomfortable dining table bench, he pulled a blanket over himself, knowing that he had a tomorrow to look forward to, and another chance to prove himself.

A MESSY MESS

After Lach fell asleep, Thanatos sneaked past him up to the deck.

Part of him felt guilty that the man was sleeping on the bench in the kitchen, but why had he invited Thanatos along if he didn't have a place for them both to sleep? It would have been much more convenient to meet in Greece.

Unless, of course, Lach had intended for them to be sharing the bed.

His stomach twisted into knots, and this time it wasn't because of the rolling of the ocean. That nausea was still there, but a mere twinge compared to the misery of the previous night. No, now he was worried that the whole point of this trip was sex.

It wasn't that Thanatos didn't like sex.

He loved sex. He had loved sex with Lach especially.

Thanatos didn't fall in lust easily or constantly like some of his brethren, chasing after every passingly attractive human he met. They had to catch his attention some other way—like being the man who refused to die, no matter how many times Thanatos felt the pull to retrieve his soul. The man who, every time Thanatos arrived to take him to Elysium, gave a cocky grin and a "thanks but no thanks, no matter how handsome you are."

Eventually, he had become the person Thanatos spent the most time with. It had felt almost inevitable the first time Lach had gone into a graveyard and summoned him without the near-death experience. The first time the human had dropped to his knees and offered to "worship" at the altar of the god of death.

The time they had spent together had been incredible in every way, and even now, imagining Lach on his knees before him made that familiar heat rise in his groin. Lach had always joked that it was as close as he came to worshipping a god, getting on his knees for Thanatos. Thanatos had always thought that if he could imagine worshipping anything, it would be in those transcendent moments when Lach loved—

When Lach had cared about him.

He sighed and stared off at the ocean. It was almost impossible at night to see the differentiation between land and sea. It was just a mass of darkness, lit only by the scattering of twinkling stars and the sliver of the new moon. In this context the rocking of the boat became comforting, reminding him that he wasn't adrift among the stars but grounded on the earth.

A tiny, hesitant part of him acknowledged that he could see why Lach loved it. It was truly beautiful.

Lach came up the stairs as the sun crested the horizon, painting the sky, and his face, in gold. Chaos, the man was beautiful. Like no other man Thanatos had ever known.

He rubbed his eyes and gave Thanatos a sleepy smile that made his heart ache. "Didn't feel like sleeping?"

Thanatos shrugged. "It was nice out, and I lost track of time."

"Easy to do," Lach agreed, sliding onto the bench next to him. They stared out at the red-orange horizon in silence for a while. That was new. The old Lach would never have managed to stay quiet for more than a minute or two at a time. Apparently he'd gained a little patience somewhere between the millennia.

"So, breakfast?"

But not too much patience. Thanatos smiled to himself. "Sure. That melon was lovely. Or are we on sea rations now? Hard tack?"

Lach snorted. "Sailing's not really like that these days. I mean, sure, after a few days without land, the fresh produce runs out, but it's not all dry biscuits and kegs of wine." His expression went distant and thoughtful. "In the old days, we even baked bread. Not sure when they stopped doing that."

Thanatos suspected it had something to do with social status or voyage length, but in so many things, he had merely been an observer to human history. Like the smartphone he carried but couldn't say how it worked—he didn't have time to understand everything.

"Afraid my skill set doesn't stretch to baking bread, though, sorry. I've got oatmeal." He frowned, bit his lip, and glanced to the side. "And I think there's some melon left, if you don't mind it."

Mind it? Thanatos was confused. Had his moan of pleasure or request for more gone unnoticed the day before? "I definitely don't mind it. It's delicious."

Lach brightened. "Sweet. I'll get on it, then."

When he stood, Thanatos did as well. He might as well earn his keep. It didn't seem like oatmeal would be that hard to make.

Lach froze. "Where are you going?"

"With you?"

Again, Lach looked conflicted. "I love that idea. Really, I do. But you've seen the mess."

Thanatos hadn't thought it particularly messy, and he was living in it regardless, so he hardly thought that relevant. "It isn't that bad. And what does it have to do with me helping you?"

A tiny line formed between Lach's brows, eyes confused, and he cocked his head. Then his eyes widened in understanding. "The kitchen. It's, ah, it's called the mess. And it's really small. Barely enough room for one person to cook, let alone two." He hesitated a moment before adding, "But you could sit on the bench down there and keep me company if you want."

So Thanatos did that. Mostly, he watched Lach mix and stir and mutter to himself, but occasionally Lach remembered he was there and spoke to him. It was mostly questions about Thanatos's food preferences, a nice neutral subject. Truth told, other than the odd meal with his brother, Thanatos didn't eat much.

That, Lach thought, was a travesty.

"But food has come so far in the modern era," he protested. "Not just different things from everywhere, but fusions of everything smashed together. The best of everything. You should be out there trying all of it!"

It was Lach in a nutshell. Out there, trying everything, confused about why Thanatos was stuck in the mud.

Maybe he was right. Maybe Thanatos should be out there trying everything.

He felt useless half the time, and that wasn't only self-doubt talking. Lots of people still died every day, but his own job didn't seem to be growing. He didn't know if fewer people were dying peacefully or if they had a better understanding of where to go when they did, but the mere fact that he'd spent more than a day on a boat without feeling as though he absolutely had to see to a soul spoke volumes about how useful he was in the modern world.

Lach was looking at him, and he realized he'd probably been asked a question. He hoped it was still about trying new food and took a guess. "I wouldn't know where to start."

Lach positively lit up. "Ibiza."

"Beg pardon?"

"Ibiza. We'll be passing right by there. We can stop off, see the sights, eat some food—"

Thanatos raised an eyebrow at him. "Starving people?"

Lach frowned for a second, but then his face cleared. "Sure, but it's still spring. We have time. And once we have the scythe, we can fix it right away. Maybe even retroactively, but messing with time might not be a great idea, even if it can do that."

It probably could fix the harvest retroactively, but Lach was right—it was a terrible idea. No one should alter the flow of time. To call such an endeavor dangerous was to call Aphrodite passingly attractive. It was an understatement of laughable magnitude.

"No altering time," he announced. "But you're probably right that one day won't make a difference."

Lach looked overjoyed, like he was going to vibrate out of his own skin as he sauntered over and set a bowl of oatmeal with honey and fruit in front of Thanatos.

"One day. We'll need to reprovision anyway, won't we?"

Silly grin still pasted across his face, Lach nodded. "Yep. We'll need to stop for food. No harm spending a few hours doing other things too."

Thanatos felt like he'd fallen into a trap, but he still couldn't see the net he'd caught himself in. He sighed and dug into his oatmeal. It was good. Of course it was. Everything was good.

Once again, they spent the afternoon on deck. Thanatos didn't know anything about sailing, but apparently it involved an occasionally shirtless

Lach climbing over every inch of the ship like an industrious ant. How he didn't lose his balance, Thanatos didn't know.

When the sun was high above, Lach looked over at him, grin on his face, and asked, "Want to learn how to fish?"

Thanatos wasn't sure he did. He'd brought death to many creatures in his life, but he'd never actively caused it. He wasn't sure he had the stomach for it. Still, that hopeful look on Lach's face had always been his downfall. He sighed and stood to join him.

Lach hopped up and started going through some small storage bins on the side of the deck, then frowning. "I'm sure I had extra gear somewhere." He stopped, sighed, and rolled his eyes. "Mis, sweetheart, can I please have the extra fishing gear?"

He pulled open the same container he'd just closed. It was twice as big as before and filled with fishing paraphernalia. For a moment, Thanatos stood there staring.

Then an all too familiar anger washed over him.

"It's a magic boat," he said, voice flat.

Lach turned to him, half smile still in place. "Sure. I told you—" His smile fell when he looked at Thanatos. "What's wrong? I did tell you she was magic. I swear I did."

"But your magical, size-changing boat somehow only has one bedroom," Thanatos spat. Because nothing could ever be what it seemed when Lach was involved. A magic boat that could probably be any size, and Lach had decided that they only needed one bedroom.

Lach sighed as though he were the victim in the situation. "I know. I'm sorry. I tried, I did, but—"

"Did you really think it was going to work? That the slightest inconvenience would make me fall right back into bed with you?" Thanatos shook his head and took a step back, almost losing his balance because he wasn't looking where he was going. Wasn't that just what he needed—to fall off the boat and make a complete ass of himself?

Lach reached for him, eyes filled with what looked like concern, but he jerked away.

He hopped back down to the bench, where at least he was unlikely to fall overboard. "Is that all this is? A convenient chance to screw a god again? What's wrong, Hermes not available?"

"He is, actually!" Lach exploded. "He practically offered last time I saw him."

"Then go find Hermes." Thanatos turned away. He should go. Where, though? He could find the pull of a soul who needed him. Or he could run. Go to a cemetery in New York and go back to see Prometheus.

There was a sigh behind him. "Thanatos. She's magic, but she doesn't always listen to me. I tried. I asked her to have a second cabin." There was a thumping sound like Lach was banging his head on the side of the boat. "Why the hell do you think I've been sleeping on that damned bench in the mess? I'm trying not to make you uncomfortable!"

He sounded sincere.

"Thanatos?" Lach sounded small and worried, and that was strange on the obnoxious, larger-than-life pirate. "Please don't go."

"I need to think," Thanatos told him, and turned to go below deck. When he got there, the closet door popped open, and there was a second cabin beyond.

Dammit.

Thanatos sighed, went into the cabin he'd been staying in, the cabin that smelled of Lach and held all the things that defined the man, and threw himself on the bed.

NO BED FOR LACH

Dumbfounded, Lach stood on the deck and watched Thanatos go below. The god could have disappeared in an instant with no way back. It could've been worse.

Or maybe he was going down to grab something he'd left behind and would be gone by the time Lach got there.

Standing there with the midday sun beating on his bare back, Lach was frozen. Helpless.

When he sighed, all the strength holding him up rushed out with his breath. He sank down onto the bench and raked his hand through his hair. It was tied back, but pieces came loose and hung around his face.

The vinyl stuck to his bare back.

"Gods damn it all."

He dropped his head back and stared up at the bright sky. No choice but to follow.

But when he got downstairs, the first thing he saw was the second open cabin. Empty.

"So now you'll help me," he grumbled to Mis.

Chances were, Thanatos was already gone. And Lach was too chicken shit to go find out for himself.

Instead, he walked into the empty cabin. Innocuous and clean,

Thanatos might've liked it better than Lach's own room. With another heaving sigh, he sat down on the bed.

"I really fucked up," he said to no one in particular. Maybe Mis. She needed to hear it.

This time, on this particular day, maybe the fuckup hadn't been his own. But he'd fucked up plenty. Three thousand years ago, he'd looked Thanatos in the eye and said he didn't want him. Because he was a dick. A complete asshole. Wrong on every possible level. And damn it, because he'd been scared.

Lach had been thirty-five, and people in his village were starting to notice that he wasn't aging. His brother, Philon—broad and hale from their improved fortunes after Lach had killed that cow and impressed Poseidon—had started to look older than Lach ever would.

There had been whispers about the influence of gods, his mother's infidelity, and witchcraft. Lach had known he had to leave Thrinacia, his family, and everything he'd known behind. And the only person he could take with him—Thanatos—he'd run scared from, because he hadn't really understood what forever meant. He hadn't thought it was possible that Thanatos might care for the thieving son of a fish monger for that long. So he'd hurt Thanatos before he could get hurt.

Just as he was getting ready to sink into a sulk to rival all sulks, the bed under him lurched. The open end lifted, folding toward the headboard, lifting Lach off the ground.

Panicked, he tumbled off. No sooner than his feet hit the floor than the bed did too. It could stay, but it wasn't for him. Mis was kicking him out.

There were two options—he could sit up there, do nothing, and risk Thanatos disappearing; or he could try.

"Fine, fine. I get it. Asshole boat." He'd have to apologize for that later.

The short distance to the back cabin felt like the longest stretch Lach had ever walked. The tight worry in his chest loosened when he knocked on the door and cracked it open to find Thanatos there on the bed, facing away from the door.

"Hey," Lach said softly.

Thanatos only grunted in return.

"I was scared you'd be gone," he admitted, leaning in the doorway.

"I just said I needed to think." All the stiffness that had seeped out of

Thanatos earlier in the day had returned in full force. Lach could see it in the rigid lines of his back, hear it in his voice.

"Do you mind if I come in?"

"It's your room," Thanatos replied sullenly.

Thanatos sat up. He swung his legs around, like he couldn't stand to lie vulnerable with Lach there in the room.

"I know. But thinking's going to bring you to the obvious conclusion that you shouldn't be here." Lach tried to make it a joke, but Thanatos didn't smile, and it only made Lach's heart ache. "I thought maybe we could talk instead."

He crossed the small room and dropped to his knees. Thanatos tucked his chin and turned away. With a single tentative finger, Lach touched Thanatos's chin and turned his head toward him. For a second, Thanatos's gaze stayed trained the other way. When he finally looked at him, Lach smiled weakly and dropped his hand to Thanatos's thigh. He knew he should've kept his distance, that Thanatos didn't want him there, but if he could hold him, maybe he wouldn't disappear. Or maybe this was his last chance to touch him at all.

"Listen, I'm *really* sorry about the misunderstanding. I could've been clearer. When we were in DC, Mis did have a second room, but it disappeared."

"Why?" Thanatos crossed his arms, and Lach couldn't blame him for wanting to protect himself. Lach had never understood why he, a god, had ever let him in, in the first place.

Lach's throat constricted. Vulnerability had never been his strong suit, but he was trying. Maybe if Thanatos knew that he could hurt Lach now, that'd make up in some part for the hurt Lach had caused him.

"Misericordia is supposed to give her captain what they need. It's . . . it's not always what I want, or what I ask for, but what she thinks would make things better for me. And she—she knows I've been . . . lonely."

Thanatos was staring at him with eyes wide enough that Lach could see the whites all around his irises. Any second now, he was going to laugh and tell him tough shit, so Lach scrambled to explain.

"But it's not her fault. She doesn't know how I hurt you. She can just tell how much I want—" Lach broke off. His stomach twisted three-hundred-and-sixty degrees right in the middle. Thanatos blinked at him, straightening and leaning back a fraction.

Desperately, Lach squeezed his thighs with both hands. "I know. I know I don't have any right to say I want you after what I did. I'm sorry. It's my fault she took away the second cabin. She misunderstood. That's why I slept out there. I really wanted you to stay, and I didn't want to push you for anything else. I just . . . I don't know. I missed you and thought maybe this was a chance to—"

Lach sat back on his heels, sighed, and hung his head. None of this was coming out well. Thanatos had the right of it—this whole plan was selfish. Lach wanted more than he had any right to ask. Everything he'd done had been manufactured to get Thanatos to give him another chance. None of it had anything to do with what was best for Thanatos.

"Doesn't matter," he said to the floor. "You should go. You're here because I said we needed to plan—we don't. Plan for what? And you're seasick, and . . . I get it. If I were in your shoes, I wouldn't want to spend time with me either. It was selfish and shitty of me to ask you to come. I thought, I don't know, that it might be fun to go together, but you've got way more important things to do than babysit my miserable ass." Lach couldn't think of a single compelling reason for Thanatos to stay with him.

Suddenly, Thanatos's fingers were in his hair. He slipped the cord out of it. It made a soft, muffled sound as it fell on the floor behind him. When his fingers clenched, pulling just enough to send needles of pleasure down Lach's spine, Thanatos coaxed him to look up.

He did it slowly. The thing about those finely made slacks Thanatos wore was that the soft fabric didn't hide a goddamn thing. Lach could see the outline of his cock, hard and trapped behind gray silk.

It was difficult to drag his eyes away, up his chest, hardly moving for his shallow breaths, to his half-lidded eyes.

"Thanatos?" Against good sense, Lach slipped his hands higher up his warm thighs.

HALLELUJAH

It was the worst idea he'd had in centuries. Maybe millennia.

But the second Lach had slipped to his knees in front of him, Thanatos had been lost to anything but him.

It was like the old days, yes, with beautiful, sweet Glaucus and his silver tongue, but Thanatos didn't lose himself to memory for a moment. Somehow, there was something as compelling about this older, newer, more measured man kneeling in front of him. Lach. He was the same man, but he wasn't.

There was an earnestness in his eyes that he had always covered in ten layers of snark and bullshit before. Maybe the years had made Lach a better liar, or maybe, just maybe, they had made him someone Thanatos could be friends with.

Friends with erections.

There was none of his usual wicked grin when Lach slid his hands toward the apex of Thanatos's thighs. He went slow, making eye contact, waiting to be rebuffed.

Thanatos wanted to tell him he wouldn't get a no, but he couldn't even form the coherence to say yes. All he could do was meet Lach's eyes and remember to breathe, and that was hard enough.

"Just—" Lach licked his lips, glancing down at where his fingers were encroaching on Thanatos's fly and then immediately back up. "I'm trusting you to say something if you want me to stop, yeah? Just a word. A push. Anything, I swear I'll be across the room in a second, hands to myself, and we can pretend I never—"

Thanatos reached out to cup Lach's cheek in one hand, and Lach turned into it like a flower to the sun. Something in his eyes opened up at the contact, and only then did Thanatos understand how guarded he'd been since their reunion. Lach had never been one to play things close to his chest, but somehow he had been, and without Thanatos noticing.

He needed the words, Thanatos realized. He didn't need the absence of refusal; he needed acceptance. That was it. Thanatos had to make a decision. The last time he'd agreed to what Lach offered, it had resulted in a few wild, joyous years together, followed by the rending of his heart into a million scattered pieces.

This was different, though, wasn't it? Lach wasn't staring up at him with those same guileless eyes, asking for everything. This was just for now. This was a mission with a time limit. They had to find the scythe and save the harvest, and then they would part ways again. Thanatos could do this, could have this, and not have his heart torn out again.

Couldn't he?

"I'm not—" His voice came out rough, and he had to stop and clear his throat. "I'm not saying no."

Lach's shoulders slumped, and for a second, Thanatos thought it was in disappointment. The way he practically dove for Thanatos said something else, though. His fingers trembled as he used both hands to undo the buttons and slide down the zipper.

He reached in and pulled at the waistband of Thanatos's boxers, uncovering his cock and staring like it was a precious artifact. He wet his lips and looked back to Thanatos's eyes, checking again for permission, granted with an encouraging nod.

The feeling of Lach's lips wrapped around the head of his dick was perfection. He had missed this so much. Not just the blow jobs, but the way the man hummed around him, the way his right hand automatically slipped down to cup Thanatos's ass, like he needed to press himself even closer.

Lach gave blow jobs like he did everything: with his whole self.

His eyes fluttered shut as he lost focus on the world around him. He slowly worked his way down Thanatos's cock, licking around it to ease the friction of lips on skin until he managed to get halfway. Then he started bobbing up and down, a tiny bit at a time, taking a little more with each return.

His left hand slipped down to mirror the right, squeezing Thanatos's ass beneath his slacks and pulling him in deeper and deeper, until Lach's nose met his groin. They let out simultaneous grunts of satisfaction, Lach humming and Thanatos having to brace himself to keep from bucking upward.

Lach didn't like that tension, though, giving an annoyed noise and pulling Thanatos into him, indicating he should go ahead and thrust forward. Like Lach didn't need to breathe.

Thanatos decided not to fight. He let Lach manhandle him, bent to Lach's need to be in charge even when giving himself completely. He planted his hands behind him on the bed and leaned back, then let himself melt into Lach, who pulled his hips up. He swallowed around the head of his cock for several euphoric seconds before slowly pulling back.

He pulled completely off to draw a deep breath, but a second later he was back, sliding his lips around the head, laving his tongue over the frenulum so lightly that it was almost a tease. When Thanatos's ass clenched in the effort to remain where he was, Lach again pulled his hips up and pushed his mouth down.

He started a quick rhythm, bobbing up and down, sucking lightly as he came up and swallowing when he bottomed out, the muscles of his throat working around the head of Thanatos's dick.

"L—Lach—" Thanatos stuttered. He wasn't sure if it had been eternity or a few seconds, but he was done. When Lach turned those blue eyes up to meet his, full of fire and want, he couldn't hold back.

His head, his whole body, fell back onto the bed, arching up into Lach as he came and came. He was left feeling as though his soul had departed his body, leaving behind a sweaty, panting husk. It was a damn sight different, and so very much better, than the last time he'd found himself in that position on the same bed.

It took him a moment to shake off the post orgasmic haze and remember he wasn't alone. He had a partner in this.

The end of the bed dipped with Lach's weight, and he looked nervous when Thanatos lifted his head to stare down at him. He opened his mouth and closed it a few times, and Thanatos thought they might be feeling the same way. He pushed himself up on his elbows and motioned toward the tent in Lach's own trousers, question in his eyes.

Lach shook his head, and his cheeks flushed. Thanatos took it to mean he either didn't want reciprocation, which was concerning, or didn't need it. It wouldn't have been the first time Lach had come without help while giving head, so he decided to give the situation the benefit of the doubt. He didn't want to think about what the other might mean.

Instead of focusing on what he was being denied, he simply let himself fall back onto the bed. He took a deep breath, then another, and in a move that he thought might be the biggest mistake he'd made in centuries, he put his arm across the empty half of the bed and looked up to meet Lach's eyes. "Nap?" He let his eyes fall back to the empty spot next to himself.

Before he could glance back up or properly ask the question he intended, Lach was filling the empty space. He pressed his back against Thanatos's side, head pillowed on his arm. The position was comfortable, but somehow dissatisfying, since it hid Lach's face from him.

Still, it was warm and present, and it felt damned good.

Less than five minutes later, Lach was snoring softly, still pressed tight against him.

He could imagine Charon's recriminations already. Calling Lach a trash pirate, a no-good fish-herder, and maybe a few slurs about his mother copulating with sheep. Maybe when everything was said and done, that was what Thanatos would need: reminders of all of Lach's failings and why Thanatos didn't want him at all.

Maybe Lach would leave him feeling used up and empty inside.

For the moment, he felt warm and soft and sated like he hadn't in so very long. He wanted to keep feeling that way for as long as possible. Was that so wrong of him?

With his free hand, he pulled up his boxers and somehow managed to zip his fly without damaging the silk underwear or skin beneath. Then he turned to spoon Lach.

They hadn't ever done that before.

Lach had always needed to be the big spoon—the one in the position of power, relatively speaking. Thanatos had never blamed him. There was a huge power deficit in a relationship between a god and a human, and he'd never begrudged Lach wanting to reclaim some ground.

This position didn't feel like he had power over the other man, though. It felt more like trust.

But that was silly. Lach had just gotten comfortable and fallen asleep. The position didn't mean anything.

Once they found the scythe, it would be over again, and Lach would be gone.

Hells, Lach would probably be gone in a few hours. He'd always been good at sneaking out in the middle of the night. Even when he hadn't been running away, he'd never liked to face the morning in Thanatos's arms.

The idea of waking up alone had him feeling cold even as he fell asleep with a warm lover in his arms.

When he woke to bright blue eyes looking into his, he couldn't stop his traitorous heart from leaping. It was too much. He couldn't hope for this. He couldn't want this. It would end with him picking up the pieces of his heart again, and how could he survive that?

Still, he couldn't bring himself to pull away when Lach leaned in and kissed him on the cheek, stale breath and all, and smiled at him. It was an open smile, less pirate and more lover, and it was the most dangerous thing he'd ever seen.

Maybe he was a weak man, but he wasn't capable of turning his back on that smile. He could feel his heart breaking already.

THE LAST OF THE MELON

Lach woke up from his nap to the soft gaze of the man he loved. He had no idea how to tell him that it didn't matter how long it'd been or what he'd said—Lach loved him. He also didn't think Thanatos would believe him. The fact remained that he had said those things and had to live with the consequences.

"Hi," Lach whispered.

"Hi."

For a moment, they only stared at each other. The more seconds ticked by, the larger the silence grew. Suddenly, Thanatos popped up.

"Hungry?" he asked.

Already, Thanatos was getting out of bed and straightening his clothes. Lach had no idea how he managed to keep them so clean—it must have been a god thing. Or a Thanatos thing. Lach had never seen him unkempt before, but he hadn't had the kind of access to him that he had now. There wasn't a ton of privacy on a sailboat.

"Yeah," Lach said, pushing up on his arm, "I could eat."

For Thanatos, eating was an indulgence; for Lach, it was a necessity. He might be immortal, but he was still human.

"Do you mind if I shower first?" Lach asked and nodded toward the door to the bathroom. There was another near the front of the cabin, but all of Lach's things were in this one. Well, and now Thanatos had to think about him wet and naked.

"Sure," Thanatos said.

Before Lach could ask him to join, Thanatos left the room. "Such a weirdo," Lach muttered. He'd had Thanatos's cock in his throat. Lach might not deserve a return on that pleasure, but he wanted the god's company anyway.

Watching someone as high-strung as Thanatos lose himself like that was something else. Lach had always loved knowing that he could do that to not just a god, but Thanatos particularly. He might not have a lick of magic of his own, but that'd always been Lach's own special brand—using his hands, his mouth, every part of himself to make Thanatos tremble and fall apart. And gods, the way Thanatos said his name as he did . . . just thinking about it, Lach might need to take care of a thing or two in the shower.

With a sigh, Lach pulled off his trousers and threw them in a hamper. Mis would take care of them. He'd never appreciated how damn convenient magic was until he had her.

Once he'd cleaned off, Lach joined Thanatos in the mess. Already, he was arranging dinner on a tray. Most of the food he'd made didn't take much preparation—the last of the melon, some sliced cheese, toast, and jam. They took it up to the deck to eat and watch the sun go down.

"Thanatos?" Lach asked as the sky turned from purple to an inky, dark blue.

Thanatos swallowed around a bite of toast with strawberry jam heaped on top and straightened his shoulders. "Yeah?"

"What's it like to die?"

On a slow exhale, Thanatos relaxed. "I don't actually know. I've never done that part. I can tell you about afterward though. It's peaceful. People spend their days doing what makes them happiest. Families are reunited."

Lach hummed. He'd never been at peace with the idea of death. Even when he'd been mortal, he'd expected to go out hard—starvation or violence would be his undoing.

"Only if they're all in Elysium," Lach said.

Thanatos shot him a measured glance. "You don't think your brother and father made it?"

Lach laughed. At their family's most desperate, his father had never been anything but a good man. Philon had been safe and comfortable for most of his life, while Lach had never been able to trust their blessings once they got them. "No. I am completely sure they both made it to Elysium."

Thanatos only stared at him, blinking his wide, gorgeous eyes. "You don't think you'd go to Elysium?"

"Do you think I would?"

"Of course!"

Lach crossed his arms and leaned away. "Thanatos, I've stolen, murdered, pissed off more than one god. Every faith in the world is pretty clear on what kind of person I am and where I'd end up."

A faint line wrinkled the smooth skin between Thanatos's brows. "I wouldn't let you go to Tartarus."

Lach started and uncrossed his arms. "I appreciate that."

Once, Lach had thought Thanatos might top the list of people who wanted to watch him suffer, but he'd always been so much better than Lach could understand—much, much better than he'd ever deserved.

Thanatos's genuine decency terrified him. The people he'd let down— his father, Philon, Thanatos—were always so damnably good. Always deserved better. And, as always, Lach crumbled under the weight of their acceptance when he'd never lived up to it.

"Guess I haven't lost all my skills in the sack, if you'd do me a solid like that."

With a heaving sigh, Thanatos pushed himself off the bench and shoved his dirty plate on top of Lach's. "Good night, Lach."

While he watched, Thanatos disappeared down below one stair at a time. Made sense. Hell, it was something of a relief to know he was still exasperating.

For a while longer, he watched the stars brighten. When he got up, he cleaned their dishes—even peeked around the corner to see Thanatos had shut the door to his room.

Now that there were two cabins, there was no reason for Lach to be so uncomfortable. He made his way to the second one.

At first, he pressed his hand down on the mattress, testing Mis's patience. Nothing happened, but when he sat down, it became clear that she'd decided he had no right to the extra bed. It folded up toward the wall, leaving Lach to scramble off the side and tumble onto the floor or become part of the ship.

For three nights after that, Lach tried the bed. Mis didn't give an inch, and he wound up sleeping on the bench in the mess every night with a crick in his neck, thinking about the god in the other room, wondering if he was sleeping. Maybe he was making his way through *3rd Rock from the Sun* with the sound turned down and the subtitles on—who knew?

On the fourth night, Lach was staring at that bench after dinner. He hadn't wanted to displace Thanatos from his bedroom, and apparently, it hadn't occurred to him to leave. That almost felt like a victory in itself—Thanatos preferred to stay in Lach's space, in Lach's bedroom, in the middle of Lach's things. Only he hadn't asked Lach to share it with him.

That left Lach with two options: he could ask to sleep in his own bed, offering Thanatos the empty cabin and potentially kicking him out of the room he'd stayed in since they started this trip, or he could continue to sleep on that blasted bench.

All trip, he'd picked the path of least resistance, afraid that if he asked for a little, it'd be too much, and Thanatos would leave. If Thanatos had wanted him in his bed, he would ask, right?

But maybe, if Thanatos meant to go, he would've already gone. He wouldn't care if Lach wound up in Elysium or Tartarus.

Stepping softly on bare feet, Lach made his way to the rear cabin and knocked on the door.

"Come in." Thanatos's voice was muffled, but when Lach opened the door, he was sitting up in the bed, wearing Lach's pajamas. Of course Thanatos had dug deep into his drawers to find the matching set of flannel pj's that Lach never bothered with. That explained some of how his clothes always looked so fresh; Mis took care of them at night.

He set a book down on the nightstand. Lach didn't have many of them, but he had a few. He leaned toward the bed to get a better look.

"*Binti?*"

Thanatos shrugged. "Your library's small. And it's a good book."

"It's a *great* book."

"Don't tell me you're looking forward to space travel."

Lach chuckled. "I've always wondered if Mis could fly."

With a shrug, Thanatos said, "Sure. Sounds like you. Can't be satisfied with a magic boat. Now you want her to fly."

Thanatos's smile didn't meet his eyes, and Lach felt a weight settle uncomfortably in his stomach. He could appreciate what he had. Sort of.

Okay, so he didn't take time to smell the roses all that often. When Lach got what he wanted—treasure, immortality, the best pizza in the city—he enjoyed it for one second, and the next, he was thinking about what else he needed to hoard and steal for himself.

Lach forced a grin. "If Mis never flew, she'd still be the best thing I've got," he mumbled, straightening.

Thanatos nodded. "Did you need something?"

At that, a weak laugh escaped Lach. He rubbed the back of his neck. "Well, a favor."

Thanatos only raised his eyebrows in invitation to continue.

"Mis, light of my life, joy of my days"—at Lach's obvious flattery, Thanatos scoffed—"won't let me sleep in the second cabin."

"What do you mean?" Thanatos asked.

"She takes away the bed."

"Sorry?" His dark brows furrowed.

"Like folds it up. Throws me off. Apparently, it's not mine. But the bench is *really* uncomfortable." Lach grimaced. That antsy, prickling feeling returned—a warning not to push his luck too far. It'd been days since Thanatos had let Lach into his bed, and after their encounter, Thanatos hadn't mentioned it at all. He'd been easier around Lach in some ways—they'd settled into a rhythm—but there seemed a firm line that Lach wasn't allowed to cross. Not a second time, anyway.

"Uh huh." That dry assessment said Thanatos thought he was up to something. He wasn't entirely wrong.

"I was wondering if I could sleep in here?"

Lach watched a cloud pass over Thanatos's face. His heart raced in his chest. This was wrong. He shouldn't have asked. What was a little discomfort?

Only Thanatos didn't look angry. "I apologize," he said, rolling out of bed. "I didn't think—do you mind if I take the book with me?"

"No! I mean, of course not. You can take it if you want, but you, um . . ." Lach swallowed hard. Forced another smile. "You don't *have* to go. If you don't want. You can. I think—I think she meant the other cabin as a space for you. But you could stay here. I'd prefer it, really."

Thanatos stared at him, the book clutched to his chest, incredulous. Heat swept up the back of Lach's neck. He shook his head.

"Not what I mean," Lach added. "Best behavior." He held up his right hand like there were something he could swear on. "I don't want to kick you out." He could see there on the tip of his tongue that Thanatos would say it was fine and be gone in a flash. "And I'd like the company," he added.

After all, their nap had been the best he'd slept in ages. There was something comforting about having Thanatos with him.

For a few moments, Lach thought he'd leave anyway, but Thanatos sighed through his nose and sank back onto the mattress. "I suppose I can stay."

Lach didn't try to stifle the grin on his face. "Great! That's great."

He stripped down to his boxers and climbed under the covers. He thought he caught Thanatos sneaking a peek, but Lach didn't comment. Instead, he dropped his head on the pillow and looked up at the god beside him.

Thanatos was content to let him have the victory. He opened the book in his lap again. "Will the light bother you?"

"Not a bit," Lach promised.

He fell asleep to the steady breathing of a god who never tired, the soft glow of a reading light, and a sense that he had half a shot in Hades of having more perfect nights like this.

In the morning, the second cabin was gone.

SWEET RED

Thanatos had been to Ibiza before, of course.

It would be difficult to find a corner of the world Thanatos hadn't visited hundreds, maybe thousands of times. He had never sailed into Ibiza just after dawn as he watched Lach eat some of the last bits of food in the ship's cupboard. He'd never imagined that crackers and jam could be sexy, but watching the man nibble a cracker was more distracting than he cared to dwell on.

One of the things that hadn't changed in the transformation from Glaucus to Lach was his keen awareness of food. The way he kept trying to feed Thanatos was a reminder of it, and he almost wanted to kick himself for how he'd forgotten.

Glaucus's family lived their entire existence in the shadow of starvation. His brother had been sickly for many years because of malnutrition, and it had almost certainly shaped Lach into the wiry, but never bulky, man that he was. Not like his bull of a father, or his brother, who'd grown to have broad shoulders and heavy muscles when their island had become prosperous.

Lach had been the one who chose to go without so that others could have, even to the point of trying to offer Thanatos the last of his breakfast. To the point where the threat of people starving was the most important thing in his universe.

More than once during their trip, he'd allowed himself to think, rather uncharitably, that Lach was less worried about their mission and more worried about what he could get out of it. He'd even allowed himself to think, just for a second, that maybe Lach had some ulterior motive for wanting the scythe.

Sure, he worked for Gaia, and finding the scythe to make the plants grow was in keeping with her agenda. That didn't mean Lach didn't plan to use it for himself somewhere along the way.

But that wasn't it at all.

The way he kept trying to press the last cracker from his breakfast into the hands of a god who didn't truly need it; that was the way Lach thought of food. Lach needed everyone well fed, always, and putting anyone but himself last made him uncomfortable.

Meanwhile, humans might not be starving yet, but the concern that they would be made Thanatos hesitant to accept those crackers, whether Lach needed them or not. Perhaps his consumption wouldn't take food from someone who could have used it better, but there was no way to know that.

Thanatos was half distracted from his brooding as he watched Lach go through the steps to moor the boat, or dock it, or whatever that was called. His lithe form flowed through the motions like the water beneath his feet. Anyone who watched him would know that he'd done it thousands of times. He grinned up at Thanatos when he finished, satisfaction and pleasure written all over his face.

Thanatos, despite his comfort with his own form, was not going to jump off the boat and trust that he would land on his feet. Lach was practically born to the sea, and Thanatos was definitely not. He stepped onto the dock hesitantly, and strangely, when his feet hit stable ground for the first time in ages, he felt even more wobbly. The wood planks beneath his feet seemed to roll like the deck of the boat always had. Was this simply his new state of being, the rolling of a boat beneath his feet?

"You'll be okay," Lach told him, seeming to read his mind but probably just noting his awkward body language. "It's always like that for a little while."

"I'm fine." He nodded as though to punctuate the sentence, but the motion made him a little dizzy, so he stopped and stood there for a moment.

Lach pretended not to notice. He pulled his phone out of his pocket and waved it around. "I've gotta stop and make a call before we get going, but then Ibiza's all ours." He lifted his free hand as though to take Thanatos's, but then his gaze skittered away, and his hand dropped limply to his side.

He turned half away and fiddled with his cell phone for a while. Thanatos wondered if he struggled to get a signal on the thing. In cellphone years, it was as old as Thanatos himself, and it was a wonder it still got a signal at all. Maybe that was Thanatos's own problem. He was so old that his receiver was broken.

"—yeah," Lach said, grabbing his attention. "We're in Ibiza, so we're a couple of days out yet. Find what you were looking for in Brazil?" He turned, and when he found Thanatos watching him, he gave a cocky wink.

Thanatos had to bite his tongue to keep from commenting on the return of the snarky sailor. It shouldn't have been a surprise, though. Lach had always been different with other people than with him. Back then, he'd thought it made him something special.

"Do you need someone to pick you up in—" Lach flinched and sighed. "Yes, I know you're perfectly capable of getting there yourself. I was offering to help is all. Okay! We'll see you in four days. Santorini. Yep." He pulled the phone away from his ear and stabbed the end-call button harder than Thanatos suspected was necessary.

"Not your biggest fan?" Thanatos asked.

Lach sighed. "Nah, it's not that. Sometimes in the field, after a while of every guy offering to help because they think she can't do her job, Martina gets defensive."

"So you offering to help was suggesting she was incompetent."

That earned another sigh. "Yeah, pretty much. My fault. I know better."

Thanatos considered for a moment, then shrugged. "Or maybe she should know you better."

He didn't know why he was feeling protective of Lach—okay, he knew exactly why—but he didn't feel like censoring himself on it. Lach was one of the only men he knew who probably deserved the benefit of the doubt in matters of sexism. Chaos knew that most of the gods didn't.

Lach gave another shrug. "It's fine. I think she's tired. And it sounds like her last job didn't go so hot."

Thanatos was about to launch into another defense, but he stopped himself. For all he knew, this woman was a lover or someone else of importance in Lach's life, and there was no reason to jump in. Instead, he turned to look at the island before them. "Where do we start?"

"Groceries," Lach said, tone definite.

"That's not the last thing on the way back to the boat?"

The pirate grin was back. "Nope. You get the boat ready to leave before anything else, in case things go pear shaped and you need to make a speedy exit. Don't wanna be stuck on the open sea without having stocked up."

Thanatos groaned. "That's happened to you before, hasn't it?"

"The real question here would be: 'How many times has that happened to you?'—don't you think?" Lach's laughter, despite the subject, was uplifting. He was an ass, as always, but he was so damned happy about it that Thanatos couldn't do anything but sigh and shake his head in mock consternation.

Food shopping with Lach was exactly what he'd expected. It was like grocery shopping with a kid who'd been shotgunning full-sugar soda. He wanted to get some of everything and didn't spend a moment thinking about cost or nutritional value. Thanatos wondered how he'd survived the years, filling his boat with chocolate and bottles of wine.

"I think man might need more than wine alone," Thanatos pointed out as Lach selected a second bottle to add to his basket. The price on the bottle was ridiculous for something that would be gone in a few hours.

Lach offered him an expression of feigned shock and turned to a nearby woman. "You believe this guy?" He hooked a thumb in Thanatos's direction. "I know he's gorgeous, but how's a guy get to be this age and think buying wine is optional when you're in Spain?"

She glanced between them and giggled before tucking her wine into her basket.

"See?" Lach asked him. "She knows what's up."

"She probably doesn't speak English."

Lach had pulled a third bottle off the shelf and paused in putting it into his basket to point it at Thanatos. "I'll have you know most of the people around here speak English. Too many helpless American tourists not to."

"So now you're a helpless American tourist?" Thanatos asked, pulling the bottle out of his hands to look at it. Sweet and red, no surprise. Lach had always loved sweet things.

Lach shrugged, clearly shameless. "It's an easy explanation. Plus it means I don't have to try telling people why my Greek slang is a few centuries out of date."

"You could try Norwegian," Thanatos suggested.

Lach turned a bright, beaming smile on him. "I knew you were listening!"

A tiny part of Thanatos was still screaming that he should deny, roll his eyes, and walk away. Instead, he sighed, set the bottle in the cart, set his hand on top of Lach's where it rested on the cart's handle, and followed where Lach led.

ACROSS THE STYX

After restocking Misericordia's larders with only the finest vino—okay, and some actual food—they got lunch at a restaurant that overlooked the water. The way the sun shone turned it a deep turquoise that sparkled at the corner of his sight. Lach might not have Thanatos's charm or wit, but when he got butter on his cheek and gave the god a saucy wink, he got a laugh anyway.

And damn if that weren't the best sound in the world. Back when Lach still thought he was human—not the half-cocked mistake he was now—Thanatos had laughed with him all the time. He'd let Lach under his careful reserve, but Lach had never understood why. He wasn't special or important. Sure, he heard about gods taking mortal lovers, but beauties and princes and magicians whose talents dwarfed Lach's very impressive skill at sailing a boat who, frankly, didn't need his help. Special people. Not the demanding, entitled sons of fish mongers who didn't know what was good for them.

Thanatos's care now, his distance, was more in keeping with Lach's expectations. But sometimes the god slipped up. He'd laugh or touch his hand—all small hints that Lach might not be as hopeless as he thought. After all, they were on land, and Thanatos had agreed to spend the day with him.

"You like it?" Lach asked, nodding toward the glass in Thanatos's hand. They'd just finished off a bottle of wine.

"What, you want to hear how right you were?" Thanatos set it down between them. Though he cocked his head in challenge, there was a gleam in his eyes. He wasn't *that* annoyed.

"Oh, I don't need to hear it. I already know." He wiped his hands off on his napkin and stood. "Since you obviously liked it, order another bottle. And something for dessert. Whatever you want."

"Where are you going?" Thanatos asked.

"Well. Human." He gestured down his own front. "I know you're extra special with your optional self-care and bodily necessities, but I kind of need the loo."

Blankly, Thanatos stared at him. "Lach, you're not British."

"No, but I have spent enough time on the queen's fair isles that I've earned the right to use any bloody slang I want."

With an exaggerated eye roll, Thanatos slumped back in his seat and reached for the drinks and desserts menu.

Lach found the restroom down a short hall on the opposite side of the restaurant. On the way back, he glanced over a community board.

Two steps past it, the only posting that mattered—maybe in the whole world—finally registered. He doubled back, snatched the poster off the wall, and rushed back to their table, where another bottle of wine had already been opened.

"I got the flaó. The waiter said—"

"Styx is playing in Ibiza."

"O-*kay*?"

"Styx. One of the top five greatest bands of all time—"

"Depending on who you ask—"

"Is playing tonight. In Ibiza. We have to go." Lach tapped the poster in front of Thanatos. "It's Styx! Have you ever seen Styx? You have to see Styx."

"I've seen the river," Thanatos offered.

Lach made a sound, high and tight in the back of his throat. This wasn't a matter for joking.

"Oh, Lach." Thanatos's dark eyes swam with concern. "Aren't most of the band members kind of . . . getting on?"

"First of all, how dare you? Second, maybe. But that's why we *have* to go. How many more concerts do you think they'll have left?"

"On this plane? Not many."

Lach froze. "Are you telling me that, in Hades, there are a bunch of great fucking musicians lounging around, giving concerts all the time? Are you saying, if I died, I could go see Tom Petty? I could go see Tom Petty in concert every gods damned day?" He dropped into his seat, his legs splayed out before him.

Thanatos refilled his wine glass, losing the battle to keep his lips turned downward. "If that's what would make Tom Petty happy in Elysium, then yeah. I guess it's possible."

Lach threw his head back. "What the hell am I doing still alive then?" he demanded. "If I get myself killed, at least I'll have that."

"Always something to look forward to."

Before he thought about it, Lach nodded enthusiastically, but as Thanatos's slow smile spread, Lach bit the edges of his tongue. Thanatos had glorious warmth in his eyes that Lach absorbed like a man trapped in the Arctic, desperate for it. Tom Petty was great; Thanatos was better.

"Fantastic as that would be, could you come with me? I mean, going to concerts alone is okay, but—you could come, right?"

Thanatos frowned. "Well, no. That's not really . . . how it works. I help souls find where they're going, but Elysium's not a place for gods to stay."

"Well, there you go. Guess I have to keep ticking."

Thanatos rolled his eyes. "You might tire of it one day."

With a deep breath, Lach tried to dislodge the heaviness that sat on his chest. Much as he didn't want to admit it, yeah, he might get tired one day. Spending every day alone, without people like him, without anybody, got old. It was hard to imagine how that feeling might outweigh his fear of what came after, especially if it meant he'd be somewhere he couldn't find Thanatos, but it could happen.

But damn it all, they were going to see Styx, and this was not the day for that kind of anguished self-reflection.

"So we can go to the show?" Lach asked, leaning forward in his seat. He clasped his hands together under the table.

"We can go."

"Awesome!"

The waiter returned with their dessert. It was fantastic, but in his excitement, Lach shoveled his half in his mouth—well, maybe a little more than his half. Guiltily, he scooted the plate with the last bite across the table. Thanatos smiled around his fork as he ate it.

"We could get another," Lach suggested.

Thanatos shook his head. "Things like that are always more enjoyable the first time."

Lach bunched up his napkin, dropped it on the table, and did his best not to think about what other indulgences might only be pleasant for one round.

After lunch, they made their way toward the outdoor amphitheater. Maybe the show was sold out, but any Styx concert would have scalpers, right? Even venues that cracked down on them had a hard time getting rid of them completely.

It'd been a while since Lach had seen a concert, but they were special. Even if he went alone, by the time the band started, he always felt like he was a part of something bigger than himself. As they approached the amphitheater, he got the itch of that feeling again.

He didn't notice the music already floating through the air around them, until Thanatos stopped to listen to it. The god stared, rapt, at a weathered man and his guitar.

"Do you want to stay and listen?" Lach mumbled after a few minutes.

Thanatos refocused on him. At the very corners, his eyes wrinkled in a grimace. Before he could apologize, Lach reached down and squeezed his hand.

"It's fine," Lach said. "You stay here. I'll get us tickets and be back before the song's over."

He let go of Thanatos's hand and slipped through the crowds. There were a few shady looking guys around, but no one he asked had tickets left for sale. Disappointment began to creep icy tendrils into his chest. Maybe Thanatos would do that god thing—push on mortals a little to get what he wanted—but Lach didn't think that he'd ever made a habit of that, and he definitely wouldn't do it so he could go to a concert Thanatos was mostly ambivalent about.

When he was about to give up, a man grabbed his arm.

"Hi. Sorry, were you looking for tickets?"

The man had hazel eyes, pale skin, and an American accent.

"Yeah. Definitely. I'd pay top dollar if you've got any."

The man smiled. "No reason for all that. I'm just looking to get back what we paid. We overdid it with all the sightseeing yesterday. Wife's got a sprained ankle, and we're not gonna make it tonight."

Lach tried to keep the smile off his face. A woman was hurt; it was nothing to be happy about. But he thought about going with Thanatos on an actual date. Music, singing, dancing under the open sky. He couldn't help it.

"Here—" Lach dug in his wallet. He was old fashioned. Cash was all right, but he didn't trust credit cards. Seemed skeevy, spending money you didn't already have. "This cover it?"

"Sure does!" The man passed him the tickets and took the cash. "I hope you have a great time, uh—"

"Lach."

"Nice to meet you, Lach. I'm Roger."

Roger shook his hand. There was something intent in the way he looked at Lach that was a little weird—just 'cause his wife was out of commission didn't mean Roger was. He could've been looking for a little something extra.

"Thanks so much, Roger! I hope your wife feels better."

Lach wasn't in the market for anything extra. He went back to Thanatos and waved the tickets triumphantly. "Got 'em!"

"That's nice." Thanatos's voice was dreamy, but the musician had stopped playing. He was taking a break, resting his fingers while one of his admirers offered to buy him a drink.

"Yeah," Lach said. "It'll be a good time. Guaranteed."

Thanatos still wasn't looking at him but far off in the distance. An old part of Lach remembered that distraction. His heart started to sink.

"I have to go."

"What?" Lach demanded.

At the sharpness in Lach's voice, Thanatos looked directly at him and frowned. "Someone needs me, Lach. It's been more than a week since I've seen to my duties."

Lach flinched. That was some kind of reprimand. "Okay. I didn't mean to keep you from anything. I thought we were going to " With a heavy arm, he waved vaguely at the amphitheater.

Thanatos softened his gaze. Gently, he reached out and brushed his fingers across Lach's forearm. "We are. I'll be back in time. No more than an hour."

"Sure, yeah. Okay." This wasn't some kind of plot to get away from Lach; it only felt that way. He forced a smile. "Someone needs you. Better get to it so we don't miss the opener."

For a moment, Thanatos simply stood there watching him. Then he gave a short nod. In a shimmer and one beat of his heart, Thanatos was gone, leaving Lach standing there with tickets in his hand and worry creeping through his veins.

It'd been an hour and two minutes when Lach wandered into the graveyard, dragging his feet between stones. He'd made it all of forty-five minutes before he stopped waiting near the venue and went searching for Thanatos on his own.

Walking between the buried dead, grass bending under his feet, he could call for Thanatos, but he'd said he'd come back. Either he meant it or he didn't, but Lach didn't think calling would make a lick of difference. If nothing else, he might get frustrated with Lach's impatience.

With a sigh, he lowered himself onto a stone to wait. The sun was going down, the sky turning a soft, powdery purple, and Lach worried he'd be going to see Styx all by his lonesome.

Wasn't like that'd be any different from most of his other experiences.

"Lach?"

He spun to see Thanatos there, as put together as ever, eyes shining softly in the fading light.

"Hi. Yeah. Hey!" Lach hopped off the gravestone. Thanatos was staring at him like he'd lost his mind. "Ready to get down?"

"Excuse me?"

"Go to the show?"

In a long, exaggerated arc, Thanatos rolled his eyes. He tipped his head side to side. "Sure. I guess we can go."

"You're gonna love it." Lach bumped his arm against the god's.

And if Lach could do anything to help it, the band wouldn't be the only thing Thanatos loved.

TEMPORAL ARTS

Music was why Thanatos sometimes thought he understood mortals. Most mortal art was made with the intention that it outlive the artist. From modern art, to renaissance paintings, to classical sculpture, to cave paintings that predated written language, humanity had been striving to leave a mark on the future for as long as they had existed.

But music wasn't like that. Sure, with music notation, modern musicians could write down compositions for people to recreate, but it would always be just that: recreation.

Because the act of creating music was the art, all music was temporal. It lasted only as long as the notes lingered in the air, and two performances of the same piece of music would never be the same.

Musical performances were like human lives. However similar, no two could ever be alike, and as long as they lasted, there was something fascinating in them. Sometimes, they were stunningly beautiful. Sometimes they were so awful that you wanted to cover your ears and forget they existed. But no matter what else was true, they were always intriguing.

So while Thanatos didn't know anything about the band Lach was so enamored of, he was fascinated enough by the prospect of music to agree to go.

Lach, unsurprisingly, was obnoxious and loud. He sang along with every song, turning his bright grin on Thanatos and holding his hand out as he sang, "Come sail away with me." All Thanatos could do was roll his eyes. He didn't pull his hand away, though.

Thanatos didn't realize he was in trouble until he caught sight of Dionysus, being held aloft by people in the crowd. The god of excess spent most of his time in Washington, DC, at his club, but he was still known to show up at the occasional party or festival to remind the mortals of his existence.

Or at least to make the event in question a worldwide spectacle.

Dionysus had always cared more about his own enjoyment than the effect it had on everyone around him.

Nine times out of ten, if Thanatos saw Dionysus show up to a party, he left. The tenth was usually a party in Hades, where he figured the majority of attendees could handle themselves, and he usually avoided imbibing regardless.

For reasons he chose not to examine, this time, when Lach handed him a cup of wine, he took it. Similar cups were making their way throughout the crowd—the work of Dionysus, no doubt.

"I told you this would be awesome, didn't I?" Lach asked between numbers, yelling to make himself heard over the crowd.

The men in the band seemed energized, strutting and playing like men half their age. Thanatos suspected the concert would be the last pinnacle of their long careers, and something about it made the experience bigger.

He nodded to Lach, took another drink of wine, and smiled. "You did. And you were right."

Lach's snarky, arrogant grin turned into his genuine pleased one, and Thanatos remembered why he'd loved the man so damned much. So few immortals found joy in simple things like good music and a cup of wine. Either they were like his sister Eris, who had always found pleasure in horrible things, or they had turned cynical over the course of millennia and found their pleasure in ways that made Dionysus's madness seem innocent.

"Come on, stick in the mud," Lach demanded as the band started their first encore. "You can't just stand there and watch a concert this epic!"

And he threw his arms around Thanatos and danced.

So Thanatos danced with him.

Dionysus caught his eye from across the crowd and winked. Thanatos, head a little fuzzy from the cups of wine Lach had kept pressing into his hands, smiled back.

The band played until the workers at the venue got antsy and started to push for an end, but even that took longer than it should have. Dionysus was quite the influence.

It was well after midnight when they finally found themselves outside, the concert over and the still-drunken revelers heading off in every direction.

Lach, sleepy and warm, grabbed his arm and clung like a barnacle. "That was awesome. Tell me that wasn't awesome."

"Are you asking me to lie to you?"

That earned him a half-hearted smack to his chest. "Funny guy. You know what I mean."

"It was good, Lach. I enjoyed it," he admitted. He didn't even hesitate. He was done lying to himself about it. What was the point? Thousands of years since he'd seen Lach, and his feelings, though slightly more fraught than before, hadn't changed all that much.

He was still in love with him.

Thanatos wasn't sure he'd ever been out of love with Lach, even when he had hated him. Both hurt, so what difference did it make?

Lach laughed into his shoulder. "Called it." He turned his head so his lips almost brushed Thanatos's earlobe, and started singing, surprisingly in tune for a man who'd had so much to drink.

Having just heard it, Thanatos knew full well how that particular ballad's chorus went, and he needed to nip the singing in the bud. He wasn't sure if he could handle Lach's low, breathy voice singing, "Babe, I love you," directly in his ear.

"Time to get back to the boat, I think," he announced aloud, rolling Lach's head off his shoulder.

"Aww, but that's miles away," Lach whined.

Thanatos looked at him, eyebrow raised. "You knew that before you went to a concert, stayed until the middle of the night, and drank all that wine."

Lach sighed like a child but nodded. Then his eyes lit up. "But you can take us there. You know, travel by god."

"You of all people know it's not that simple. I could take us to the cemetery between here and there, but it's still a long way from there." Thanatos looked around and realized he didn't even remember which way the marina was. Maybe it would be easier to go back to the cemetery.

Or maybe . . .

He closed his eyes and thought of the boat he'd spent the last two weeks of his life on. Surely a connection had formed, even if he weren't exactly being worshipped there. He reached out and drew himself toward its thread, allowing his physical contact with Lach to draw the other man along as well.

A second later they were standing in front of the boat, and Thanatos felt rather accomplished.

Then he remembered the reason Lach had said they had to travel by boat. He turned, worried, half expecting him to be bringing all that wine back up, but Lach was just staring up at him, lazy smile on his face. He didn't even look dizzy, much less sick.

Thanatos's blood turned to ice. "You lied to me. Again." He took a step back from Lach, his fists clenching so tight they ached. Lach stumbled, and the urge he had to reach out and help made him even angrier. "I can't trust a thing you say, can I?"

DARK BELOW DECK

Thanatos jerked away from him, and Lach staggered to close the distance. No luck—like two magnets with the same polarity, Thanatos shifted, maintaining the distance between them until Lach stopped trying.

"What are you talking about?" Lach asked. Just a few minutes ago, they'd been at a fantastic concert. It hadn't been a date, but it was the closest Lach had gotten to one in decades. It should have been a date, really. If Lach had any sense, he'd have asked Thanatos out for real—not weaseled his way into spending a day together but been upfront about what he wanted. Now, Thanatos was looking at him like he'd kicked Cerberus.

Lach held up his hands placatingly. "Whatever I did, Thanatos, I'm so sorry."

"Whatever you did?" Thanatos scoffed. "You can't even keep track of your own lies."

All Lach could do was stare at Thanatos as fury darkened his features. He'd never had cause to be afraid of Thanatos before, and he wasn't now, but perhaps he should have been.

"I don't know. I think I've always had a pretty good grip on—"

Thanatos cut him off with a glare, marching toward him and jamming his finger in the center of Lach's chest. "You said we couldn't travel my way

—that it'd make you get sick. Instead you let me spend days *miserable* on that damned boat—"

"Hey!" Lach cut in, anger rising to match Thanatos's. "You can be mad at me, but don't talk about Mis that way."

Thanatos rolled his eyes. "Of course you care more about that boat than you do about—" He caught himself. Fell silent.

What was there to say to that? Lach did care about Misericordia. She'd been his partner and best friend for decades. But it wasn't a contest. His shoulders sagged. "It's not like that."

Another scoff from Thanatos. Crossing his arms, he turned to look out across the water.

The quick rush of anger, then its dissipation left Lach feeling sober and empty. He reached for Thanatos's hand, resting on his opposite elbow. Thanatos shrugged him off, so Lach stuffed his empty hands into his pockets.

"I'm sorry I lied to you. I didn't do it to hurt you. I just wanted—" Whatever he'd wanted, he'd been selfish about it.

Thanatos still wouldn't look at him, so Lach leaned over to try and catch his eye. "If I had asked you to travel with me, to spend any time with me at all, would you have said yes?" Lach asked.

Silence hung between them, Thanatos's eyes hard and wary. Didn't matter how close he was—Lach could've reached out and held him in his arms, and Thanatos still could've disappeared with a thought.

"No," he admitted. That was the answer Lach was looking for, the one that would give him half a shot of getting himself out of this mess, and it still hurt to hear it.

Swallowing past the tightness in his throat, Lach nodded. "I get that. You're completely right. I lied. I did it because I . . . I wanted the chance to show you I'm not the same man I was the last time you saw me. Guess I fucked that up right off the bat, huh?"

Thanatos didn't laugh. He still wouldn't look at Lach. The distance between the god he'd known and the one that stood in front of him now struck him. This wasn't the first time they'd stood on a dock, one of them imploring the other for mercy.

Back then, Thanatos had looked at him, eyes wide and guileless, and been ready to do anything to close the distance between them. And Lach had shoved it in his face. He'd hurt Thanatos on purpose. Why should he give Lach the benefit of the doubt now?

That wasn't the point, though, was it? If he wanted to be the kind of man who deserved someone like Thanatos—a powerful god and so, so much better than Lach could ever hope to be—he needed to take the lesson from Thanatos back then. He had to be willing to do anything.

"Listen," Lach said quietly, hanging his head. "I'm sorry I lied. I wish I hadn't. If there was some other way to see you, I'm—I'm too thick or careless to figure it out. But you deserve better than that. If you want to go, I get it."

Thanatos finally turned away from the water and back toward him, and Lach tore his eyes from the planks underfoot and met the god's hard gaze. "But I'm not sorry you came," Lach continued. "However I got you here, these last couple weeks have been the happiest since . . ." Lach bit his tongue. He couldn't think of a time he'd been happier since before he'd completely wrecked his chances with Thanatos by abandoning him on those docks.

"I never should've left you back then," Lach said. "I was an idiot, and cruel—a complete pile of shit." He forced a smile, hoping it'd get Thanatos to crack one. No luck. "I'm so sorry."

Maybe it was the human in him that made him fill the silences Thanatos left. He'd say immortality made Thanatos patient—and no doubt he was a lot older than Lach—but Lach had plenty of time to figure that out. To figure anything out.

He'd been trying his luck with Thanatos this whole time. Every smile, every glance or moment that Lach thought he was making some headway toward winning him over—every small victory was built on lies.

"Thank you for coming with me this far," Lach whispered.

"I'm not leaving." Thanatos's words were as blunt as a baseball bat.

A real grin turned up Lach's mouth. The god before him didn't return it, but Lach couldn't quell his pleasure.

"You sure?" He stepped in, reaching out to cup Thanatos's cheek. The god turned into his palm like he didn't have to think about it.

"There's a world to save."

An excuse. They both knew it. Thanatos could've met him in Santorini. Hades, he was a god. Maybe he could sense the scythe and Lach was entirely redundant to the whole enterprise, despite his adventurous spirit and skill with a pistol.

Thanatos was staying.

Unable to help himself, Lach leaned in and kissed him. It was the first kiss he'd shared with the god in millennia, but a familiar warmth flooded him. Thanatos's lips were every bit as soft as he remembered—sweet silken heat—and yielding.

Too soon, Thanatos pulled away from him. He tucked his chin down, denying Lach a second chance at kissing him. Didn't matter. He was *staying*.

"And one pathetic man to keep out of trouble," Lach added.

Thanatos shrugged. "And one pathetic man," he agreed.

Before Lach made sense of what was happening, Thanatos seized the front of his shirt. There was a sensation like his feet being pulled off the ground, then a great tug through the world. To his credit, traveling the godly way *was* disorienting, but it didn't lay him out flat like he'd implied.

They came to a stop in Lach's room below deck, though they could've been halfway around the world for all he knew. In the dark, he felt Thanatos grab his hips, slide firm hands up his chest.

"Do you want a light?" Lach asked. He couldn't see for shit in the dark, and there were only tiny windows up high on the wall. Curtains blocked out any light.

But Thanatos had been born to chaos. He moved freely in the underworld and didn't seem to mind the dark now. Lach, for his own part, was in a mood to give him anything he wanted, and if that left him fumbling and sightless, so be it.

"You weren't *really* miserable the whole time, were you?" he asked.

Thanatos was tugging Lach's shirt up, fingers brushing the heated skin of Lach's torso until his breaths came short and shallow. "Hmm?"

His fingertips traced the ridges of Lach's chest and swirled in featherlight circles across his nipples.

"It was the melon that ruined everything, wasn't it? Should've gotten a melon baller."

"What in chaos are you talking about?"

"Nothing. Doesn't matter." Lach's thoughts scattered as Thanatos leaned in. The air from his breath rushed over Lach's skin. His lips finally closed on Lach's collarbone, and a low rumble of a moan worked up his throat.

When he reached for Thanatos, though, the god was slippery. With little more than a shrug, he escaped Lach's arms before he could wrap them around his waist. They closed around air.

"What are you doing?" Lach asked.

"Taking what I want. Don't tell me you mind now?"

A slow stream of air filled Lach's lungs as he sucked in slow, trying not to let his chest shake with the effort. "I definitely do not mind."

"Good."

Seeing only Thanatos's shadow was bound to drive him crazy, but his thoughts spun when the god reached for his belt, undid his pants, and slipped his hand inside.

Lach cursed under his breath as Thanatos wrapped firm fingers around him. There was a muffled thump as the god fell to his knees, then the blissful wet slide of his tongue.

He was only teasing, licking and kissing and working his hand just enough to get Lach throbbing.

Too soon, Thanatos pulled away. Lach heard his nightstand drawer open and Thanatos rifling around inside. Somehow, he didn't mind the thought of Thanatos searching through his drawers when he'd been alone in here—not if it led to this and the memory of Thanatos cozy in his pajamas.

Rifling clothes, a moving shadow, and the sound of the mattress sinking under Thanatos's weight were all Lach had to go on. He could imagine what the pop of the cap meant—the low moan a second later.

"Coming?" Thanatos asked, his voice sharper than a moment ago.

Lach didn't have words for that, but he crawled onto the bed on his knees. In the dark, he had to feel around for his place. He touched Thanatos's calf first, brushing his hand up the back of his thigh as the god arched toward him. There was a subtle movement. When Lach leaned in close, he could feel Thanatos's wrist as his fingers smoothly worked in and out of himself.

Thanatos was facing the headboard, propped up on it with one hand while he worked himself open with the other. What Lach wouldn't give to see him like that. Instead, he had to content himself with tracing the backs of his thighs, the curve of his lower back.

"Feel good?" Lach whispered against his shoulder.

"Not as good as your cock will."

Lach cursed, burying his face against the back of Thanatos's neck and sucking a mark. He never tasted like salt and sweat, but like something holy and sweet and far, far beyond Lach's comprehension.

"What are you waiting for?" Thanatos demanded, knocking Lach out of it.

"Nothing," he muttered, sliding his hands around to touch every inch of the god he could reach. Already, Thanatos was pressing back against him. He moved his hand, pressing both palms against the headboard. The smooth curve of his ass pushed against Lach's dick. He thrust against him, but that wasn't enough. Not for either of them.

With one hand to steady it, and another on Thanatos's hip, Lach found his hole. The blunt head of his cock slipped between Thanatos's cheeks, and when he felt the slick ridge of it, he pushed inside.

Thanatos's moan was soft and low: the kind of sound that filled his dreams. Gods could do that with their voices—fill a whole room and drag mortals' attentions their way. Lach's entire world narrowed to that soft sound and the point where Thanatos's body wrapped around him in electric pleasure.

He started with a slow rhythm. Thanatos could take anything Lach threw at him, and for a human, Lach had always been demanding. Now, he wanted something soft, something that felt good, something that showed Thanatos how much he cared.

Steadily, he thrust into that clenching heat, until stars sparked behind his eyes. Each time, he sank deeper, searching for that place where they could meld together.

Fantastic as it felt, it wasn't enough. Lach needed more of him.

Craning over Thanatos's back, feeling the heaviness of the god's breathing all along his front, he slipped his hand around to touch his jaw and tilted Thanatos's head back. Lach leaned in for a kiss, but before he touched his lips, Thanatos pulled away.

"Don't." It was a breath, soft and airy, but with all the sharpness of a knife.

Lach blinked, staring at the outline of Thanatos. He was wrapped in his arms, with Lach's cock inside him, and he still pulled away.

"Oh," Lach said. "Okay. I'm—I'm sorry."

" 'S fine."

He was frozen for a second, until Thanatos pressed back against him. Lach didn't know what to do with his hands anymore. They settled on Thanatos's hips for lack of a better place.

"Do you want me to stop?" Lach whispered. He didn't think he could manage anything louder without his voice cracking.

"No."

"Okay."

Lach tried to find his rhythm again, but all of a sudden, the room was too quiet. The slap of skin on skin was uncomfortable. All the cozy warmth before, heightened by only finding his lover through touch, had disappeared.

Why couldn't Lach kiss him? He could fuck him. He could run his hands over his skin and feel Thanatos shiver underneath him. But he couldn't kiss him.

"Shit," Lach hissed. His dick slipped out. He tried to shove it back in, but it slid past Thanatos's hole, soft and useless.

"Sorry. Just—just give me a second," Lach gritted out. He sat back on his heels. With quick, efficient strokes, he tried to get his dick to cooperate.

Thanatos made an impatient sound, and after half a minute, Lach had to accept his dick wasn't going to get there.

Before Thanatos could turn over and demand to know what the blasted fuck was wrong with him, Lach sucked three digits into his mouth and worked them into Thanatos instead. When the pad of his thumb pressed that soft place behind his balls, Thanatos finally shuddered. He sank down, pressing his face into a pillow.

"That's it," Lach whispered over his back, teasing the shell of his ear with his lips.

For all his faults, Lach was thorough when it counted. He hooked his fingers, rubbing Thanatos's prostate until the god quivered under him. He spread his fingers and dragged his lips down Thanatos's back, blowing a stream of cool air over his heated skin. Thanatos whined.

Only when Lach was certain that Thanatos couldn't take anymore, he reached between his legs and tugged his dick. Against Lach's calves, Thanatos's toes curled in. He tried to pull his knees together, but Lach kept them apart with his own.

"Let go, Thanatos," he growled.

With a few more strokes, the god's dick twitched in his hand, spurting come over the sheets.

Slowly, Lach pulled his fingers out. Thanatos huffed out a shaky breath and rolled over onto his side to avoid the wet spot.

Lach wasn't sure if he should go. They'd fought (sort of) and fucked (sort of), and Lach didn't know if Thanatos wanted him there, or never wanted to see him again.

Sighing, Lach turned over and leaned against the headboard.

"What's wrong?" Thanatos asked. His tone was careful. Lach really couldn't imagine what he was worried about.

"Nothing's wrong."

The mattress dipped. Thanatos leaned over and flicked on the bedside lamp. When he turned back, he looked at Lach with a furrow between his brows.

"It's okay, Lach. That kind of thing—it happens to everyone sometimes."

"Not to gods."

Thanatos laughed. "You'd be surprised."

Lach rolled his eyes and shrugged. He pulled the sheets over his lap. He didn't think he'd ever disappointed Thanatos before—not in bed, anyway. Felt like a new low.

Thanatos got up on his knees. With a steady hand, he cupped Lach's cheek. "Will you talk to me?"

With the god he loved there, imploring him, Lach couldn't help but look at him. His skin was lightly flushed, a little darker than it normally was, and his eyes were swimming with concern.

"About what?" Lach asked.

"You seem upset."

"I don't mean to be."

"But you are."

Lach took a slow breath. "You didn't want to kiss me."

Thanatos flinched.

"It's okay," Lach hastened to say. "I get it. You don't want to get hurt again, and I hurt you. So I'm probably not . . . not a guy you want to kiss." He reached out and touched Thanatos's chin, turning his head gently to look up at him again. "But I don't want to hurt you."

The skepticism in Thanatos's eyes broke his heart.

"I don't. I know I—I did. Want to hurt you. Definitely. What I said, that I didn't want to be with you because you're Death? I knew it'd hurt you, but I didn't mean that. I'm not making excuses for saying it—there are none. I got scared. I ran away. I knew if I said that, you'd let me go."

"So you wanted me to live thinking you felt that way?" Thanatos's voice was chilly and distant. There was a gap between them that Lach no longer thought he could cross.

"No. Yes. I—Thanatos, I was stupid, and so fucking young."

"Plenty of mortals get their lives together by thirty-five. They don't disappear for months without word or lash out at people they've been with for years."

Lach grimaced. Some mortals did that, but that didn't make them worth emulating. "Yeah. But you don't think the Fates gave me immortality because they knew I'd need more time?"

Thanatos scoffed. "I don't think the Fates gave you anything."

"Yeah. You're right. Whatever I am now, it's some kind of mistake. I mean, I've got a pretty impeccable track record of fucking up. Hurting you—that's the worst thing I ever did. And I'm so, so sorry. But Thanatos, I don't want to be the man who can fuck you but can't kiss you. I can't—" This was absurd. He should've taken what he could get and been grateful for it. Plenty of other gods would've smote him already. "I can't pretend this doesn't mean anything to me. I love you."

Thanatos let out a breath like Lach had punched him in the gut.

"I know," Lach continued. "I'm not saying I think you should love me back. But I love you, and I can't do that halfway."

ONE BAD TURN

Over the millennia, Thanatos had occasionally fantasized about this scenario.

On one level it felt silly, as though a being his age should be long over such childish whimsy. But sometimes he wondered if he'd really changed all that much over his eons of existence. Prometheus had made humans like the gods, so the similarities were many, but it seemed to Thanatos that humans gained in wisdom quickly while the gods languished in their excesses: a sort of indefinite arrested development because they had no reason to move forward, learn, and grow.

For so many years Thanatos had imagined this moment, when Lach came back, insisting that he'd been wrong and saying he still wanted him, still loved him.

At first, he had always taken Lach back, wrapping him in his arms and holding him as every bit of him wanted to.

Later, he had spent the fantasy tearing Lach apart the way Lach had done to him, insulting everything from his attitude to his prowess as a lover. It had all been lies, of course. Thanatos might be incapable of gaining the wisdom mortality bestowed, but he wasn't ignorant enough to think Lach wasn't perfect, even—and perhaps especially—in his imperfections.

That Lach saw himself as a mistake was astounding, and like every damned thing about him, oddly endearing. Thanatos didn't think the Fates had decided Lach's future because Lach had always brashly forged ahead, making his own path where there had been none. To call him a mistake was to call a tornado a mistake. They weren't planned, certainly, but they decided their own fates from start to finish, and even the gods couldn't predict their actions.

Lach was staring at his own sheet-covered lap, looking as downcast as Thanatos had ever seen him. He was responsible for that. It was like the fantasies where he'd spun tales of better lovers, told Lach how he had never truly satisfied him with his wildness and his demands. The truth, of course, was that the unexpectedness of everything Lach did was why Thanatos loved him.

He sighed, but even as he did it, he reached for Lach's hand.

"I love you," he whispered. It was so quiet he could barely hear it himself, but Lach's head snapped up, eyes bright and hopeful. Thanatos cleared his throat. "I don't think I stopped loving you, as pathetic as that is. I kept telling myself I wasn't going to fall into this trap again. I wasn't going to let you hurt me again."

Lach flinched, and maybe it was wishful thinking, but everything about him did seem regretful about how things had ended between them. He was so earnest. Thanatos had always loved that.

He had always loved Glaucus, but this Glaucus, Lach, was somehow even more than the scrappy, stubborn man he'd known. The man he had become was different, but everything Thanatos had loved was still there. And now there was a little more self-reflection, a little less cocksure arrogance, and more unflinching loyalty, all hidden beneath that same dashing pirate smile.

But could that loyalty apply to Thanatos in a way it hadn't before?

Glaucus had clung to those he loved, like his brother and father, but it hadn't extended to Thanatos then. Could it now?

"I don't want to," Lach said, his eyes shining. He grabbed the hand Thanatos had rested on his. "I don't ever want to hurt you again. It's not a trap. I swear, Thanatos. I won't—"

Instead of letting Lach make promises he might not be able to keep, Thanatos leaned forward and cut him off with a kiss. Maybe it was doomed to failure. Maybe there was no way to make it work, and Lach would always leave him. But right here, right now, he could have this. He could have the Lach who said he loved him, whose emotions seemed so easy and transparent.

Lach returned the kiss with force, his tongue sweeping into Thanatos's mouth and claiming. He wound his left hand behind Thanatos's neck and pressed their bodies tight together, bowling him over and landing on top.

He didn't break the kiss until he had to gasp for breath, and then he pulled back, eyes sparkling. "You wanna try this again, lights on, full kissing?"

What could he say to that? The same thing he always said to Lach in the end. "Yes."

Lach gave him that brazen grin and reached out for the lube that had been discarded to one side.

Thanatos wasn't sure more was necessary, but Lach was careful in ways Glaucus had never been, too. He caressed instead of groping, built a rhythm instead of a frenzy, and focused on Thanatos's body more than his own. Maybe it was a side effect of millennia of experience, and Thanatos had to chase away a flash of jealousy at the image of Lach having sex with thousands of men and women over those years, but whatever it was, the result was kind of nice.

He still hit like a tornado, but his touches were less force and more care than they had been before.

Lach ran his hands up and down Thanatos's chest, soft and almost tickling, at the same time as he used his knees to press Thanatos's legs open and settle between them. He slid their cocks together, reaching one hand down to wrap around both and stroke a few lazy times before slipping the same hand down to press at Thanatos's hole. The first finger slipped in easily, and Thanatos let his head fall back against the pillow.

It had been good, feeling Lach in him again, even when he'd given up and used his hands instead of his dick. There was a moment's self-consciousness at the memory of it, a niggling reminder than nothing like that had ever happened to Lach in their previous lovemaking. Did he want Thanatos less now, or had it truly been simple shock at the idea that he didn't want to kiss?

No, worry was for later, when Lach wasn't pressing a second finger inside him. He pushed into the hand, even though it wasn't what he wanted. He wasn't going to pretend to be demanding again. It wasn't him, and hadn't worked anyway, so he let Lach take over.

After a few more pumps of his hand, Lach took his fingers away and replaced them with his cock. Thanatos was grateful for the extra lube, because the position was a bigger stretch.

Lach leaned down to look him in the eye as he pressed inside, slowly and inexorably pushing himself into Thanatos in the way that only he had ever managed.

Thanatos didn't try to pull away again when Lach wrapped his left hand around the back of his neck. He pulled their faces together so close that Thanatos's vision was distorted, full of nothing but bright blue eyes that seemed to drill into his very soul, if he had such a thing. It was moments like these, with Lach so close that Thanatos could feel every part of him, that he thought maybe he did.

How could he feel this tremor in his entire being if he didn't have a soul?

When he was fully seated in Thanatos's body, Lach let out a breath and leaned in for another kiss. And then another and another, as he pulled back out and built not a rhythm, but a slow, gentle glide that felt like it could be suspended forever between them. He pushed all the way into Thanatos and slid slowly back out, their breaths syncing up and bodies working in tandem, like they were parts of a single being.

This would be his Elysium, if creatures like Thanatos were allowed eternal rest. This moment, with Lach, forever.

They were so aligned that when Lach slid his hand between their bodies and wrapped it around Thanatos's dick, it felt like a natural extension of his own will. It wasn't Lach's sometimes impatient need for Thanatos to get off so he could as well. Instead, Lach stared into his eyes as he slid his hand up and down, more invested in Thanatos's pleasure than his own.

When Thanatos saw stars and his vision whited out, Lach's face mirrored the ecstasy that rolled through him. He pushed all the way in and froze there, breathing in Thanatos's ear.

Quietly, so very quietly Thanatos wondered if he'd intended to be heard, he whispered, "Stay with me."

The trip across the Mediterranean wasn't long enough, Thanatos decided two days later as he and Lach sat on one of the benches on deck watching the sun rise. Not that he wanted to put off their search for the scythe, but part of him wanted to stay right here, doing exactly this, forever.

He couldn't put off work indefinitely, but he wanted to, a little. Other gods had hired—or created—help over the years, and for the first time, he was tempted to do the same.

A small, cynical part of him kept pointing out that the mission had a time limit, and no matter what Lach said, their rekindled relationship probably did too. Lach needed Thanatos to help him find the scythe. Thanatos was a titan like Cronus, and he could locate magic that resonated with his own. That was all Lach wanted from him.

After that, once again, what did any man want with Death?

A glint on the horizon caught his eye, and from the way Lach leaned forward, he figured Lach had noticed it too.

"What is that?" he asked.

"Another boat."

They continued sitting there together, but as they did, tension bunched Lach's shoulders.

Thanatos raised a brow at him. "Do you not run into a lot of boats? Seems like something that would happen all the time."

Lach leaned forward and opened a small storage bin, pulling out a set of binoculars. He stood and leaned forward as though the extra foot would make a difference in what he could see. "Maybe so," he said, distracted and concerned. "But not usually boats headed directly at us."

He went to the wheel and made a few adjustments, changing their direction for the first time in more than a day. Fraught moments passed before he checked the other boat again and cursed under his breath.

"Lach?" Thanatos asked. He felt out of place and useless. He was the closest thing to a pacifist among his kind. He was possibly the most useless person to have on your side in a fight, and the way Lach was tensing up, it looked like a fight was imminent.

Lach, still wearing nothing but a pair of loose sweatpants, ran below deck and came back up a moment later, holding a gun. Thanatos wasn't conversant in modern technology, but the thing looked like it belonged in a museum.

"What are you doing with that?" he asked, and shamefully, his voice squeaked on the last word.

"They're not just heading this way. They're coming at us. They changed course to intercept when we turned." Lach's voice was tight with concern, but he looked more angry than frightened, and that worried Thanatos.

"I could take us—"

"I'm not leaving Mis."

Right. That was an excellent point. Thanatos had grown to like the boat over the course of the previous few weeks, and he was sure she was a sentient creature, as Lach kept saying, and not simply an object that he was inordinately attached to. The way she and Lach occasionally argued was unmistakable, and he sympathized with her frustration toward her capricious partner in crime.

He stepped up next to Lach, blanket still wrapped around his shoulders. "Lach, that gun is ridiculous. It belongs in a collection, not a firefight."

Lach snorted and waved him off. "You should go dress. They don't get to see you in your underwear."

Thanatos thought he muttered something about wishing he had a cannon as he headed below deck. As much as such a thing might help them, Thanatos did not like the notion of Lach with access to a cannon.

"I hope you don't have a cannon," he told the boat as he searched for his socks. "He'd get himself killed with it."

There was a rattle above him, and he looked up to find a DVD from Lach's collection shaking itself loose. It fell to the floor a few feet in front of him. *Quantum Leap*, the cover said.

He looked at it for a moment, trying to decide if he was getting the right message from it. "He doesn't want to leave you."

The cabin door opened, as though inviting him to depart.

He nodded, then stopped and looked at the nightstand where Lach's wallet and phone sat. Better safe than sorry, he supposed, grabbing them and tucking them into his own pocket. "I understand. I'm not going to do anything drastic unless it's called for, though. We'll wait and see." If a ship could sigh, he was pretty sure Misericordia did.

By the time he found his way back onto the deck, fully dressed, the other boat was mostly visible. It had come from in front of them, likely because if they had come from behind, they couldn't have caught up with Misericordia. She was every bit as fast as Lach had claimed, after all.

Lach was trying to change course to avoid them still, but it looked as though they were at least fast enough to compensate for that.

"What do we do in a fight?" Thanatos asked.

Lach pulled the pistol out from where he'd tucked it into the waistband of his sweats—Thanatos cringed at how close it had been to rather sensitive bits—and waved it around. "I shoot them."

"And you've got how many shots with that gun?"

Lach frowned in a way that Thanatos could only call a pout. "One."

"And how many people would they need to run that boat of theirs?"

The responding scowl was enough to tell Thanatos the answer was more than one.

The deafening noise followed by an immense plume of water to their aft made Thanatos freeze for a second. Chaos, they were being shot at. He'd never been shot at in his life.

Lach yelled an incomprehensible battle cry and went to the edge of the deck, pointing his tiny gun in the direction of the huge boat. There was another explosion, and this time the crunch that reverberated through Misericordia made his heart lurch. The living being beneath his feet had just been shot, was damaged.

"Get below deck," Lach said, turning to look at him. "Maybe you can— can . . ." He trailed off, wild-eyed and panting. There was a sharp crack, nothing like the thundering sound of whatever they were shooting at the boat, and Lach jolted forward, pressed against the mast. When he drew away, his shoulder was bloody.

Thanatos took a step toward him, not sure what he could do but knowing he needed to do something.

Terrifyingly, the look in Lach's eyes changed from angry terror to acceptance. "You should go. Go to Santorini. Find the scythe. You can get it to Gaia and fix this."

Thanatos was more inclined to throttle Lach than leave him to his fate and go looking for the scythe, but Misericordia had other ideas. A rope that tethered her boom came loose just as Lach stepped past it, and it swung around to hit him in the back and knock him into Thanatos.

Thanatos grabbed him and righted him as there was another ear-splitting crash, and a hole opened up straight through Misericordia's starboard side. She listed wildly to port, and the motion of the water exaggerated the movement. For one breathless second, they were weightless as the boat reached a crest and instead of falling back, it continued the roll.

As Misericordia capsized beneath their feet, Thanatos wrapped his arms around Lach and transported them to Santorini.

WHITE GRAVESTONES

The sun had risen, they were miles away, and Misericordia was sinking. Unprepared for the stable ground, Lach's legs overcompensated. He listed starboard, toward white paving stones. Light reflected off every nearby surface, turning the riot of flowers on headstones and monuments into stark shadows in the bright white light. For the first time, Thanatos was steadier than him and squeezed him close.

Lach had felt the tilting of the ship, even before the boom had sent him tumbling into Thanatos's arms. His stomach had slid up into his throat as the whole world rolled. For one horrifying moment, they'd been weightless—nothing under their feet but a deck tilting perpendicular to the ocean swells that were swallowing Mis. All Lach had seen was the deep blue. Then, they were gone.

Closing his eyes, Lach tried to get a grip on where he was. He could hear the distant crashing of ocean waves, the squawking of seagulls. Nothing like the violent explosions and roaring sea spray. The gentle breeze that cut between the graves on the hillside rushed salty over his skin. They were in Santorini.

"Lach—" Thanatos reached for him gently, touching his shoulder. "You're bleeding."

His fingers barely grazed the wet spot on Lach's shoulder. Distantly, he remembered the shock of the spinning bullet tearing through his flesh.

He'd hardly felt it then, but now, when Thanatos touched him, he felt the bruising force and sharp sting of pain.

Lach had gotten into a gun fight in nothing but a pair of sweat pants. Lucky he didn't have worse. A single bullet wound, barely a graze, was forgettable.

"We have to go back," Lach rasped, gripping Thanatos's arms and pinning them to his sides.

Thanatos was staring at the blood on his shoulder. Lach had never seen Thanatos bleed, he was too careful, but he'd seen other gods do it—Poseidon and Ares and Artemis. If Thanatos were hurt, he'd bleed golden. Heal quickly. Lach's skin still sported an angry red gully.

"Thanatos," he said sharply.

Shaking himself out of it, Thanatos met Lach's eyes. Bleakness shone out from those golden irises. The shake of his head was so small that Lach nearly missed it. "We need to get you to a healer."

Lach scoffed. "This is not the first time I've been shot, Thanatos."

Paler than he'd been a second before, Thanatos straightened. "Is that supposed to make me feel better?"

"It looks worse than it is." Impatience had sharpened the edge in his voice.

Thanatos hollowed his cheeks. Gritting his teeth, Lach squeezed his eyes shut. What use were reason and talking now? He had to do something.

"Lach—" One soft syllable, and it was too much. Anything other than "okay" was too much.

Lach's eyes flashed open wildly. "Take me back!"

Seagulls took flight at Lach's shout, but Thanatos only started. After all, he was a god—what power did Lach have to command him?

"I can't."

With Lach gripping his arms, Thanatos could only lift them so far, but he settled his hands on Lach's hips. His thumbs brushed over the ridges of Lach's hip bones.

"Bullshit." Lach's voice broke, and he took a moment to swallow and clear his hoarse throat. "You just did. You have that . . . that god-connection thing to her now. Come on. We have to go back."

"There's nothing to go back *to*."

Lach shook his head. "You don't understand. Mis is magic. She's fine."

Had to be. Mis was created by a god to give her captain what they needed, right? She'd helped him get Thanatos to look at him twice, kept him company for years out at sea, whisked him around the world and back. All Lach needed right then was for her to be fine. So she was.

Thanatos had considerably more strength than he appeared to, and used it to shrug out of Lach's grip. Rather than pull away once he was free, he wound an arm around Lach's waist. His other hand—silky soft as ever—cupped Lach's cheek. Lach didn't realize his lips were trembling until Thanatos touched them.

"If we go back now, you'll drown," Thanatos mumbled.

"So I'll drown!"

Thanatos blinked.

Lach shouldn't have shouted, but he could feel the pounding in his chest, the panic that turned his skin pale and sweaty, the shivering dizziness of lost blood, and the searingly bright sun bouncing off every surface.

"I can't leave her," he whispered. "She's my home."

"I know she is." The soft movement of Thanatos's fingers on his cheek was as gentle as his words. "But there's nothing you can do now."

Lach tensed, everything in him rejecting the idea that he was powerless. Every time he'd been held down, he'd squirmed his way out of it. Arrogance, brashness, and blundering had never failed him. They'd saved his family, made him immortal, won him the eye of a god. Desperate, he shook his head.

"Calm down," Thanatos said. It was only a breath, but the words carried that low resonance only gods could achieve. They swept over Lach, curling around the back of his neck, easing into his frantic heart until it beat steadily again and his whole body went lax in Thanatos's careful arms.

By the time he realized what Thanatos had done, he was too languid to give a damn. Later, he'd only remember flashes of Thanatos helping him down the hill, his own feet dragging, the god's fingers stroking his side while he murmured assurances. The small inn with its door surrounded by bright red flowers. Offering to pay, and Thanatos waving him off. Gentle hands easing him into a bed on stable ground. No rolling waves beneath him.

TOE TO TOE WITH GODS

Martina disliked flying. There was nothing to do but sit and hope the movies that'd come out that season were good. Driving, she could control the car. Walking, there were sights to see. Horses, camels, motorcycles—all offered advantages. Yet here she was, prepping for another twelve-hour flight, because there wasn't a better way to get across the ocean. Lach and his boat were ridiculous.

Just before boarding, her phone buzzed in her pocket. She pulled it out and glanced at the screen. It was Roger. She picked up.

"I'm about to get on a plane. What's going on, Roger?" she demanded.

"I need you to check on Lach." Roger's voice was tight and strained. She could almost see him standing there, hand on his hip, expression pinched and serious. With a sigh, she leaned back against a column near the check-in counter, hand on her suitcase.

"Why?"

"We sank his boat."

"You did what?" Marty demanded, voice chilly. Why the blasted fuck Roger had authority to command the Fidelis Filii and she didn't was completely beyond her. No doubt, it had something to do with cocks. Penises, after all, were *very* important to a person's leadership character.

"We sank the boat."

"Why the fuck would you do that? *How* the fuck would you do that?"

The boat itself was relatively new, but Marty had been on it, had drinks, thrown potato chips off the side for seagulls to snatch. And every time something weird happened, Lach would give her a cheeky wink. That boat was enchanted.

"Stuck a tracker on him in Ibiza. Blew up the boat."

"Roger, we need him. You can't go fucking drowning the only immortal in the world who can contain Cronus *and* doesn't have the power to smite you on the spot."

Marty had spent years of her life forging a bond with Lach—Glaucus. Decades ago, when her and Roger's father was young, they'd met. They'd been friends, even. Until they'd disagreed. Lach, Marty had learned from personal experience, was pretty damn lonely. And lonely men talked. He might've beaten around the bush a little—not spoken explicitly about gods to her—but she knew he'd been born in Greece. And her father had a picture of the two of them from decades earlier. He looked exactly the same.

"Not all gods are that powerful," Roger said. Marty would like to see him face one down. Even Hebe—Martina followed her on Instagram. Her page was full of flowers, carefully staged selfies, and feminism. The goddess of youth would absolutely wreck him. "Anyway, we didn't kill him. I think. We were *going* to snatch him out of the water."

"We have a plan, Roger!" He entirely lacked the patience to see it through. Now, that was her problem. "Why didn't you get him?"

"Don't know. He disappeared. He was with some Black guy in Santorini. Maybe he's a mage."

"Or maybe you fucking drowned him!" Marty hissed. A little girl, holding her mother's hand in line and waiting to get on the plane, stared at her with enormous eyes. Marty forced a smile. The girl pressed her face against her mother's thigh.

With a groan, Marty rolled her eyes. "Sure, whatever. I'll call him and let you know if you murdered our only good lead." She hung up. "Fucking asshole."

With quick thumbs, she dialed Lach. The phone rang three times, a chill creeping further up her back with every shrill tone. Finally, he picked up.

" 'Sup, 'Tina?"

Martina exhaled slowly. Lach sounded groggy, but at least he'd picked up.

Of course, she couldn't let on that she knew anything was the matter. "If you ever call me that again, Lach," she snipped, "I'll cut your tongue out."

"Apologies, Martin-ha." He snickered. "What can I help you with?"

"Just wanted to let you know I'm about to get on a plane," she said. "Are you okay? You sound kind of off."

"I'm good. I'm *good*. I got shot."

"You got shot?" she echoed. Sure, they were going to pluck him out of the water. No problem. No reason to leave the guns at home.

" 'S okay. Hermes is here to patch me up."

"Shut up, you dink," another voice snapped in the back. "Stay still."

He hissed into the receiver, his breath the sound of a shell pressed to her ear. She jerked the phone away.

"You gonna go get me some trousers, aye?" Lach demanded, putting on a deep brogue that Martina hadn't heard before. "You gonna find me some pantaloons, Hermes? Don't wantcha to get *in* my pants, just get me some pants. Don't get any ideas. I've got a *boyfriend*."

"Are you drunk?" Martina asked.

"Are you sober?" Lach challenged. He laughed again and ended on a long sigh like he was lounging back in a sun chair. "My fella talked to me like Morgan Freeman and now I feel *really* good."

Martina pinched the bridge of her nose. "I don't want to know what you mean by that."

"Ariadne thinks Morgan Freeman's voice is sexy."

In the background, she heard a muffled, "Ariadne thinks everything is sexy."

"Okay, so you got shot. How'd that happen?" Martina asked. "Are you in trouble with someone?"

He was. The Fidelis Filii wanted his immortal body as a vessel for their master. The whole thing sounded shady, sure, but they were trying to make a better world. And Lach had had a long time to enjoy the current one. That was what Marty told herself when she thought about throwing potato chips off the side of his boat or the rush she got after narrowly escaping danger with him. She was his friend, but the world had gone off track, and it needed their master more than it needed Lach at the moment. But there was no reason for him to know that, and if he did, they were in deep shit.

Logical as she was trying to be, her heart clenched when he made a small, broken sound. She'd never heard Lach *hurt* before.

"It'll be okay, Lach," someone said on the other end. This wasn't the same voice as before, but a steady, deep, empathetic one. There was a rustle—apparently the sound of Lach passing off the phone and possibly the muffled sound of a sob—and then, "Hello? This is Thanatos."

FEAR OF THE UNKNOWN

Thanatos set the phone down on the bedside table with a sharp plastic clack. Lach's friend the archaeologist had seemed nice enough, and quite concerned for his wellbeing, but he'd hardly wanted to chat with her while Hermes sewed Lach's shoulder closed and Lach's lips trembled. While Hermes wasn't the ideal choice for the job, he was the one god Thanatos knew had experience helping injured mortals who didn't hate Lach on principle.

Well, and if Lach were to be believed, he was also friendly with Poseidon, but Thanatos hadn't been willing to gamble his life on that.

Hermes was faster anyway.

"There ya go," Hermes said, ruffling Lach's hair as he stood. Lach was barely awake and gave a soft whine as Hermes wandered over to where Thanatos stood. "He's gonna be fine. But what about, uh . . . he said he has a boyfriend. Just now. He said that."

Thanatos rolled his eyes and huffed a sigh. "I suppose he did."

"And?"

"*And* we've been discussing things." Thanatos looked over at Lach, whose eyes had slipped shut. He was probably going to be angry when he woke to remember that Thanatos had forced him to calm down. Maybe their reunion would be over as quickly as it had started. He shrugged and turned back to Hermes. "Maybe. I don't know."

In a surprising show of emotion, Hermes furrowed his brow and pursed his lips. It made him look older, more like his father and brothers than he usually did. "You sure you know what you're doing? I like Lach as much as the next guy—hell, probably more than most—but if I've ever met two people more different than you, I couldn't name 'em."

It was a good point, but Thanatos had always seen their differences as a benefit, not a drawback. And either way, he wasn't going to sit here and discuss it with Hermes. "As much as I appreciate your concern, Hermes, I'm older than you by quite a lot. I'm completely capable of making my own decisions."

Hermes threw up his hands defensively. "I know, I know. And you're usually the most sensible guy I've ever met. But you have a history of making not-the-best decisions when it comes to this one thing. Just, you know, be careful. I'd hate to have to kick Lach's ass on your behalf."

"Eons older than you," he reminded Hermes. "Eons. I can defend my own honor."

"Yeah, but you're kind of like a golden retriever, all sweet and innocent and—"

"Are you comparing me to a dog?"

Hermes glanced quickly to one side and then the other, then lifted his brows and tried to look innocent. The expression was very much like Lach. "No?"

Thanatos sighed. "Go on, Hermes. I can handle this from here. Thank you for the help."

Hermes offered a bright grin. "Anytime! I'm always happy to help the people who don't want to kill me." He headed for the door without turning his back, still smiling. "So I'm gonna go before you change your mind about that whole not wanting to kill me thing. Maybe I can find Lach some pants in town. Call me anytime and all that."

Almost the second his hand touched the knob, Hermes had opened the door, gone out, and closed it behind him. With Zeus for a father, the poor kid was in a regular state of almost-fear, but the idea that he still found Thanatos frightening was odd.

He scrubbed the back of his neck with a hand and sighed. When he glanced over, Lach's eyes were open and on him.

"You're nothing like a golden retriever, you know," Lach told him.

He supposed it was reassuring Lach didn't think he was a dog. Unless he was about to say he was actually a chihuahua or something like that. "Oh? Some other kind of man's best friend?"

Lach shook his head, and his eyes went distant. "Nah. You couldn't be a dog. Or a cat, either. They don't get sad like you."

Oh, well that was better, clearly. "I'm not sad."

"You are. People make you sad. People like me." He sighed and rolled his head, so he was staring back at the ceiling. "It's because we're scared of you, a little. You hate it."

He wasn't wrong. It was part of why Thanatos had spent millennia cultivating the softer aspects of his personality, but it didn't seem to matter how calm he was, how gentle, how soft-spoken. People still feared him simply because he was, and he was Death.

"I'm sorry we make you sad," Lach whispered. "I don't mean to."

Thanatos sat on the edge of the bed next to him and brushed his fingers across Lach's cheek. There was no point in denying it or asking why people feared him. He knew the answers, and knew they wouldn't change. "I wish I could convince people," he said, pushing Lach's wild hair off his face. "But nothing I do helps. You all insist on being frightened, no matter what I do."

"Who would ever want to die? I mean, we have to leave everything and everyone behind. It's terrifying." Lach shuddered and didn't meet his eyes.

"But you're Greek, Lach. You know where you're going. You know what's waiting for you, and it's better than anything you have here."

Lach met his eyes and reached out to grab his hand. "I don't think it is."

And that was unexpected. Did he mean . . . ? Thanatos took a deep breath and forced himself to go on. "Your father is there. Your brother and mother. Eternal spring and sunshine, sailing into the horizon forever if that's what you want."

"But it's not. Don't get me wrong, I'd love to see them again. All the friends and family I've lost. But how could Elysium be what I want? There's no adventure in a place where everything's perfect and nothing ever goes wrong." Inexplicably, Thanatos was disappointed in the answer. It was classic Glaucus, though. Lach cleared his throat. "Besides. Not everyone I've ever loved is there. You're not there. You'll never be there."

"You can't keep yourself from eternal happiness for one titan,"

Thanatos denied, despite the fact that the words made his heart jump crazily in his chest.

Lach snorted. "I'm not suited to eternal happiness." His eyes narrowed thoughtfully. "But you wish you could go, don't you? It's why you're so dead set on Elysium for everyone all the time. Why you're so bothered when people don't want to go there. *You* want to go."

No one had ever pointed it out so starkly before. Hades had expressed concern for him over it, and other death gods thought him weak because of his feelings for the dead and their rest, even if they didn't say it aloud. He tried to shrug it off. "Gods don't get to rest. It's not in our nature. Elysium was made for mortals."

"Well there ya go," Lach announced, loud and obnoxious. "I'm not a mortal, so I'm not allowed. Guess I'll have to stay with you. I'll find some way to cope, I'm sure." The lascivious grin on his face left little doubt as to how he intended to do that, but in the mental state Thanatos had left him, Lach was basically drunk. Having sex with him would be inappropriate. Not that Lach would understand and accept that fact. He probably didn't think it was possible for anyone to take advantage of him, self-loathing being what it was.

Thanatos sighed and leaned in to press his lips to Lach's forehead, briefly, before pulling away and standing.

Lach opened his mouth to protest, but Thanatos felt the barest hint of a tug. It was so weak he was sure the dying mortal was more than capable of finding their own way, but it would be better for everyone if Thanatos left Lach to get some sleep.

"I have to do some work," he said, trying to pretend he didn't see Lach's face fall. Still, he mumbled, "Sorry. Try to get some sleep, okay?"

Lach glared at him and started to say something about how he didn't need any sleep, but he was cut off by a huge yawn. He glared even harder, as if Thanatos had caused it. If only he could, his life would be so much easier, but that trick belonged to Thanatos's brother Hypnos.

"I'll be back in a while," he promised, and before Lach could protest any further, he turned and let the thread pull him away.

A GOLD WATCH

Sleep came too easily once Thanatos disappeared. It'd be great to blame it on some kind of godly influence, but truth was, getting shot was work. The panic, the tension in every muscle, coming down from the adrenaline rush—all of it left Lach's human body completely wiped, and the pillows propping him up were so soft.

He slept fitfully without Misericordia's gentle rocking beneath him. In his dreams, he imagined the attack. More than once, he jerked awake with the sense he was falling, gravity losing its pull like it had as Mis tipped over.

However fitful, a couple hours of sleep did him well. He woke to the sound of the door opening.

Blinking his eyes open, he expected to see Thanatos there. Wasn't like he could appear in the inn's bedroom unless Lach, like, worshipped him. Maybe if Lach prayed, but he hadn't been able to do that since finding out the gods could hear him. Always felt like asking too much.

It wasn't Thanatos at the door, but Hermes with a pile of clothes slung over his arm.

"Was that unlocked?" Lach asked.

Hermes smirked. He was handsome—'course he was—most of Zeus's children were startlingly attractive. Golden-hued and perfect, they darted around the world stacking up conquests.

Thanatos was the opposite—lovely brown with honey eyes and endless patience. Though strong, he wasn't a conqueror. The first time Lach had seen him on that beach, having nearly drowned, he had thought Thanatos was the sort of god he'd have to beg for mercy. Instead, all he'd ever had to do was ask for what he needed. Sometimes he didn't even have to ask. When Philon had gotten sick, Lach had told Thanatos to fuck off entirely, thinking that might stay the fate that came for his little brother. Instead, Thanatos had returned with help, had healed Philon.

He was kind when Lach hadn't been. Yielding when Lach needed to feel in control. And all the while, sad, because Lach couldn't appreciate him the way he ought to have appreciated him.

As Lach's fingers twisted in the blankets, Hermes scoffed. "No. You think I need a key to pick a lock?"

Lach arched a brow at him. "Depends on the lock."

"No, it doesn't," Hermes challenged. "God of thieves. They haven't invented a lock that can get in my way."

In any case, the wooden door was old, and the burnished hardware looked original. The lock was simple. Easy to break into, if Lach were afraid of that sort of thing.

"They haven't invented a Lach, huh?" He snickered.

"Shut up," Hermes griped. "Where's Thanatos?"

"Dunno. He said he needed to work."

"He left you right after you got shot?"

Lach didn't like the way that Hermes's brows were creeping up toward his hairline. Thanatos had to work; it didn't have to mean anything. "He wanted me to rest. You've seen him. How much sleep do you think I'd have gotten if he stayed?"

Hermes laughed—a puff of a breath. "Forgive me if I don't buy that Thanatos is incapable of controlling himself."

"He can. I can't."

"Fair enough." He crossed the room and unloaded the clothes at the end of Lach's bed.

"What's all that?"

"Well, you said you needed trousers. Unless you're in the mood to walk around Santorini naked but for a pair of salt-crusted sweatpants?"

"Probably not the best look," Lach admitted.

"Much as I'd appreciate the show, no." Hermes waggled a pair of shoes in the air once he set down the rest of the clothes. "Had to guess your sizes. Figured they're similar to mine." Hermes's assessing gaze flicked down Lach's form under the covers. "Think I got pretty close. Could size you up for myself . . ."

Lach narrowed his eyes. "You testing me, Hermes?"

Hermes shrugged. "Thanatos isn't like us. I don't want to see him get hurt again. And frankly, I don't want to watch Charon turn you inside out."

Though he clamped his mouth shut, Lach's sigh escaped through his nose. He couldn't say he and Hermes were nothing alike—flippant, untrustworthy thieves, the pair of them. Shit, Lach was every bit as self-destructive as Hermes was, and just as prone to running away when things got rough.

"I'm not going to hurt him." He might have to say it every day for the rest of his life to convince anybody, but he intended to follow through this time.

"Uh huh."

Well, Hermes wasn't the first god he needed to convince. "So," Lach pivoted, "how much do I owe you?"

Hermes started. "What?"

Lach nodded toward the pile of clothes. "For those?"

"Oh." Hermes waved him off. "Don't worry about it."

"Seriously, it's no big." Thanatos hadn't let him pay for their room either. It hadn't occurred to him that anyone might think he was every bit as destitute as he'd been on Thrinacia. Sure, he didn't go around living the life of Riley, but he'd been ticking a long time. "I'd rather be square with you."

"Lach"—Hermes waved a hand down his body as if Lach needed an introduction to his very existence—"god of thieves. Don't worry about it."

"Oh, uh . . ." Once upon a time, Hermes thieving him a new wardrobe wouldn't have bothered him in the slightest, but Thanatos wouldn't like it. Lach didn't want to face his disappointment, even if he hadn't done the actual stealing. Already, being with Lach was a compromise for Thanatos—a human who wouldn't die, a man who wouldn't settle down, and kind of a prick. If Lach wasn't as close to perfect as he could get, the miraculous shot he had at being with Thanatos again wouldn't last. "So where'd you get them then?"

"Main street in Thera. Couple different shops. Why?"

"No reason. They seem nice, and I lost everything. Might need more clothes."

Hermes was looking at him like he'd gone crazy. "Okay. Well . . . You good?"

"I'm good." Lach didn't think it wise to ask a god, even a relatively friendly one, to run any more of his errands. "Thanks."

With two fingers to his temple, Hermes saluted him. In a flash, he was gone.

Lach was surprisingly sore when he sat up. He shrugged his shoulder, and the pain that exploded in his head was so overwhelming he had to blink spots out of his vision. It'd been decades since he'd gotten shot, and modern guns were nothing if not efficient. Goddamn cowards hiding behind their technology.

He got out of bed. Hermes had a pretty keen eye, and the first shirt he pulled on fit fine. Trying everything on right away was out of the question —hard enough to get dressed trying to only use one arm.

Thank goodness Thanatos had grabbed his phone and wallet, so he stuffed those into his pocket. He left the little inn, making note of the name so he could get back, and had the woman behind the desk call him a cab.

That afternoon, Lach went around to the stores in Thera, trying to pick out ones he owed money to. Of course, he could've planned it better. By the time he got there, Lach had forgotten what most of the clothes looked like. When he described Hermes to the clerks, people just looked at him funny. Nobody'd seen him—of course they hadn't—he could move faster than they could see.

Denied the chance to make true repayment, Lach settled on buying things he saw and liked. Until he walked past a jewelry case and saw a watch glinting in the display. It had a leather band, subdued and classic except for the large Roman numerals and the peculiar warmth of the gold casing. Thanatos didn't wear jewelry that he'd seen, but Lach would put money on him favoring gold. Quite a lot of money, in fact.

"How much?" he asked the clerk in Greek.

He bought it without haggling. The sun was starting to go down when he stepped outside. It was probably time to get back.

Thankfully, Thera was less than half an hour from Oia, where they were staying. His bags fit with him in the back seat, but hauling them out again was a pain.

When he got back to the inn, up to the room Thanatos had gotten them, he struggled to get the door. Suddenly, it pulled in. On the other side of the threshold, Thanatos stared at him.

"Where were you?" Thanatos demanded. "I came back, and you were —" He cut off abruptly.

Lach frowned. He shifted the bags. "Little help?"

With both hands, Thanatos snatched them all from him. "Where were you?"

It took Lach a moment to realize what was wrong. His heart sank. "You thought I left?"

A fair assumption, but it hurt how easily Thanatos could jump to it. "I'm sorry," Lach blurted out. "I should've left a note. Let you know where I was."

"Because you needed to go shopping?" Thanatos asked, shaking the bags. "You got shot, Mis sank, and you, what, needed to work it all out with some retail therapy?"

Lach's spine straightened. His shoulder gave a dull throb. "No." He took one slow breath, hoping that would give him the chance to come up with a perfect response. No luck. "Hermes brought me clothes, but he stole them. I thought you wouldn't like—I don't know. Figured I should try and pay. When you rip my clothes off, I don't want you thinking about how they're stolen." He tried to pass the last off as a joke, but Thanatos only blinked at him. "I really am sorry I worried you."

"I wanted you to rest." Thanatos's voice was small and hurt.

Lach bit his lip. "I know, but I'm not good at that. I did for a while, but I didn't know when you'd be back, and . . . I don't know. I fucked up."

Thanatos shook his head. "You don't have to run everything you do by me."

"Well, maybe not all the time," Lach agreed, "but I think we both know today wasn't the day to just disappear. I was thoughtless."

Again, Thanatos shook his head. "I figured you might be . . . I don't know, upset with me?"

"Why would I be upset with you?" As much as Lach had wanted to go back for Mis, he couldn't fault Thanatos for trying to keep him alive.

"I manipulated you."

"You mean when you calmed me down? Thanatos, that doesn't matter." Maybe the idea of someone having that kind of power over him should've freaked him out, but it wasn't like Thanatos had ever made a habit of it. On that dock all those millennia ago, Thanatos could have commanded Lach to stay. At any point, he could have used his formidable power to bend Lach's will however he wanted. He hadn't; he'd only done it for Lach's own benefit. "I needed it."

Thanatos grimaced. He looked unconvinced as he dropped the bags at the foot of the bed.

"I got you something," Lach said.

As he straightened, arms crossed, Thanatos frowned. "What?"

Lach stepped in close, bent to search through a bag, and came up with the jewelry box. He held it out to Thanatos.

"I figured after New York, I owed you one."

"You didn't have to do that," Thanatos said softly as he opened the box.

Lach swallowed. He wasn't a fool—a god didn't need a watch, even a Cartier one. But what could Lach give Thanatos that he genuinely needed? "Sure, but I figure, I don't know, that it'd look nice with all your, uh, suits and stuff. Do you like it?"

Thanatos smiled softly. His thumb brushed over the watch face. "It's nice. Too expensive."

Lach laughed. "So? What, you think I'm destitute?"

The god blinked at him like he'd never considered an alternative. "Well, you steal."

"From people who deserve it. When they have too much to pay attention. Thanatos, I've been working for the literal earth for millennia. Gaia's got gold veins and gems running through her entire body, and she likes me. You think I'd still be working for her if I didn't get paid? That sound like me?"

He leaned in and took the watch out of its box. He held it out for Thanatos to slip his hand inside, then clasped it shut around his wrist.

"Are you trying to seduce me with your riches, Lach?" Thanatos asked, and finally, Lach felt some of the tension in the room disappear. He might've startled Thanatos, but the damage he'd done wasn't permanent.

"Maybe," Lach admitted, smirking. "Is it working?"

Thanatos rolled his eyes.

Lach looked at the shining metal on his arm and shrugged. "I know it's stupid. I just wanted to give you something," he said. "I can't be Elysium, and I don't guess I can give you peace like that, but I can make being here a little better for you. Well, I can try. I'd like to try—"

Thanatos cut him off with a gentle hand around the back of his neck. He pulled him in. The god's lips were soft but unrelenting. His tongue slid into Lach's mouth, and the second his lips parted, Lach groaned.

He fumbled with Thanatos's shirt, pulling it from his belt, reaching for the buckle. Thanatos leaned back, out of reach of his lips.

"You're hurt," Thanatos whispered.

"I don't care," Lach huffed. Thanatos shook his head. When Lach bent his head to kiss his neck, he felt Thanatos swallow. How often had Thanatos denied him anything? "Please, Thanatos."

"No."

Lach's face fell. It was absurd, but he needed to feel the connection. Without Mis, he was listless. Adrift. The very last thing he could stand was to "rest" while Thanatos rushed off to work again.

Before he started to sink into that worry, Thanatos cupped his cheek. "Get on the bed," he whispered.

All too eagerly, Lach complied. Thanatos rarely took the lead in the bedroom. It'd been a surprise—a revelation—to find that the god bent to his demands back when he'd just been Glaucus, son of a fishmonger and general louse. Now, even when Thanatos crawled onto the bed with him, there was something soft and accommodating about it.

With careful hands, Thanatos undressed him. When Lach reached for him, Thanatos tutted and shook his head. "I'm only doing this if you relax."

Lach narrowed his eyes, but when Thanatos sat back on his heels to wait, he took a deep breath and relaxed back onto the pillows, slipping his hands under the small of his back. "Don't trust myself," Lach admitted.

"Better," Thanatos said, pressing gentle kisses down Lach's collarbone and lower, across his chest, down his stomach. Every brush of his lips was soft, tingling, leaving a trail down his torso that had heat rushing into Lach's cheeks. In the past, he'd always pushed for more, demanded what he wanted, because he thought that was the only way he'd get it. But here Thanatos was, offering, if Lach could only relax enough to let him.

His eyes fluttered shut as Thanatos licked a stripe from the base of his cock to the tip. He sucked Lach off gently, his hand moving in slow strokes in tandem with his mouth. When Lach tensed under him, arching his back, Thanatos paused. He didn't pull off, didn't chastise him, but instead slid a hand up his chest, all the way, till it settled on Lach's cheek, firm and steady.

He peeked down and saw Thanatos staring at him, light brown eyes molten as he hummed around the tip. Lach whimpered. The smooth brush of Thanatos's thumb over his cheek reminded him to breathe through it.

Lach's peak wasn't explosive, but the slow, hot rise of magma. When he came, shuddering, into Thanatos's warm mouth, it felt like Thanatos had wrung him dry. He eased his arms out from under himself, only distantly aware of the pang in his shoulder.

Thanatos was still dressed. Lach reached for him. But the god cocked a brow, and Lach dropped his hand, empty. Only then did Thanatos release his cock from his trousers. He stroked himself where Lach could see him. His balls tightened toward his body, and Lach's gaze flashed up to watch pleasure wrinkle his brow. He came across Lach's belly, but all Lach could do was watch his lips part, that shudder of relaxation work its way up his spine.

Thanatos leaned over to lave his tongue over the wet streaks of come on Lach's skin. "Fucking Hades," Lach cursed as he watched. Thanatos smirked up at him and caught another spot on his tongue.

"It's a little weird when you use his name at a time like this," Thanatos said, his voice a low rumble.

Lach wasn't to be put off so easily. "Thanatos—"

"What?"

Lach bit his lip. "Will you stay with me tonight? I want to feel—"

He could ask—he knew he could ask—but this was soft and selfish. Thanatos didn't have to sleep. He could, but he could also disappear. Go help lost souls. Do about a thousand things more important than holding Lach all night because he was lonely.

Already, Thanatos was shedding his silk shirt, kicking off his trousers. His skin against Lach's was warm and soft and felt like home. Only that silly watch's metal clasp was cool as Thanatos slung his arm over Lach's middle.

"Yeah, Lach." He leaned over, and the kiss he gave Lach was soft and chaste and tasted downright sinful anyway. "I'm staying."

Lach swallowed past the lump in his throat, nodded, and tucked his head in the crook between Thanatos's neck and shoulder. "Me too."

AL FRESCO

Thanatos woke with the morning sun pouring in the window, and the first thing he felt was amazement.

Lach was there.

He hadn't been sure when he went to sleep that he'd wake alone, but it wouldn't have surprised him. Waking with Lach by his side on the boat had been novel and comfortable, but really, when they were trapped no more than a dozen yards from each other in any direction, where was there to escape to? Now, there were miles of island Lach could be off exploring. Or shopping, which was apparently something he sneaked off to do now.

Lach had money. Somehow it was both shocking and not a surprise at all. It only made sense after all; Gaia could pay better in mortal riches than most gods, and she had never been miserly. At the same time, it was hard to imagine scrawny, scrappy little Lach, who was determined to work too hard for everything he got, ever amassing a fortune. But he'd had millennia in which to do so.

He glanced down at the watch on his wrist. It was beautiful: pink-tinged gold with a leather band, and a round face crowded with bold Roman numerals. If he'd wanted such an accessory, he might have chosen it himself.

But Lach had thought of him and bought it.

The man had wandered around the island buying things to fix an imaginary debt incurred by Hermes stealing things in his name. How very like Hermes. And how very unlike the Glaucus of Thanatos's memory.

He'd done it for Thanatos, clearly. Did that make it any less sweet, that he'd been thinking about Thanatos's feelings? Definitely not.

Lach's beautiful eyes cracked open, a little red and irritated from the previous day's stresses, but he smiled. "Hi."

"Hello."

They stayed there like that for a long while. Thanatos didn't want to break eye contact, much less pull away when Lach was lying there in his arms, warm and sleep-ruffled and smiling up at him. When Lach's gaze drifted off to one side and sadness seeped into his expression, Thanatos knew precisely what, or who, he was thinking about.

Misericordia. Lach's best friend for who knew how many years, taken from him in an act of violence.

He tightened his hold on Lach, pulling him tight against his chest and petting his hair rhythmically.

They were interrupted some time later by Lach's phone ringing. As much as Thanatos didn't want to let him go, they still had a job to do. He loosened his grip, and Lach twisted to answer his phone while Thanatos sat up and stretched his loose muscles.

Lach had a quiet conversation that Thanatos didn't listen to as he found his clothes and took his time dressing. Lach, meanwhile, dropped his phone on the bed, hopped up, and started buzzing around the room grabbing clothes. It was easy to see the moment he remembered his injury, when he reached for his shirt draped over the back of a chair and cringed. He slowed his rush to dress after that, thankfully.

"Something wrong?" Thanatos asked.

He sighed. "Martina got in this morning, and she's kinda waiting on us."

Thanatos frowned at that. He'd been unaware that they had things to do, or he'd have made better use of their morning and ensured they had arrived to pick up Lach's friend on time.

As it was, Lach likely wouldn't have a chance to eat, and that was no good. He might be immortal, but all that sticky red blood had been the worst reminder possible that Lach was not a god. He still needed human things to survive, like food, sleep, and not being shot.

Lach glared at the shirt he'd picked up for a minute before sighing and setting it aside. He groped through the previous day's purchases before coming up, triumphant, with a different one. A short-sleeved button-down shirt. Thanatos wasn't sure buttons were great for Lach's shoulder, but maybe lifting his arm to put on something over his head was worse.

He watched as subtly as possible as Lach slipped the shirt on with relative ease and made surprisingly quick headway over the buttons. It was impressive, and made Thanatos wonder how often he injured himself and had to do things one-handed. Either way, as long as Lach was fine, there was no reason to injure his ego by offering to help.

When they finished and made it out to the street, though, and Lach made to get a taxi without considering food, Thanatos had to say something.

"You need breakfast."

Lach grinned at him and nodded. "Yep. We're going to meet Martina at this place in Thera with the best view on the island. Also, maybe the best pancakes in the world. You've gotta try them."

That was better. Maybe Thanatos had wanted to keep Lach to himself for a while longer, but he couldn't complain when the man was so easily agreeing to his demand. It helped that once they were in the cab, Lach leaned against him, pressing their sides tight together.

The island was small, so the cab ride was all too fast, and then Lach was pulling away to go inside. The view was beautiful; it was true. It still wasn't as nice as that last morning on Misericordia, just the three of them and the sunrise.

They met Lach's archaeologist friend at the table. Martina Paget was a substantial woman with a curvy figure, well-toned arm muscles, and a no-nonsense tone. Thanatos wasn't sure why he took an immediate dislike to her. Maybe it was just that she was there, and as such, she took some of Lach's attention. He wasn't used to being so childish, but stranger things had happened.

"Babe," Lach said, giving Thanatos a wicked grin, eyes sparkling, "this is Martina Paget, archaeologist extraordinaire. Martina, this is my boyfriend, Thanatos."

She blinked at Thanatos for a second, eyes cloudy with confusion, brows drawn together. Then she gave a tiny, private smile and stuck out her hand. "Nice to meet you, Thanatos. That's a rather unusual name."

He inclined his head. "I suppose it is. My parents are rather unusual."

"I know the feeling," she sighed.

"Not me," Lach said, grin still in place, guileless and adorable as ever. He caught Thanatos's eye and winked. It was all Thanatos could do not to forget about breakfast and drag him back to their room for the rest of the day.

Regardless of Thanatos's own distractions, the moment they sat down to breakfast, Martina was all business. "I assume since you wanted my help here, we're going to visit Akrotiri?" At Lach's blank look she quirked an eyebrow. "The island's excavation site? Enormous Bronze Age settlement?"

"Oh!" Lach motioned off to the south. "You mean—Yeah. Akrotiri. That place. With the . . . settlement."

All Thanatos could do was try to hold down his laughter. Lach was exactly as awkward as he might have imagined when dealing with impossible-to-obtain historical information. Thanatos didn't know what the mortals had called the island in ancient days, but it didn't shock him that Lach remembered. And had a hard time pretending he didn't.

Martina chewed on her bottom lip for a moment, clearly wanting to ask something, but then she shook her head and looked down at the table. "I'm not sure exactly what you're expecting here, Lach. This dig site is incredible, but it's more than fifty years old. They're still working, but I haven't heard of any major finds here in years."

"So it's a city on the south end of the island," Lach said, staring off into space. "Big one? Looks like it was evacuated, right?"

She nodded, eyes narrowed to slits. "They think it was probably evacuated before the volcanic event that buried the city in ash, yes."

Lach turned a meaningful look on Thanatos. He hoped Lach didn't expect him to know about the island's history. There was a reason he hadn't already known about the scythe's possible location: he didn't commit things like place names and historical events to his memory unless they were enormous and pivotal, like Athens, New York, or the rise or fall of a major empire.

"Some people still think Akrotiri is the source of the Atlantis myth, you know," Martina offered, out of the blue.

"Do they really?" Lach asked brightly, and thank goodness, that was when the waiter arrived to take their order. Any more awkwardness might have been terminal, and Thanatos didn't want to be distracted by work.

The table was quiet for a while after that, with Lach trying to gather his thoughts and his friend giving him time. They didn't have much to go on, just her awareness of the island's historical importance and Thanatos's hope that if they got anywhere near the thing, he'd feel it. It was an object of power; surely it would be obvious?

The settlement had been buried in volcanic ash, she had said. Was that something Zeus had done to keep people away from the scythe? He'd have needed help to do that, but alignment against Cronus was one of the few things the gods could usually agree upon. The universe was a better place without Cronus running amok.

"We can go visit the museum after breakfast," she said, her patience finally cracking. "It has a lot of the art taken from the settlement. Or we could go straight to the dig site."

Lach glanced at Thanatos, and back at Martina. "The art—that's like, frescoes and stuff, right? Not objects?"

Her eyes narrowed. "There have been a few objects, but like you said, they evacuated. They didn't leave a lot behind unless it was too big to move. Something in particular you're looking for?"

Lach shook his head vehemently. "No, of course not."

Both Thanatos and Martina looked at him dubiously. She rolled her eyes after a second when Lach clammed up. "You're a terrible liar, you know. What makes you think there's a heretofore undiscovered artifact on the island?"

"We're not certain," Thanatos interjected as smoothly as possible. "What we have is hearsay, a friend who vaguely remembers seeing something once."

"And on that, you came all this way? Hired me? What if we don't find anything?"

Lach sighed and scrubbed his hands over his eyes. "Then we're all pretty screwed," he muttered.

She didn't get a chance to respond right away, since their food was delivered. After the waiter left, she looked up at him for a moment, brows drawn together and frown on her face, but she didn't say anything.

Lach had been right—the pancakes were delicious, a fact he kept pointing out all through breakfast. Thanatos thought he heard a couple of tourists order them specifically because of the "loud American" extolling their virtues. Lach seemed to enjoy cultivating the feel of an

American tourist, and it was the most on-brand thing he'd ever done. Only Lach would choose to garner a reputation as being loud and slightly annoying.

Good as the pancakes were, Thanatos couldn't help thinking that he'd enjoyed Lach's lopsided attempt at making pancakes more.

After breakfast, Martina took them to Akrotiri. It was a strange place: a whole city buried under layers of ash, perfectly preserved, like Pompeii. Unlike Pompeii, it had no remaining feeling of terror and death. It wasn't a dead place, simply an empty one.

Thanatos had no love of Pompeii. He had helped Hermes in his work that day; so many people dying at once had been too much for any of them to process at the time. It wasn't a kind of death Thanatos saw often, and he wished no one ever had to live it.

She led them around the dig site, pointing out interesting things and chatting with people involved in the dig. She was well educated, polite, and helpful. When she put her hand on Lach's arm, Thanatos still had to keep himself from growling at her.

Lach, the asshole, noticed and winked at Thanatos. He also reached out and grabbed his hand, so he could be forgiven.

"Aren't you hot in that?" she asked him as they leaned against a railing looking over the abandoned city. "I mean, the Armani is nice and all, but all black in this climate? And long sleeves?"

Thanatos looked down at himself. He supposed he was the only person he'd seen wearing so much black. Mortals seemed to favor light colors when in the desert. He shrugged. "I don't mind the heat. Maybe I run cool."

"That's my Thanatos," Lach said in his very best "I'm about to say something obnoxious" tone, grinning over at him. "He's always been the iceberg to my Titanic."

Martina saved Thanatos from having to respond by snorting loudly. "How very like you, to compare yourself to one of the biggest disasters of all time. I guess no one can say you don't know your own faults."

Lach seemed entirely satisfied with the conversation and kept bantering with her. Thanatos wasn't terribly comfortable with the way he talked himself down so much; it had always seemed like a self-fulfilling prophesy, but it wasn't up to him.

He stared out at the city and worried, because as fascinating as the place was, filled with history and information and an odd kind of serenity, there was one thing it wasn't.

A repository for a powerful magical artifact.

Thanatos didn't know if he'd be able to find the scythe by its energy, but he doubted it would feel as quiet and mundane as this abandoned place. Akrotiri might hold secrets, but Thanatos knew in his gut that the scythe was not one of them.

So what now?

"Shall we go to the museum?" Lach asked, seeming to sense Thanatos's shifting mood. "I mean, this place is amazing, but I guess they removed some really interesting frescoes to the museum. Took out a whole wall to get one of them."

"They're really impressive," Martina agreed, motioning for them to follow her back the way they had come.

The museum was fascinating in the way all history museums fascinated Thanatos. Mortals were more passionate about the things that had happened before their births than most Olympians were about their actual lives. The way they dug, discovered, and extrapolated—sometimes in bizarrely incorrect ways—was amazing. It made Thanatos feel small, maybe in the same way it did to them. He liked it.

Like the dig site, however, the museum felt quiet and peaceful, not like there was an object of power lurking in the shadows.

Martina led them through, explaining the frescoes, what they depicted, and what the humans who had discovered and studied them thought they meant. Some were simple, like a beautiful depiction of spring. A few were harder to understand.

When they came to the last in a long line, her face changed. A dozen emotions flitted through her eyes faster than Thanatos could track before she straightened her back and turned to them. "This is the most recent one found."

The painting was stark and less detailed than most of the others. It simply depicted two men in combat, hunched toward each other as though they were wrestling. Above them, there was a lightning bolt in the clear sky. Below them, stuck in the ground, a scythe. They were surrounded by fire on both sides, and the ground beneath their feet was cracked, flames flickering through.

In the context of history, it made no sense. There had been no humans to witness the Titanomachy, let alone to know where its battles had occurred or what they had looked like. In the context of reality, and their presence on the island, it was everything.

"Is that . . ." Lach breathed, reaching for the flaking paint before remembering himself and pulling his hand back. "It is, isn't it?"

"It is," Thanatos agreed. It was the first sign that they were in the right place.

I COULD TELL YOU

Lach caught Thanatos's gaze, a slow smile spreading across his face. There always came a point in every adventure where things got real—intangible ideas hardened into something he could grasp, find, take. Gaia might've sent Lach after the scythe, but it'd felt like a story until that moment. And damn if he hadn't needed the win.

"It is what?" Martina demanded, staring between the pair of them. She crossed her arms, cocked her pursed lips, and raised her eyebrows, unwilling to let them sideline her.

Lach chewed his tongue and considered her narrowed eyes. So far, they'd been playing things close to the chest, but Lach had called on her because she was the best archaeologist he knew. He trusted her, and nothing about giving her the information she needed to be effective required him to disclose that he was standing beside a god he'd personally known for millennia. And she couldn't help if she didn't have all the facts.

"Cronus's scythe," he said.

With wide golden eyes, Thanatos stared at him. Lach hooked his thumbs in his belt loops and gave a little shrug. Shoulder still hurt, but the thrill of a lead was enough to distract him.

Martina stared too. For a few seconds, she was frozen. Then, she let out a bark of a laugh. "Cronus as in the titan god of time? That Cronus?"

"You don't believe in gods?" Lach asked.

"Do you?" she shot back at him. "Which gods? There are thousands all over the world from hundreds of unique cultures. Who's to say if any of them are real?"

Don't look at Thanatos. Don't look at Thanatos.

Lach bit the sides of his tongue and shrugged. "Okay, not literal gods. Metaphorical. We live in a world of magic. There are powerful artifacts everywhere. Why not an ancient one?"

"A scythe wielded by a god that can control time?"

"And harvests."

"And harvests," Martina echoed hollowly. She breathed in slow through her nose and let it out in a sigh. "Okay, say this scythe does exist. You're talking about a weapon that would've been in play in the Golden Age before Cronus fell—which we have no *real* conception of, if it happened at all. You're looking for an artifact that's conservatively ten thousand years old, and you think you're just going to find it lying around Akrotiri?"

"We got a tip," Lach said.

"Oh yeah? Got an eye-witness account, did you? There's no way it's here. The earliest evidence of habitation here is from the fifth millennium BCE, and it's decidedly human," Martina said.

"But what's under that?" Lach asked.

"Who the hell knows? Ash. Volcanic deposits. I study people, Lach. Geology is an entirely different field."

Lach chewed his lip. Old as he was, he didn't predate people. Thanatos did, but his lips were firmly shut, and he looked less than thrilled at Lach having spilled all that to Martina.

She was pinching the bridge of her nose. "I'll do some research," she offered. "I mean, if you're going extremely metaphorical, I guess the entire island could be a scythe—"

"I don't think we're *quite* that far gone yet. We're looking for an actual tool."

Martina dropped her hand. Her eyes narrowed skeptically. "Why?"

"Professional curiosity," Lach offered at once. "Think about the kind of money you'd make on something like that. The papers you could write."

"Uh huh." Martina remained completely unconvinced. "Well, supposedly Zeus defeated Cronus and threw him in Tartarus with the rest of the Titans who stood against him. Then Prometheus made people—modern people. I wouldn't know where to look for something that old."

"An object of power, you'd think Zeus would make some kind of edifice for it or put it somewhere safe."

"Seems unlikely that a god would leave a weapon that powerful unattended where anyone could pick it up," Martina agreed.

"Well," Thanatos cut them off, reaching for Lach's arm. "Thank you so much for bringing us, Martina. That was enlightening. Now, I'm famished. Join us for lunch?"

"I think I'd better check out the archives. I'll touch base with you as soon as I find something," she said.

"Sounds great," Thanatos replied.

Lach frowned. There was no way Thanatos was hungry; something was up.

"Thanks for all your help, Martina. Call if you find anything," Lach said.

"Will do."

Lach let Thanatos pull him out of the museum. They were walking fast enough that Lach had to double time to keep up.

"What's going on?" he asked, tugging on Thanatos's arm and pulling him to a stop at the edge of the road.

"Nothing."

"You're hungry?"

A line puckered Thanatos's brow. "I wanted a minute alone with you."

"Okay." Lach waited a breath, then two, before Thanatos huffed.

"You told her everything."

Lach chuckled. "Well"—he turned and slipped his good arm around Thanatos's neck—"I didn't tell her you could kill her with a look." Thanatos scowled, so Lach pressed on. "Or that the last time I was here, it was to pillage the town before Hephaestus had his wicked away with the place."

Thanatos's frown cleared at once. His contemplative look spoke to the deep well of patience and intelligence that allowed him to solve a problem rather than crash straight through it. Lach fiddled with a lock of his black hair while he thought it through. "Did he have his way with the place?" Thanatos asked.

With a tilt of his head, Lach shrugged. "I guess not. When my crew docked, pretty much everyone was gone already, and they'd taken all their valuables. Usually, when a god goes all fire and fury, it's not done so cleanly."

Gods all had their moments—regrettable behaviors when they overvalued their own importance or undervalued mortality. But maybe, this time, Hephaestus hadn't been trying to hurt anyone. "You think he warned them? Why would he do that?"

"I don't know, but we should find out."

"Now? We just got here."

Thanatos shook his head. "You can't come."

"Like fuck I can't."

"Hephaestus is not a fan of company. He might tolerate me, but . . ."

"I'm too loud?"

Thanatos's smile was pure, sweet indulgence as he leaned in and brushed his lips across Lach's. "You're kind of loud."

Lach rolled his eyes, but what could he say to that? Hephaestus was so reclusive that he was one of the few gods that Lach hadn't actually met. If Thanatos could get more intel from him on his own, then they should split up.

"Fine. You can go alone. I'll see if Martina needs any help with her research."

Thanatos grimaced.

"What?" Lach asked.

"Nothing. I just—maybe you should do some research on your own."

"That's ridiculous. Way more doors open for Martina Paget than they do for me. She gets the *good* primary source material. I'll be stuck trolling Wikipedia all day."

"And while you're with her, are you going to tell her all the secrets of the universe?" Thanatos asked.

"Do I know any?"

"You know a lot more than you think you do."

Lach's frown was deep. He'd shared his secrets with mortals before, and Thanatos was right—it'd bitten him in the ass. But this was different.

"She can't do what we need her to if she doesn't know what we're after, Thanatos."

"She knew too much. Way too fast. If I asked you to believe in the gods —our gods—for the first time ever, would you be able to pick it up like that? She was talking about Zeus like he's real."

"He *is* real."

"She shouldn't know that."

Lach shrugged. "Martina's smart. And we were talking in hypotheticals. This is probably some kind of thought exercise for her, and in the morning, she'll have somebody lock me up for spouting nonsense."

Thanatos continued to look skeptical, so Lach cupped his cheek. "It's fine," he mumbled, satisfied when Thanatos closed the distance between them.

If he'd had his way, Lach would've coaxed him back to their room and said they could work it out in the morning. But there was time for that after, when they'd found the scythe, fixed the crops, and had nothing left to worry about but getting to know each other again.

Thanatos's hand carded through Lach's hair, combing it back from his face. "Can you make it back to the hotel on your own?"

"I think I'll manage. I *have* survived a few thousand years on my own," Lach said. Maybe he should've been affronted, but after being shot and losing Mis, it was nice to have someone worry about him.

"I honestly don't know how." Thanatos kissed his cheek, and in a shiver of air, he was gone, and Lach was left to see what trouble he could stir up at a dig site before lunch.

FATHERS AND SONS

For all that it was a part of Hades, Hephaestus's lair was loud and bright. It was to be expected of a blacksmith's dwelling, perhaps, but it was always a little jarring to step from the silent halls of the underworld into Heph's realm.

It was also arranged by a man who clearly didn't want company: the brightest, loudest, hottest part of the smithy was right near the entrance. One had to really want to see the god of the forge to force themselves past it.

Hephaestus glanced up when he walked in. "Poseidon send you?"

"Poseidon?"

After meeting his eyes for a long, uncomfortable moment—as Hephaestus was wont to do—he shrugged and looked back to the object he was working on. "Not important. I'm just not going to make him anything unless he asks himself. What can I do for you?"

"I hate to be the sort of man who only visits in order to make demands," Thanatos hedged. It wasn't his style, though, beating around the bush, so he shrugged and laid it out. "I've been on Santorini. Thera. I'm not sure what they called it a few thousand years ago, but you evacuated it."

Hephaestus sighed, and his shoulders slumped. "Don't tell me you're here for Zeus." He set down his tools, along with whatever he'd been working on, and left the forge. His unusual gait was more pronounced, as it generally was when he was angry or agitated, and he ran his hands through his hair, stopping to rub the back of his skull as though he had a headache. "I'm not doing it again. It was bad enough for the whole damn world the first time. The caldera isn't there to bow to his whims."

Thanatos blinked and stared for a long time, watching Hephaestus look tired, old, and stressed. Then he shook his head and took a breath. "I'm not here for Zeus either. I may actually be here against him."

That seemed to catch Hephaestus off guard. "You're siding with Hera over him?"

"Chaos, no!" Thanatos threw up his hands to ward off the notion of taking any side in the eternal war between the goddess of marriage and her errant husband. He liked her rather better of the two, and if forced to take a side, it might be hers, but he always thought himself better off out of it. "This isn't really about them."

Hephaestus gave a wry laugh. "Don't tell them that. They might die of shock."

They might, at that. The two were well matched in their enduring belief that the universe revolved around them. Really, they were well matched in everything, and Thanatos didn't understand why they weren't happy together, unless they simply didn't want to be.

Of course, given the situation with Lach, Thanatos was starting to realize how little he understood anyone.

"Come on, then," Hephaestus said, when Thanatos spent too long trying to gather his thoughts. He waved for Thanatos to follow and led him into the living area of his home. It was simply decorated, with a sturdy wood-and-steel table that somehow managed to look both simple and like a piece of modern art. The chairs matched in a way that was rhyme more than precision, as though they were the table's varied children.

"Sit down. Have a drink." He poured two goblets of water from a decanter, putting one in front of Thanatos and downing the other before refilling it. He settled himself into one of the chairs and threw his feet up on another, looking comfortable as he only did when he was in his own home and in the company of someone he trusted.

The level of comfort he displayed was a reminder that while Thanatos was there to ask for help, he and Hephaestus were not at odds. He had rarely disagreed with the god of the forge, if only because Hephaestus was singularly sensible among his brethren. Thanatos often felt as though they were just different generations of the same weird uncle no one wanted to hang out with.

He picked up the goblet, sipped, and sat down in one of the chairs. It was strangely comfortable for a thing of metal and wood, almost like it was made to hold him.

"What are you doing on Thera?" Hephaestus asked after they had been sitting there for a few moments.

Part of Thanatos wanted to answer the question with a question—ask why Hephaestus had evacuated people from the island. Instead, he sighed and nodded. "I suspect it has something to do with your evacuation. They were your worshippers?"

Hephaestus nodded, a bitter smile turning up the corner of his lips. "Of course they were mine. How better to choose a place that's not important to my father?"

"He asked you to activate the caldera?" It was almost more of a statement than a question. He wasn't sure, but it was all starting to make sense. "It's where he defeated Cronus, isn't it?"

Hephaestus rolled his eyes but nodded again. "The scene of his greatest triumph. It's a wonder it took years to occur to him that it was a bad idea, telling his sons that his greatest moment was destroying his own father."

Thanatos winced. It was very like Zeus to see only his own side of a situation, and doubtless, he thought it obvious that Cronus had been the enemy, while he himself was the hero of all stories. It made a person wonder if he realized most humans thought of him as a force of nature at best, and often as an outright villain.

It was also very much in Zeus's nature to think himself smarter than everyone else, and that it was terribly clever to leave the scythe in the most obvious place: right in the spot where it had fallen.

Thanatos sighed and downed the rest of his water. "He didn't want to move the scythe, so instead he buried it."

Hephaestus gave a deep, exhausted sigh, and nodded "Right in the middle of the battlefield."

"But then it resurfaced?" It was a pointless question. Thanatos could see it all so easily.

Zeus had put the scythe underground, because to a creature who adored the clouds as he did, it was the worst possible place to be. But the scythe was an object of massive power, and like its wielder, it didn't want to be hidden. Unlike a prison in the underworld, an earthen grave wasn't enough to hold something that powerful. It had found its way back to the surface and forced Zeus to deal with it again.

"He demanded that you bury it, right there, by whatever means necessary." Thanatos spoke as softly as possible, but Hephaestus still winced.

And why not? He'd never been the most widely worshipped of gods, and he'd had to take his followers out of their homes, make unreasonable demands of them, on the whims of his father.

"You can say it," Hephaestus said, his voice low and filled with self-loathing. "I'm like an abused dog. He kicks me whenever I come near, but I keep coming when he calls."

Thanatos set the goblet down on the table so hard that it let out a metallic clang and water sloshed over the side, but it didn't even make him hesitate. Clearly, Lach had been rubbing off on him. And would've giggled like a child at that double entendre.

Hephaestus, seven-foot-tall mountain of muscle, god of volcanoes, flinched. It made Thanatos feel awful for a fraction of a second, before he reminded himself that the flinch hadn't been his fault. It wasn't about him.

He turned to stare at Hephaestus. "And do you blame the dog for that? For being so loving that they can forgive anything?"

"It's different for them. It's in their nature. A god should be made of stronger stuff." The words had the feel of something repeated over and over until it had lost all meaning.

"The ability to forgive doesn't make you weak," Thanatos insisted. His mind immediately related it back to Lach, of course, because he was all Thanatos could think about anymore. Forgiveness wasn't a weakness unless you allowed yourself to be taken advantage of, and Lach had changed. Whether he had changed *enough* remained to be seen, but dammit, Thanatos had let himself wallow in bitterness for too long. "And a man who kicks a dog is no kind of man at all."

"I shouldn't forgive him."

"No, you shouldn't," Thanatos agreed. "He's used up more than all of his chances to have a relationship with his least annoying son."

Hephaestus snorted into his goblet at that, but he didn't say anything.

"I'm not saying you should forgive, or that it makes you a better person to do it. I'm saying that forgiving him doesn't make you the problem here. It's still—*it's always*—him."

Hephaestus closed his eyes and let his head fall back, and for a moment, he just breathed. His eyes were clearer when he opened them, and he looked hard at Thanatos. "You're looking for it. The scythe."

Thanatos nodded.

"Why? Are you planning to free Cronus?" Disturbingly enough, he didn't look horrified at the idea, more like thoughtful. Thanatos wondered when Zeus had pushed his son so far that he would entertain the notion of freeing Cronus.

The room was silent for a moment, both considering the ramifications of the question, and the concept. Finally, Thanatos shook his head. "No. He was worse, believe it or not. Demeter has broken her promise to humanity, and crops are failing to take. We need it to ensure a harvest."

"You're making sure there's not a famine?" Hephaestus asked, one eyebrow raised.

Thanatos looked away for a second, but shrugged and looked back, determined. "It's the right thing to do, and I'd be doing it even if it weren't. We do funny things for love."

That brought out a smile. Hephaestus looked at a pair of filigreed golden wings hanging on his wall, a sad sort of nostalgia in his eyes. They were stunning, and no doubt, a gift from his one-time wife, Aphrodite. If anyone knew about falling in love outside of their comfort zone, it was Hephaestus. Thanatos would have to remember that if he ever needed advice.

Hephaestus nodded and turned back to him. "It won't stay down. It keeps pushing its way back up. I can feel it there, like a splinter that's almost worked its way free. For now, it's only making the shoreline bleed. If the wrong person gets their hands on it though . . ."

"I won't let that happen."

"Be careful, my friend," Hephaestus told him, voice soft and gentle, as he stood and set his goblet on the table. "The things you're involving yourself in are dangerous. The hatred between father and son is bad enough. Love can make the most painful wound, intentionally or not."

And with that, he left Thanatos alone in his dining area and went back to his forge.

FOR A FRESH START

L ach and his friend—and *Thanatos*—knew about the scythe. Martina sat on the edge of her bed, staring at a wall. Thanatos.

There was no way, was there? Sure, he was incredibly handsome and had an uncanny ability to wear a black suit in the desert without looking uncomfortable, but could the man actually be *the* Thanatos?

And if he were Thanatos, what was he doing hanging out with a reprobate like Lach? Marty liked Lach, but he wasn't exactly the target market for the god of merciful death.

That was a continuing problem, though. Marty liked Lach.

She'd read the texts. She knew that to raise Cronus, they would need an immortal vessel. It was Lach's destiny, to be the container for the king of the titans.

From childhood, she had been taught to look forward to the rebirth of the Father. He would arise, put down those who had wronged him, and make the whole unjust world right. The brotherhood's writings were vague about what it meant to put the world right, but given how things were shaping up, Marty wouldn't mind if it meant wiping the face of the planet clean and starting over.

A fresh start sounded nice.

For that to happen, Lach had to be sacrificed. It hurt a little. He was one of the few beings who might deserve better. She certainly didn't.

She stood and shook herself free of the doubt that tried to drag her down, struggling to breathe. It was obvious from the fresco, and from Lach and Thanatos's reaction to it, what had happened. She didn't need to check any archives.

Some two thousand years ago, long after the volcanic episode that had forced Santorini to be evacuated, two new islands had pushed their way out of the ocean in the middle of the caldera.

The eldest of the two islands, Palea Kameni, was still smaller than its sister isle, and little grew there.

It was the scythe. Damn Zeus had left the scythe there, maybe even caused the volcanic eruption that had buried the island, and it was trying to make its way back to the surface.

It would rise, and they would use it to help the Father take his rightful place.

She shuddered but made herself pull out her phone to call her brother. He would screw everything up again, so she had to make him understand that she could handle things.

"What?" He answered on the fourth ring. He'd been acting more and more like their father since he'd taken over the day-to-day running of the Fidelis Filii, as though he thought himself better than her.

She let the line go on, silent. She accepted a lot from their father; Roger was not her father.

"Marty?" Roger asked after a while, less certain and slightly annoyed. He finally huffed a sigh and used actual words. "What's going on, Marty?"

"Oh good," she said, voice as terse as she could manage. "For a second I thought you were expecting a telemarketer."

He sighed again, loud and theatrical. "Of course not, Marty. But my time is—"

"They know about the scythe."

"What?" His voice was shocked, strained, and she heard him moving around in the background. "Do they know where it is? Have they found it?"

"Yes, and not yet. We have to beat them there, obviously."

Something banged on the other end of the line, like he'd hit something, angry child that he was. "Tell me where. We'll stop and get the cockroach, and then—"

"Don't." She stopped and waited for him to deny her, to complain, but he was quiet. "Don't come for Lach. I'll bring him. You get the brotherhood to Palea Kameni. I'll meet you there."

THE PAGET FAMILY TREE

The site afforded no more clues. He hoped Thanatos fared better, but when he returned to the hotel room, it was empty still. He sighed, sinking onto the bed, and wondered if he should get dinner alone. It was getting late, and Thanatos didn't need to eat, but Lach liked taking him places, watching the small variations in his expression every time he discovered a new delight.

He'd determined to wait when his phone buzzed in his pocket. He flipped it open. "Lach here."

"Hey, it's Marty. I found something. On Palea Kameni." There was a reason he and Martina got along so well on expeditions—she didn't beat around the bush for a second.

"Great! Let's go look."

"Now?"

Lach stood up to glance out the window. It was still light enough. The days were getting longer. They could pop over to the island and be back in a couple hours. Then he'd grab a late dinner with Thanatos. Better than sitting around twiddling his thumbs, waiting for someone else to make things happen.

"Now," he confirmed. "For sure now. We haven't got time to waste. If things don't start growing, the season'll be gone. Too late. Kaput. Starvation station."

"Sorry, what?"

Right. Martina wasn't trying to save the world—she was trying to get a paycheck. "Nothing. Don't worry about it. Thanatos isn't back yet, so we might as well check it out. See if we can get some good news. Where can I meet you?"

"I'll pick you up."

Ten minutes later—after grabbing his gun and leaving a note to let Thanatos know he was with Martina—he was in the back of a taxi with her, headed west. "What'd you find?"

"Well, everything suggests that Cronus's scythe has something to do with volcanoes, a split in the ground. There are hot springs on Palea Kameni that stain people's skins red. It's not dangerous, but active. And worth checking out. It's a short boat trip."

It'd be shorter on Misericordia. The aching loss in his chest sharpened when he saw the harbor. Martina paid off a boatman to take them across before Lach shook himself out of it. Well, she could put it on his bill.

The rocking of the boat was familiar and saddening enough that Lach didn't think too much about it when he saw a flicker of flame on the island. Otherwise, it appeared to be uninhabited. When they disembarked, the sky was already turning a deep purple.

"We're not going to find much in the dark," he said. Already, some of his earlier resolve had dissipated. It'd been a while since he'd mourned anyone; he'd forgotten how the devastation came in waves. One second, he'd be fine. The next, he'd realize how ridiculous it was for him to go adventuring at twilight when he could be in bed, staring into the abyss.

"We'll be fine," Martina said. She pulled a flashlight out of one of the pockets of her taupe cargo pants and waved it in the air. "And there are lights up ahead."

They climbed the black rocks, only to find when they got there that they weren't alone on the island—there were about a dozen men. Lach frowned at them. They were standing around in a wide arc. With stiff chins and narrowed eyes, they had the look of men with purpose—a single purpose, if the implication of their matching robes was to be believed. Lach grimaced. Nothing good ever came from a group of best buds getting together and donning their supersecret club's favorite creepy costume.

"Friends of yours?" he asked Martina.

"I wouldn't say that," she replied. But the way she spoke was reserved.

She tipped her chin up and refused to look directly at him. A chill crept through him, even before she said, "I'm sorry, Lach."

"Sorry for what?" he demanded.

"For bringing you here," a man said. He stepped forward into the light, and Lach frowned. He had familiar hazel eyes. "For the sacrifice you will have to make to restore the Father."

"I remember you. You're Roger. You sold me those concert tickets," Lach said.

"And put a bug on you, yes. How *did* you manage to get off that boat?"

Everything snapped into place—how they'd found him, how Martina had tipped these people off about where he was going when he'd left New York and maybe even what he was after. They'd shot him. They'd sunk Mis.

"I'm going to kill you," Lach said casually.

In response, the man grinned. "I'm not surprised you think so. It is nice to finally make your acquaintance, Glaucus. I'm Roger Paget."

Paget. Like Martina Paget. Like Charles Paget.

Lach hadn't thought about Charles in years. Eighty years ago, Lach had fallen into Charles's circle. Charles had been taking a world tour after college. He'd had bright, hungry eyes and big ideas, and Lach had spilled his entire past to him. Why not? He was lonely, and Charles was the first person in an age who really listened. He'd seemed so interested, and Lach had been desperate enough for company to try and keep him on the hook.

And he was Martina's father. Years of friendship, and she'd been playing him the whole time.

Lach finally looked at the man in a wheelchair beside Roger and saw behind the thin white hair and loose jowls that youthful man who'd wanted the world, so long as he could keep it for himself.

"You're looking well, Charles." The last time Lach had seen the man, he'd been young, hale, and determined to restore the world to what he thought it ought to be, with people who looked and thought like him making decisions for everyone. It'd taken Lach an embarrassing amount of time to realize that Charles was an enormous dick.

Didn't hurt that he'd been pretty. But now, looking at him—at his son, who had the same frail handsomeness that money could buy—Lach realized that was nothing. Nothing to Thanatos's gorgeous eyes, his soft amusement, his genuine care.

"Not as good as you," Charles replied. His voice wavered and cracked, the effort a strain after nearly a century of aging.

Lach chewed his tongue. There were men all around him—some formidable, some who looked like they were on spring break from the Ivy League university their fathers' checkbooks had gotten them into. But there were way, way too many for Lach to handle on his own.

Didn't mean he had to roll over. He pulled his gun from his belt and leveled it at Roger Paget's pretty face. There was a shuffle, and something crashed into his side as he pulled the trigger. Roger shouted—not dead, too bad—and Lach went tumbling into rocks. The man who tackled him slammed his hand into the ground, and he let the gun go. Another joined in dragging Lach to his feet.

Yards away, Roger was clutching the side of his face, bleeding through his fingers. Lach laughed.

"What the *fuck?*" Roger demanded.

Lach shrugged as well as he could with men gripping his arms. "Dunno. I had one shot, and I don't like the way you look."

A guy—one of those sorts who were so broad his arms didn't touch his sides when they hung down—stalked toward him. He raised his fist, telegraphing every move, but all Lach could do was jerk in the grips of the men behind him, which did nothing to stop the blow from cracking against his jaw.

His teeth clacked together, he tasted blood, and his head swung toward Martina Paget.

"Martina, you really need to diversify your friend group."

She flinched, barely, one second before another blow landed and Lach sagged. The men held him up. Muscle mountain in front of him cocked his fist one more time, but Roger's droll voice stopped him. "Don't ruin him yet."

"That sounds promising," Lach said. Well, he thought he said it, but his tongue was thick and his ears were ringing and he couldn't be trusted to use his mouth for anything other than incomprehensible moaning.

"Tie his hands behind his back. Put him on that altar there," Roger commanded.

Lach was manhandled over to a rock, his arms jerked behind his back and tied at the wrists. When they lay him down, his arms were trapped achingly behind the small of his back. He arched up.

"Hold him down," Roger said.

Lach expected hands on his legs to keep him from squirming, not a small boulder lowered onto his thighs to pin him down. But if Palea Kameni had anything in abundance, it was rocks. He groaned, bracing his heels and trying to push off the massive weight. It didn't budge.

Could've been worse though—they could've put the boulder on his chest. He took a deep breath and closed his eyes. He could think his way through this.

If he were a god, he wouldn't have to. With a twitch of his little finger, he could throw the rock off, crush his enemies, see them driven before him, and hear the lamentations of their loved ones. Yet here he was, a long-lived human but nothing more, with an empty antique gun and a sharp tongue.

It would've been easy to admit that his death was inevitable. He'd had a good run, more than he deserved, and he'd spent his last weeks in the company of the god he loved. If he died now, at least he'd be guaranteed to see Thanatos one last time, when he took Lach to Elysium. Even knowing that was what awaited him, Lach chafed at the idea of giving up.

A long time ago, he'd have been able to shout Thanatos's name and the god could've found him anywhere. Now, with the gods' powers waning, it didn't work like that.

Except that it had. With Mis. Thanatos had been able to take them back to that boat with a thought after the Styx concert. And why? Because Misericordia was his place. That small room below deck with Lach's movies and pajamas was Thanatos's as much as it'd ever been Lach's. Lach wanted to fill that boat with the sound of Thanatos laughing, the sight of his smile, the warmth of his skin after sitting all morning in the sun.

And damn it all, Lach was his person. The gods weren't weaker now because they were older; they were weaker because people didn't believe in them as ardently as they had. Lach had never been much for praying, but if there was a single thing left in the world that he believed in, it was Thanatos.

He closed his eyes and tried to reach out. After all these thousands of years, it still felt ridiculous. Someone like him couldn't hope he was strong enough or loud enough or important enough to catch the attention of a god, even one who loved him. But he shook off that doubt. He had to try anyway.

Thanatos, he thought as hard as he could, until the syllables throbbed in his aching head. What would he say? Help, I've been kidnapped by an archeologist and the Wonder Bread brigade? That wasn't a prayer. Wasn't belief or trust or anything of value.

He took a shaking breath, adrenaline and pain making his chest jump as he heard the movement of wheels across the uneven ground. *Thanatos, I need you. I need your wisdom and your mercy and your help. Come find me. Don't leave me here. Don't let me leave again.*

"Old friend," Charles said, his voice low and his breath sweet as peppermint candies as he leaned over Lach's face.

Thanatos, please.

"Tell me again how you won your immortality," Charles continued.

Lach swallowed. His mouth was dry, his throat like sandpaper as it flexed. Finally, he opened his eyes. A smirk tilted his lips as he turned to look up at Charles. His pale white skin was wrinkled and sallow, marked with spots. But his eyes were lit with the same hunger and a desperation Lach recognized. He did not want to die.

"I killed a cow, because I was hungry."

For a moment, a smile smoothed out the lines of Charles's lips, and he nodded. "Kill the meat, inherit the power." He paused a moment to lick his lips. "Will I have to eat you?"

"Father!" Martina sounded horrified. "He's just a vessel. For Cronus. Not for—"

"Shut up, Marty," Roger hissed.

For Cronus, she'd said. With a chuckle, Lach rolled his eyes. Martina couldn't pick and choose the parts of this she wanted to support. It was all or nothing, and when someone was monstrous, it was foolish to think they weren't a monster all the way through.

"Charles, I really think you ought to. Wouldn't want to risk it not taking. I bet I would go *amazingly* with a Sangiovese. But you should ask Cronus for a recommendation when he gets here. He's pretty well versed in cannibalism."

With knobbed hands, Charles braced himself on the edge of the rock. He pulled himself out of his chair, leaning his knees on the rock for stability. Roger offered him a knife, long and silver and sharp, that caught the moonlight and reflected it coldly. Charles couldn't have help killing him.

What if he made his troll of a son immortal on accident? It wasn't a gift Charles would be willing to share.

"You won't make it forever," Lach warned. "Cronus will tear you apart."

"We will set the world back on track. Together," Charles said with the stubborn surety of the deluded.

He did not lift the knife so much as drag it across Lach's chest. His hand shook, even as he positioned the knife above Lach's heart. He didn't stab, too weak to lift the blade on his own; he leaned his weight against the blade to push it in.

Lach's mouth fell open. The air, despite the season and the hot springs nearby, felt cold in his lungs. His head fell back, and he looked up. He wouldn't have his last sight be Charles, brow furrowed with the effort of murdering him. For one brilliant second, the stars twinkled brighter than ever, honey hued and perfect. And then everything went dark.

LIVING ON A PRAYER

He had the information they needed, and some part of him thought he should be pleased. Excited, even. Instead, all he could feel was a deep sense of foreboding.

Thanatos had never liked Cronus; he doubted that he'd like the scythe any better. Even if Hephaestus's information did lead them to it, and that seemed likely, he wasn't sure he wanted it.

They were almost there, almost done, and yet his heart was shouting that it would be a better idea to throw themselves on the mercy of Demeter. Admittedly, the goddess of the harvest wasn't known for being merciful, but anyone was preferable to Cronus.

The feeling of wrongness in his gut wasn't relieved by the note he found in their hotel room. *Gone with Martina.* Great, because Thanatos trusted Martina as much as he trusted his own people. Sure, she hadn't given him any particular reason to be suspicious, and he knew he wasn't being reasonable, but the concern prevailed.

Thanatos.

He turned toward the door, for a moment thinking Lach had returned. His relief soured a second later when there was no one there, and he realized Lach was praying. Lach was praying to him.

How dire did things have to be, for Lach to resort to that? The words were surprisingly traditional sounding, almost like Lach knew how to pray. The last part, though, sent a chill shivering down Thanatos's spine.

Don't let me leave again.

An image swam up in his mind from all those years ago. Lach—Glaucus—and when had that name been so entirely eclipsed by the new one?—standing on a dock, looking at him with nothing but annoyance. Saying he didn't want to tie himself to Death.

And now he had latched on so hard that he could pray, and Thanatos heard him, as he had only heard the most devout priests in history.

When pain lanced through his chest, he dropped the note and reached for the prayer, for Lach, with all his power. He could feel the universe give under his grip, almost as though he were ripping a hole through it instead of moving it around himself.

He landed heavily, still on his feet but slightly off balance. When he reached out to steady himself, his hands hit stone.

It was an altar, and Lach was pinned to the thing under an enormous rock. An old man stood, shakily, across the altar from Thanatos, trying to slide a wicked looking knife into Lach's heart. He'd missed, but not by enough to reassure Thanatos. Lach was pale and unconscious, and the sight of him made Thanatos's chest constrict.

At Thanatos's appearance, the old man looked up, wobbling and having to let go of the knife to hold the altar so he didn't tip over. "Who are you?" Then he shook his head like it had been a silly question, and motioned to a beefy man behind him. "It doesn't matter. Kill him."

Thanatos had never been a creature of violence, and for a fraction of a second, he froze with indecision. The man started around the altar toward him, but it was Lach's pained breath that broke the stupor. Lach was, as yet, alive. Thanatos wasn't going to allow his hesitation to change that.

He stared at the musclebound man. "If you have an ounce of self-preservation, you'll stay where you are." The man hesitated at the certainty in his voice, but the old man flailed an arm at him.

"Now!"

A day before, Thanatos might have considered himself a pacifist.

It turned out that when a certain pirate's life was on the line, he was not. He made a motion, like shooing someone away, and brushed the man's spirit out of his body. The body dropped like a stone, and the spirit stood there, staring down at himself in shock.

That seemed to make the old man reconsider his position. He'd been reaching for the knife in Lach's chest, but instead he took a step back and stumbled into a wheelchair, glaring at Thanatos, teeth bared in something between a grimace and a snarl.

"Father," Martina and a man called, practically in unison. Thanatos glared at her. He'd known they couldn't trust her.

They didn't have time for her, though. He looked back at Lach.

His Lach, only just returned to him after so long apart.

He didn't know if they could make it work this time, but he couldn't allow it to end like this. Reaching up, he cradled Lach's head in one hand. A drop of blood slipped from his lips and trailed down one cheek.

Thanatos understood, suddenly, why one Olympian after another had selfishly chosen to make their lovers immortal. If he let Lach leave him, that was it. There was no reunion in Elysium for them. If Lach left, he couldn't follow.

And a world forever without Lach was too horrible a thing to contemplate. Not now. Not like this. He could not allow it.

Leaning down, he kissed Lach's forehead.

"Hermes," he called, in his most resonant tone. He didn't call on his Olympian counterpart often—never twice in a handful of days—but the man had always—

"You called, boss?" Hermes paused and looked at the tableau before him. A dozen angry men, the withered old bastard who'd stabbed Lach, and that damned traitor Martina. "Well, this is awkward."

"Forget them," Thanatos said, waving a hand in their direction and ignoring it when they all stepped back. All but Martina, hands firmly planted on her father's shoulders.

He shoved the boulder off Lach's legs, toward the others, and turned to Hermes. "You have to heal him."

Hermes stared, horrified for a fraction of a second, before he jumped into action faster than Thanatos could see, muttering to himself about how many times he'd warned Lach that his mouth was going to get him into trouble. He hopped onto the altar, straddling Lach, and first tore his shirt off, then pulled the knife out, keeping pressure on the wound and working quickly to try to minimize the bleeding.

Thanatos didn't know as much about medicine as Hermes did; he was prone to arriving when it was far too late to help. Still, he stepped up to the side of the altar, prepared to offer his hands, when Hermes waved him away.

"I've got this. You handle the Ivy League. What the hell did he do, tell them Nietzsche was overrated?"

"You are not a part of this," the old man said in their direction, glaring at Thanatos. He was so angry, his words so staccato, that spittle flew from his lips as he spoke. But his body seemed to be failing him, since he was trying to look and sound impressive, but his volume didn't manage to rise above an average speaking tone. "Leave at once!"

Thanatos stared at him, drawing himself up to his full height and pulling his power around him like a mantle. Perhaps he was no Ares to be feared for his martial prowess, or Hephaestus with his impressive size, but damn them all, he was the god of death. If he couldn't use his power to frighten a few mortals, what good was it?

All Hermes needed—all Lach needed—from Thanatos, was for him to stand between them and the enemy. He could do that.

He marched around the altar, past the beefy man's body. His spirit was trying desperately to get back in, yelling for it to get up.

Thanatos reached out and gripped the spirit's arm. "This place is not for you anymore. I gave you an option, and you chose this." He closed his eyes and called to the Keres with his mind. A scant few seconds later, the man's soul was being borne away in the claws of one of his sisters.

"It's not possible," the old man muttered, almost to himself. "*You* can't be a god."

Thanatos offered the most serene smile he could muster when Hermes was in the middle of trying to keep Lach alive. "My godhood isn't relevant to you. Well, except in the sense that most men only meet the god of death once in their existence. I don't foresee you being an exception to that rule."

The old man waved a weak hand to a man behind him and turned. "Now."

The man looked at his superior and then over at Lach, so Thanatos deliberately stepped between.

"We don't have any more time for that," the old man ground out. "It's time to destroy this pretender. We can worry about the miscreant later."

At that, the man nodded and held out his hand as though reaching for Thanatos. He could see the magic the man released, simple corpus stuff that didn't pose a threat to Thanatos. Neither, though, was it aimed at him.

It hit the ground, followed by a low creak that sounded almost like a pained moan. The earth between Thanatos and the men split open, and there was the sensation they had been searching for.

A queasy pit opened up in Thanatos's stomach, nausea and longing and a warped kind of nostalgia for a time when he'd been miserable and alone. The scythe slid out of the crevice like a slimy swamp dweller, dripping blood-red water, and placed itself in the old man's grasp.

He grinned at Thanatos. "Who is the god of death now, fake?"

UNION

This couldn't be more wrong if it were an actual nightmare.

Marty had planned to lose Lach, even if she liked him more than her father and brother combined. A new, just, hopeful world was worth any price, even if it had been her own life.

But this wasn't a new world.

This was murder for the sake of her father's own selfish wishes—preserving his life past natural boundaries that existed for a reason. Killing Lach for his immortality had no part in the plan the Fidelis Filii had always claimed to aspire to.

They were supposed to retrieve the scythe and sacrifice an immortal vessel so that Cronus could inhabit it.

If they killed the immortal, where was Cronus supposed to go?

Don't you know yet?

The feminine voice shocked her, and she looked around. She had always been the only female member of the Fidelis Filii. As her brother liked to remind her regularly, they were the faithful sons, not daughters. She hadn't bothered telling him that the term could just as easily mean the faithful children. He didn't care. She saw no one looking at her, and no overtly feminine forms in the group.

"No," she whispered. "Where?"

The voice was sad when it came again, almost resigned. *Into your father, to bind the two of them forever. Your father thinks he can partner with Cronus and become the ruler of his brave new world. It is unfortunate, but however much we love them, some are beyond saving.*

Marty wanted to throw up. She'd never considered saving Roger or her father before. They simply were what they were, and she'd accepted it.

But this was too much.

This wasn't a fresh start. This was a shameless power grab.

Her father pushed himself up from the chair again, holding the scythe aloft, and began to speak the words of the spell. He'd learned them in English, because his Greek had never been particularly good, and his Latin even worse. Half of the men looked rapturous, staring into the heavens as though a creature imprisoned in the underworld would descend from above.

Did you not imagine something similar, when you pictured my son's ascension?

Son. Oh gods, it was Gaia. The very earth beneath Martina's feet was speaking to her. "He was supposed to bring a new Golden Age," she whispered.

Somehow, her father heard her and turned his head. "We shall do exactly that, he and I together." His eyes narrowed at her. "Or do you wish to deny your father continued life?"

When had he finished the chant, to be speaking to her? Surely he hadn't interrupted ritual magic in order to rebuke her.

"I've never denied you anything, Father," she told him softly. She suddenly wished she had. She wished she'd never told him about meeting Lach, or Santorini, or anything at all.

The Fidelis mage next to her father cleared his throat and whispered, "The spell, sir."

Her father turned to go back to chanting, only to frown down at his hand and shake it as though trying to dislodge something. A dozen red strands had seeped out of the scythe, fine as silken threads, and wrapped themselves around his hand as though to attach the thing to him.

When the flick of his wrist didn't remove them, he reached over with his left hand and tried to brush them away, only to have them stick to it as well. He started muttering under his breath, increasing in volume and anger until the threads started winding their way up his arms, and his voice turned high and hysterical.

Cronus will not share with your father. He will destroy him. And, dear child, the Golden Age was not what you think it was.

Images flooded her mind: an angry, cruel titan, ruling with an iron fist. Lashing out at any who questioned him—mother, sibling, and other titan alike. Swallowing his own children to keep them from supplanting him the way he'd done to his own father. Say what one might about Zeus, when confronted with the prophecy that one of his sons would kill him, he hadn't tried to destroy them all.

If that is the Golden Age you wish to see again, by all means, allow this to continue.

"Allow?" Martina asked. She'd have worried she was being too loud, but no one was paying attention to her anymore. Everyone focused on trying to help her father. Or just watching him with horror. A few had even run off. "Allow implies I can do something else."

I am giving you a choice, child. I have not walked in a form such as yours in many millennia, but I make the offer. Do as your father has attempted to do with my son, and become my avatar. I will end this.

"Will you take me over entirely?" she had to ask. She wasn't sure it would change her answer, but in a way, Gaia's response would give her a measure of the goddess.

Such is not my intention, but I do not know. It has been ages since I experienced this existence on two legs.

"Lach said something about a harvest. It's why he was looking—" Members of Fidelis Filii were starting to glance her way with confusion and mistrust, but it didn't matter anymore.

I sent him for the scythe because of the coming famine. We will stop this and restore the harvest together, you and I. Perhaps that will be enough of a new world for you.

"Yes. I agree to your terms."

Yes.

A golden-green light shot up from the ground around her and carried her aloft. She could feel her whole body filling with it, and along with that warmth came a sense of peace and serenity. The millennia were long and vibrant ahead of them if they could stop these fools from destroying everyone with their selfishness.

They would start with their father and their son. Charles and Cronus.

They reached out to their newly combined power and found it to be something new, different, and more powerful than either of them had experienced before. The part of them that was Martina was proud to offer such an ancient creature a new feeling.

Using the energy of the planet itself, they cut the red strands tying their father to the scythe, attempting to summon Cronus from the depths. Charles collapsed to the ground in a heap, and even the part of them that had been Martina could not worry about him.

With a simple motion, they sent the scythe flying high above, only to explode into a shower of a million, million pieces, like a great red-and-gold firework that covered the whole sky, as far as the eye could see.

When they pushed, the energy of the scythe spread across the whole globe, diffused into little more than the odd ember on the wind. Where the specks drifted down to touch the barren ground, plants revived and grew, and the very soil teemed with previously missing vigor.

"*None shall dictate my growing seasons but I,*" they announced, voice booming and resonating on a godly frequency, that their children might hear it as well as those present on Palea Kameni. The cultists needed to know it, but so too did Demeter, their recalcitrant grandchild who thought to starve an entire world for the sake of a tantrum.

They smiled. For the first time in their existence, no husband or son or daughter would control their fate. They had infused the magic of the scythe into themselves, and they would control their own destiny in a way that had never before been allowed.

"Dammit," a tiny voice said, apparently uninterested in her newfound power. "You can't do this to me, Lach. Or to Thanatos! I mean, you've spent all these years trying to figure out how to make it up to him. You can't do that and then bail, can you?"

Their most loyal child and friend was lying on a stone altar, covered with his own blood. They held so much responsibility for this. They had sent him for the scythe. They had brought him to this place to use as their son's new avatar. He was their friend. Both of their friend.

If all of that hadn't been enough, the broken expressions on the faces of dear sweet Thanatos and clever little Hermes spoke of how important this single child was to the whole world.

They moved forward, the small and thinning group of cultists parting before them, and went to Lach's side. So many centuries, he had been their loyal man. So many years, a good friend.

They reached out and laid a hand on his forehead, filling him with their magic, restoring his body to its proper state. Wounds closed and cells repaired—his slow heartbeat gaining strength as his eyes opened.

"We are sorry, friend, for all the pain we have caused you this night. It was not our intention."

Lach blinked up at them for a moment, closing one eye and then the other, as though he could see each of their halves in turn. "Holy crap," he muttered hoarsely. On top of him, Hermes collapsed into a fit of hysterical laughter.

"Gaia." A hand touched their arm, and they turned to see Thanatos, eyes shining with emotion. "How can I—"

"We are pleased to see you happy, sweet one. Like us, too long have you been alone." They leaned forward to kiss his cheek. *"We shall speak again, but at this moment, we wish to taste food for ourselves."*

"French fries," Lach croaked. "You're gonna love 'em."

They resolved to put French fries at the top of their list and reached for the thread of a place where the Martina part of them remembered having had excellent food. They were ready for a new adventure.

AFFIRMATIONS

Lach shut his eyes and took stock of his body. Somehow, he was still occupying it. Charles hadn't even had a nibble.

He felt like he'd had his heart torn out then stuffed back in—there was a phantom ache and the peculiar feeling that every heartbeat was a cheat against death.

Or maybe it was for Death. He took a deep breath, imagining the scrape of metal on his bones, sharp against his ribs. But nothing was there. He was fine. And his eyes fluttered open on the best thing he'd ever seen.

"You came," he whispered. He didn't think he imagined the glassiness of Thanatos's eyes or the thick way he swallowed when he nodded.

Lach tried to sit up, but a firm hand held his shoulder down.

"You should really take it easy. You lost a lot of blood," Hermes said. Lach wasn't sure he'd ever seen the trickster look concerned before.

"I'm fine," Lach assured him, but Hermes didn't back off until Thanatos approached. As Lach tried to sit up again, Thanatos slipped an arm behind his shoulders. A second later, his other arm slid under Lach's legs, and he had a sinking suspicion the god was about to carry him.

"Thanatos, I'm f—"

One look up at him, with his dark brows crinkled with concern and worry swimming in his golden eyes, brought Lach up short. What was the harm in this? For so long, he'd chafed against the idea of being a burden, being unworthy, but it'd never been about that. Lach might be an asshole, a thief, and yes, he had done a legitimate stint as a pirate, but it wasn't up to him to decide he wasn't what Thanatos wanted. He didn't get to push happiness away just to sate that broken part of him that felt like he hadn't earned it—not if it meant hurting the person he loved.

His inhale shook, and he smiled faintly at Thanatos. He slid his arm around the back of Thanatos's neck, using the leverage of his hand curled under his hair to lean in and kiss his cheek. "Thank you."

Thanatos made a short sound, something like a hum that vibrated against Lach's side. Something unwound in Thanatos's wary gaze when Lach accepted his help. Their eyes caught for one impossible heartbeat, then another, before Thanatos looked up. "Hermes?"

"You go on," Hermes said, waving his hand. "Two gods to round up a bunch of humans—even with an island-splitting mage—is overkill. Leave me my fun."

He smirked and darted off, but not before Lach realized his hands were stained with blood—Lach's blood. Shivering, he buried his face in Thanatos's neck. "Can we go home?"

Once Thanatos transported them to a graveyard near the hotel, it was something of a letdown to remember that "home" meant their room there, but when Thanatos carried him upstairs and lowered him onto the bed gently, Lach was grateful for something soft.

Before Thanatos could straighten, Lach grabbed the lapel of his jacket and dragged him in for a kiss. He tasted salt and sweat—mostly his own—and Thanatos's sweet lips under all that. "Don't go," he rasped, hardly willing to part for even that long.

"Not going anywhere," Thanatos promised, cupping his cheek. Lach's eyes slipped closed at the soothing brush of his thumb. "But you need to rest."

"Because Hermes said so?" Lach laughed.

"Yes, because Hermes said so." Right then, Thanatos looked so stern that it was a struggle for Lach not to roll his eyes.

"I was healed by the literal earth mother—"

"From a six-inch blade to the heart."

"Charles missed. I'm fine."

Thanatos pursed his lips. For a second, Lach thought it was just because he was being stubborn. Then Thanatos asked, "You knew him before tonight?"

Lach sighed, sinking into the pillows behind him. "I guess we have some things to discuss before I jump your bones."

Though the look Thanatos gave him was thoroughly unimpressed, he nodded, toed off his shoes, and started working on Lach's less comfortable clothing. "So talk," he said as he untied Lach's shoelaces.

Everything Thanatos did was so methodical that it took a while to undo Lach's laces and twist them up so they wouldn't get tangled. While he worked, Lach had the luxury of leaning back, looking up at the ceiling, and recounting how he'd befriended a bigot.

To his credit, he hadn't known Charles was a bigot at first. He told Thanatos how he'd met Charles in Paris, where Charles was on tour after graduating from Banneker College of Magic. He'd had big ideas about how to change the world, make it better, but Lach hadn't realized that he was only talking about making the world better for himself and people like him. Charles's issue with the status quo wasn't that injustice remained, but that people had begun to make feeble attempts to dismantle it.

"Sounds like the kind of man who'd appreciate Cronus," Thanatos said mildly. Lach got the impression he was trying very hard not to pass judgement.

"Well, as soon as I realized, I told him where to stick it. The world doesn't need more entitled assholes. But by then, I'd already told him everything. About me. How I became immortal. What the world had been like. It was stupid." Thanatos frowned at him, but before he had the chance to say anything, Lach continued. "I don't know. I guess I was lonely. He made it seem like he was listening, that he cared, and the idea of a better world—it sounded good. But I gave him all the information he needed to get here tonight. I set him on that path."

"You're not responsible for him, whatever you said. You could've told him to burn the world down, and if he'd listened to you, that'd be on him."

He didn't know what to say to that. Maybe Lach should be defending himself still, but Thanatos didn't seem angry. There was nothing to defend himself from.

"Pants on or off?" Thanatos asked once he'd taken off Lach's belt.

Lach wiggled his brows. "Off, obviously."

It was a wonder that Thanatos didn't scoff at him—Lach wouldn't have been so strong. "We can have sex tomorrow. Or the next day. Or the day after that," he said steadily, his gaze boring into Lach as heat swept up Lach's neck.

"That sounds good. Sex tomorrow. And the next day. And the day after that," Lach teased. He gripped the front of Thanatos's shirt and pulled him in for another kiss. All Lach had ever had to do was ask, and Thanatos came for him. "And tonight." His voice cracked. "I know it's silly, but I thought I'd—" Lach blew out his cheeks, and his breath puffed out of him. "I thought I'd only see you one more time after tonight. To go to Elysium. And I—I wasted so much time being so *stupid*—"

"Stop saying that."

Lach furrowed his brow.

"It's inaccurate," Thanatos clarified. "And offensive. If you had a smartphone, you'd know that."

Lach sighed, but a smile crept onto his lips. "Okay. What I'm saying is that I wasted a lot of time without you, and I need you tonight. If—If you're up to it, I mean."

With his lips screwed to the side, Lach realized he might've been asking too much. However the night had affected him, Thanatos had been there too. He might need time, or space, or—

When Thanatos swept in to kiss him, he did it without a second's hesitation. A moan rose from Lach's throat when Thanatos's tongue parted his lips. When he broke the kiss, he tipped his forehead to lean against Lach's. His eyes were closed; Lach wished he'd open them.

"I didn't know you were lonely all that time."

"Oh." Lach shrugged. "I did that to myself. I didn't have to be." He bit his lip, reaching for the hem of Thanatos's shirt. He didn't have patience for the buttons and tugged it over his head. "I'm not now."

Thanatos leaned back to allow him to pull it off. He still looked tortured, worried about a time that had already passed, but he didn't say anything.

Words were hard sometimes, so Lach sat up and moved to the edge of the bed. "We'll go easy," he whispered. "Okay?"

Thanatos nodded. He let Lach strip him of his trousers and kicked them off on the floor. Without Mis there, they were going to need to go shopping again, or, Hades forbid, do laundry themselves soon. Maybe

Thanatos's impervious god charm was transferrable and Lach would never get dirty again. A pirate could dream.

Right in front of him, naked and perfect, stood the best god in the whole pantheon, and Lach was overwhelmed with the sense that he could keep him. After running for so long, that actually sounded pretty damn good.

"I love you," he said, running his rough hands over Thanatos's silken hips.

Thanatos ducked his head, hiding a faint smile. "Love you too."

And that was it—Thanatos the way he'd been before. Oh sure, he was a god, perfectly capable of killing someone with a wave of his hand. But he was Lach's Thanatos—generous and kind and soft. And this time, Lach would care for him better.

"Come here?" he asked lowly.

Thanatos shook his head. "Scoot back?"

Before he did, Thanatos helped him shimmy out of his pants. Then, when Lach's shoulders hit the headboard, Thanatos crawled into his lap.

There, like that, there was hardly a part of each other that they couldn't touch. Lach took his time, tracing Thanatos's graceful limbs, the lines of his stomach, like he had eternity to memorize him. Gods above, he hoped he did.

When Thanatos leaned over and searched out the lube, he pressed it into Lach's hand. "Now," he keened.

Lach didn't have it in him to refuse Thanatos anything. There'd be other times for teasing. Other times to drive him to the edge and leave him hanging there. Now, he sank his fingers into Thanatos and spread him open. His own breath hissed as Thanatos rocked, the friction of their bodies making the whole world shrink to just the space between them.

His own patience shattered, and he lifted Thanatos up. With one hand, he steadied his cock. Thanatos's arms twined around his neck for balance, and he sank onto Lach steadily.

They moved slowly, bent as they were and curled around each other. There wasn't much space, but Lach could hardly lament that it forced him to stay buried in the man he loved. It was a gentle rock, and Lach kissed everywhere he could reach—Thanatos's sharp cheeks, the line of his jaw, his fluttering eyelids. When Thanatos gripped his shoulders hard, arching his back, it changed the angle of Lach's thrust. The sound Thanatos made when he cried out—Lach couldn't imagine ever wanting to hear anything else.

"Lean back," Lach said, pressing a hand to the center of his chest. Biting his lip, Thanatos did as Lach asked. He had to hold himself up on his hands, braced on either side of Lach's calves on the mattress, with his legs bent beside Lach's chest. Like that, he was completely open to Lach, all smooth, gorgeous skin. Unable to help himself, he glanced down to watch his dick sink into Thanatos. He thrust deeper, gratified at the low rumble of a moan. "You're so beautiful," Lach breathed, catching his eye again as Thanatos worried his bottom lip with his teeth.

With Thanatos over him, covered in a thin sheen of sweat that looked as gold as his eyes in the light and trapped prone by the effort of holding himself like that, Lach was lost. He reached out to wrap his hand around Thanatos's dick. He stroked in time with his thrusts, losing himself in that tight, clenching heat until Thanatos cried out, spilling over his hand and dragging Lach over the edge with him.

His arms shuddered and gave out, and Thanatos collapsed, panting, on top of his legs. Lach grinned. It was an enormous ego boost to think he could wear out a god, even if it was only because Thanatos let him.

He shimmied out from under Thanatos only to curl around his side and bury his head in the god's shoulder. His arm looped around Thanatos's waist, and he pressed a short kiss against the corner of his jaw. The mess could wait; the world could wait. All Lach needed was right there in his arms.

LIKE JAWS

It was not a surprise that Lach slept quickly. Even with Gaia's intervention, he'd lost a lot of blood. And been stabbed.

Some small part of Thanatos wanted to blame the mess on himself—to say that if he hadn't been there, Lach wouldn't have gotten into trouble. It simply wasn't true though. Lach was good at getting himself into trouble, and it was likely that even without Thanatos, he'd have found himself on Palea Kameni.

But if they hadn't spent the last few weeks together, if Lach hadn't thought he could reach out to Thanatos . . . That didn't bear thinking about. He shivered and pulled Lach closer, as though to warm him.

He was almost angelic in his sleep. Gold-tipped brown lashes so long they rested against his cheeks, no tightness around his eyes or mouth to show the tension he constantly carried inside. No anger or fear or worry, as he'd cycled through over the last few weeks. He let out a little snore, then snuffled and buried his face against Thanatos's chest.

Thanatos ran a hand through his hair absentmindedly. It was probably socially unacceptable to lie there and watch his lover sleep, but considering his night, what he'd almost lost, he thought he'd earned a bit of a pass. It wasn't as though Lach would be offended.

He spent hours like that, holding Lach and thinking about what had happened and how it all could have gone wrong. Sometime in the middle of the night, his thoughts turned into something else. They turned to what came next. What he and Lach could do together.

There were so many places they could visit, things they could do, gods he could introduce to Lach. Charon would have to come first, and it would take some careful work to do that. His brother was going to go protective, no doubt, given how it had gone the last time they had spoken on the subject of Lach.

Charon would get over it. He would have to.

Then there was Hebe. It wasn't that the goddess of youth needed to convince Lach about the merits of a smartphone—though she did—there was the matter of Lach getting injured twice in less than a week. Thanatos couldn't live with that kind of fear, and for the first time in his existence, he was going to be completely selfish about something.

He was going to ask Lach to give up Elysium forever. Well, he could visit, as Thanatos did. But once one partook of ambrosia, they forever gave up mortality and its benefits. Even though Lach had expressed disinterest in the afterlife, part of Thanatos felt as though he were asking for too much. Lach would laugh and roll his eyes, but it wasn't simply immortality. It was forever.

Not much could truly kill a god, and for those few who had died, no one knew if anything came after. Thanatos doubted it. They had come from nothing, and it seemed reasonable that they would return to nothing when they faded or were killed.

He would have to make all of that crystal clear to Lach, not that he'd listen. He'd wave it away and tell Thanatos he was worrying too much. It was possible; Thanatos did that. But there was still a big difference between a few thousand years and forever.

That didn't matter, in the end. Thanatos was going to offer, because he wanted Lach forever. After that, it was all up to Lach.

In the gray hour before dawn, there was a soft tap on the door.

Thanatos carefully peeled himself away from Lach, jostling him as little as possible. He took the pillow he'd been resting his head on and slipped it into Lach's arms. Lach squeezed it, then grumbled something unintelligible but vaguely displeased. He didn't sit up, though, so Thanatos slipped into his pants and tiptoed over to the door. The lock clicked loudly when he slid it open, but there wasn't much he could do about that.

He opened the door to find a manic-looking Hermes, bouncing on the balls of his feet as though he could barely contain himself.

"I take it the, um . . . cultists are all in custody? They are some kind of cult, right?"

Hermes gave a sharp nod. "Sure are. And I think I got them. At least most of them."

Thanatos narrowed his eyes in the other god's direction. "Most of them? You realize what they were trying—"

"I don't think they got away," Hermes corrected. "Just a couple of them got to their boat and gunned it for the island."

He brought a hand up in front of himself like he was a toddler playing with toy vehicles. He zoomed one along in front of himself as though it were a fast boat. Thanatos half expected him to make a little "vroom" noise.

"Then the weirdest thing happened."

With his other hand, Hermes mimed something coming up from beneath the imaginary waterline and smashing into the first. "It was wicked cool, like *Jaws* or something," he exclaimed, like an excited child. "But the thing is, the boat capsized, and I have no idea what happened to the dudes. Water is so not my element. They might be dead. Can humans swim for miles?"

Thanatos stared at the second hand, ostensibly some kind of submarine that had rammed the cultists' boat. A thought started to form in his mind, but around Hermes, nascent thoughts were rarely able to come to fruition.

"So anyway, I gave Dad the cultists. He's still all pissed at me, but he hates his dad way more than Hera, so maybe I'm a little out of the doghouse." He looked so hopeful that it broke Thanatos's heart. Zeus was a better father than his own had been, but no good father produced sons who feared him as much as they were desperate for his approval. And really, it didn't take much to be a better father than a man who ate his children.

"And the cultists?"

Hermes sighed as though put upon, but there was still mischief twinkling in his eyes. He was so much like Lach, sometimes. "I guess there are more who didn't make it for the sacrifice. Lach-rifice?" He shook his head. "Anyway, Dad told me to track down the rest of them, 'cause we can't have people trying to free Cronus around."

A little of the energy went out of him, and he frowned at the floor.

"Hermes?" Thanatos prodded.

Hermes looked back up, offering a half smile for a second before biting his lip. "I dunno. Something seemed off about the way he was acting. If I didn't know Dad better, I'd say maybe he was, like . . . scared."

Things were getting stranger and stranger as they went, but at least for the time being, Thanatos was done with godly infighting and plots to destroy all humanity. He hoped he was, anyway.

"If your father is nervous about it, I hope you'll do your best to be careful, Hermes. Zeus isn't easily frightened, and they might have been easy to round up, but those cultists almost succeeded in summoning Cronus."

Hermes frowned at that but nodded. "I will be. And if things go bad, I'll call you and Lach. I mean, not right away, because you guys are going to be going at it like—"

"Good night, Hermes," Thanatos said, stepping back and closing the door.

Just before the door clicked shut, Hermes said, "But it's morning!"

Thanatos rolled his eyes and turned to see Lach watching him from the bed. This was getting to be a habit. "Sorry. I was hoping we wouldn't wake you, but Hermes is . . . Hermes."

Lach grinned at that. "Hey, I like him. Most of the time. Didn't know he liked me, but he's fun."

"Didn't know he liked you?" Thanatos asked, staring in disbelief. "You didn't think the god of tricksters, thieves, and travelers would like you, the thief and trickster who's spent the last few millennia traveling around the world on boats?"

Lach didn't answer, just shrugged and kept grinning at him.

That was when he remembered Hermes's odd story about the cultists' boat. "You want to get dressed and take a walk?"

Lach quirked an eyebrow. "A walk? Why would we go for a walk when we have a perfectly serviceable bed right here?"

"Humor me. You're going to have to get used to that."

Without further argument, Lach hopped out of bed and set to dressing. There was no struggle this time; it seemed that while Gaia's healing hadn't replenished his energy, it had definitely healed both the knife wound and the previous gunshot.

Thanatos had always been a little bitter toward Gaia for keeping Lach's loyalty when he couldn't, but that evaporated like so much dew in the dawning light of Lach's bright grin. Gods didn't worship other gods, but Thanatos sent off a tiny mental thank you to the earth for preserving the man he didn't know how to exist without anymore.

MELITINI

Lach had never been the sort to take early morning walks or even late morning walks. Whenever he strolled, it was with an eye to what he could get out of it. Now, his prize was slipping his fingers through Thanatos's, which was definitely worth getting out of bed for.

They stopped at a bakery for breakfast and got melitini. The pastry was golden and flaky, the sweet, creamy cheese melting on his tongue. Thanatos insisted he eat first, and Lach indulged him by taking the first bite. Then he held it out in front of Thanatos's lips.

"You have to get over the idea that I'm so fragile, I need pastries to keep me alive," Lach chided, earning a faint glare.

"You almost died. You need to get your strength up."

"Not sure this is the most nutritious option, Thanatos." When Thanatos furrowed his brow as if he were considering dragging Lach off for a dozen eggs and a rasher of bacon, Lach laughed. "It's fine. It's good. Try some."

Watching pleasure bloom on Thanatos's face when he took a bite made Lach wish they'd bought a dozen rather than four, carefully wrapped for later.

They walked along the edge of the coast, and Thanatos narrowed his eyes out at the water. In the distance, Lach could make out the shape of Nea Kameni, but Palea Kameni was hidden behind it.

"Are we looking for something?" Lach asked.

"No," Thanatos said. "Maybe."

"Well, let me know when you figure it out." They'd gotten to the harbor. Lach let go of Thanatos's hand, but only to extricate another pastry for himself.

He was looking down the row of boats wistfully, and a sick pit in his stomach opened up when he thought about Mis. She should've been there with them. How was it possible to be so happy and so miserable at the same time? Didn't feel fair to have anything he wanted when Mis was—

Mis was there. At the end of the dock, and no mistaking. She was a little different than before—a little sturdier, a little bigger—but there wasn't a damn thing she could ever do that'd make him mistake her for another boat.

He made a sound, high and tight, in the back of his throat and dropped the bag of pastries. The one he'd been reaching for lost flakes on the deck. Thanatos blinked at him. "What?"

"Umpf," Lach said, best he could manage, and rushed onto the dock. He got close enough to touch her side—white and shining and perfect. His arm span wasn't quite large enough to hug a boat, but damn if he didn't want to.

"I was beginning to doubt you'd show," a droll voice said from above them. Charon sat, legs crossed, all in black with a brown paper bag at his side. Looked like the kind of thing you'd carry when you were trying to sneak booze onto the subway.

"Brother," Thanatos said. His voice was tight, like he was nervous. In the years they'd been apart, he hadn't considered that it wasn't just Thanatos he had to impress. Thanatos might want him, but that hardly meant anyone else would be pleased with the match.

"Isn't it a little early for that?" Lach asked as Charon lifted the bag and took a swig of whatever was inside.

Charon scoffed. "No rules on the high seas. And I knew I'd be dealing with you. Certain measures had to be taken."

"Did you come all this way to bring me my boat, Charon?" Lach asked, grinning.

Charon scowled, crossing his arms. "You're her captain."

Lach's smile faded. He was sure what came next would be the implication that Charon shouldn't have *had* to reunite them.

Instead, Charon shrugged. "She told me what happened," he said, setting the brown bag down beside him again.

If anyone could talk to Mis, Lach supposed it would be Charon, who'd spent millennia ferrying souls across the Styx with no one to talk to but his ferryboat.

"You didn't abandon her," Charon said stiffly. The way he avoided looking at his brother was as blatant as if he'd stared directly at him.

"No, I didn't." Lach wanted to say that he'd changed, but he'd been around long enough to know that actions were way more important. It'd take time to prove himself to Charon. It'd take time to prove himself to Thanatos, too, but he'd finally realized that he could—Thanatos wanted him there, so they'd find a way to make it work.

"I realized some things are worth sticking by," Lach added, and he settled his hand on the small of Thanatos's back. From the corner of his eyes, he saw Thanatos's skin darken in a flush, so he gave his hip a little squeeze.

"Uh huh." Charon stood up and turned around. "Well, there's nowhere in the underworld to stow the soul of a vessel like Misericordia. And for some reason, she wanted to come back to you."

Above them, Charon gave a pronounced eyeroll and stepped back to disappear below deck.

"He hasn't smote me yet. Does that mean I'm in?" Lach asked.

Thanatos stared at him. "I sincerely doubt that's what it means."

"But it definitely means I haven't been smote."

Finally, Thanatos's lips began to creep into a smile. "Reasonable assessment," he agreed. Lach hazarded to guess that even if Charon were in a smiting mood, Thanatos wouldn't let his brother hurt him.

"After you," Lach said, extending his arm toward the boarding ramp connecting Mis to the dock. Thanatos hesitated, a frown overtaking his soft smile, but Lach understood—Thanatos wanted Lach to have this moment.

He smirked and shook his head. "Seriously, you go first," Lach insisted. "I want to watch your booty."

If it were possible to look charmed and completely exasperated at once, Thanatos managed it. They climbed aboard. Everything was mostly the same, but the bench they'd sat on to watch the sunrise now bent in an angle with a table at the corner where they could set their breakfasts.

Already, Lach was thinking about abandoning their lumpy pancakes so he could lie Thanatos back across the bench and feed other urges.

They followed Charon below deck. Now, there was room in the kitchen for both of them to cook, though Lach imagined they'd brush against each other often enough to get distracted.

And above the dining room table's bench, there was a small grim reaper. Lach burst out laughing when he saw it. He leaned over to get a better look at the thing. It was plastic, nothing special, and completely perfect.

"Yeah, I noticed that. It's grotesque," Charon said, as if he were determined to be unsatisfied by everything.

"Is not," Lach protested. When he tapped the grim reaper's head, the whole thing bobbled like one of those hula girls people stuck on their dashboards in the nineties. He grinned. "It's an icon." He spun toward Thanatos. "A little piece of death so you can always find us."

"I do not look like that," Thanatos said softly.

Of course, the grim reaper in common wisdom was terrifying. Thanatos was anything but—sweet and gentle, with no pale, stretched features and promise of doom.

Lach gave him a once over, from his silk suit jacket to his polished black shoes. Where he was luminous, the little grim reaper was so pale he was almost gray. The icon was absurd in its difference, but that was the point. There was nothing in the whole world that could mirror a god like Thanatos.

"No, you don't," Lach agreed. He sidled up to Thanatos and slipped his arms around his hips. "But you can't expect a toy to capture how gorgeous you are. Anyway, it's cute."

"Not creepy or terrifying?" Thanatos asked. His eyes had begun to twinkle, and when he smiled, Lach thought they might get to keep the bobble grim.

"Not even a little."

He leaned in and stole a kiss. He'd gotten close to dying, but right there on the edge, the scariest thing had been losing this—losing Thanatos when he'd only just gotten his second chance.

"I cannot stay here and watch this," Charon griped, grabbing his things, which amounted to a half-drunk bottle of the wine that Lach had picked up in Ibiza.

Lach frowned. "You drank our wine?"

"I returned your boat," Charon replied smoothly.

After a moment, Lach shrugged. That seemed more than a fair trade. He looked up at Thanatos and bit his lip. "You up for another trip to Spain to restock?"

Thanatos took a slow breath and looked up like he was considering it. "I *suppose* I could make time for that."

Charon groaned, tucking the bottle into his jacket. Though he and Thanatos shared a color palate, Thanatos's appearance was immaculate. Charon looked like a bum and sported the kinds of pockets you could tuck entire bottles of wine into. "Thanatos, you staying?" he asked, shifting his oversize jacket back into place.

"Yeah," Thanatos said. Lach was gratified when he left his arm around him, even though his brother was clearly less than pleased.

Before Charon made it to the stairs, Lach stopped him. "Hey, Charon?"

The ferryman turned around and cocked a brow.

"I imagine you're pretty familiar with the concept of spending a lot of time alone on a boat, right?"

Charon looked at him like he'd gone crazy. "Sure. Think I've got that down pat."

"Really puts things in perspective, don't you think? A lot of time to mull things over when you're out on the water."

For a few long seconds, Charon considered him. Finally, he inclined his head. "A lot of time to think, yeah."

"I might make a mess of everything, but I won't make the same mistakes twice." Lach meant it to sound like a promise, but he chewed his tongue. "Okay, sometimes I make the same mistakes twice. But not here. Not with this. You know. Something important. Some*one* important."

Okay, speaking frankly about his intentions and making promises he intended to keep were not Lach's strong suits; he was bound to be awkward at it. But there was no reason for Charon to groan and roll his eyes like he did.

"Thanatos," he said, refusing to acknowledge Lach's earnest pledge and turning to his brother, "lunch next week?"

Thanatos bit his tongue to try and hide his smile. He didn't manage it. "Sure. I'll bring the pirate."

LUNCH PLANS

"So..." Lach said. Charon had left some time earlier, and Lach had been wandering around Misericordia, reacquainting himself with all of her altered and unaltered aspects. Now, though, he looked like Hermes when he wanted a favor, and it was unsettling.

"Yes?" Thanatos asked when Lach didn't continue.

"Is there any way you could talk to Gaia? I mean, I know you can all talk to each other, I just—I'm worried about Martina."

For a moment, all Thanatos could do was blink at him. Then he remembered why that was a strange request. "She tried to kill you!"

Lach gave a half-hearted shrug. "You gotta give her a break on that. I mean, Charles was nuts. Imagine having a father like him." He made a face as though he'd just remembered that Thanatos's own father was the primordial entity of darkness, and shook his head. "Anyway, I'm worried about her, you know? I mean, I love Gaia. She's always been awesome to me. I've known her for ages, but can Martina be okay in there? Did she have a choice in all this?"

Thanatos sighed and sat down on the bench in the mess. "You're serious." The look he got in return was so very Lach, all he could do was sigh again. He cleared his throat and took a deep breath. "Gaia."

He'd never imagined he would do that. He rarely summoned any gods, or even spoke to them at a distance. He certainly hadn't ever considered summoning a goddess as ancient as his own parents.

Truth told, he didn't expect her to answer, let alone show up. She'd said she planned to go looking for food, which Thanatos could understand. Most gods spent all of their time chasing worldly pleasures, but Gaia had been the world itself for so long, he doubted she truly understood what the term meant.

He was trying to decide whether to bother calling again when she appeared in the middle of the room.

She had changed from Martina's pragmatic cargo pants into a flowing beige dress reminiscent of something from ancient Greece, and there was a serene smile on her lips.

Lach rushed over to her, and Thanatos had to struggle not to stop him. Dammit, the man had almost died, and he was determined to go around acting like he hadn't. Like he hadn't almost bled out right there in front of Thanatos and Hermes. Thanatos was taken by the dual urge to grab him and shake him, and to wrap him in so many layers of armor that nothing would ever touch him again. Perhaps Hephaestus would be willing to make something for him.

"We are pleased to see you well," Gaia told him, smiling and brushing a lock of hair out of his face in the most maternal manner Thanatos had ever seen.

Her voice sounded less like a goddess and more like a person, but she was clinging to the royal we, which seemed like a good sign for Martina. At least, to Thanatos it did. Lach bit his lip and kept his gaze trained on the floor.

There was no hesitation in Gaia; she knew Lach and knew what he was worried about. "You are concerned for the half of us that was Martina."

Lach looked up at her so fast Thanatos was worried he was going to give himself whiplash. "I don't mean to be disrespectful or anything. It's just that she's my friend, and I know how we mortals tend to get torn up in service to the gods—not that I'm talking about you or anything, but—"

"We understand your concern," she said, leaning in and patting his cheek. "The part of us that is Martina is surprised that you aren't angry with her."

"Puh-lease," Lach dismissed, waving the concern away. "Everyone who's ever worked with me has wanted to kill me at least once, and you didn't even follow through. Plus, you know, you guys kinda saved my bacon."

Gaia cocked her head to one side. "Bacon?" Without any explanation from them, she nodded. "Ahh, bacon. And a colloquialism. We put you in the situation that nearly cost your life. Both of us. It was the least we could do to extract you from it."

"Well the least you could have done—"

"He means thank you," Thanatos interrupted Lach with a glare. "He appreciates your help. Now if only we can continue to keep him from getting himself killed with his own sheer carelessness."

"Hey!" Lach said, ready to protest.

Gaia turned to Thanatos and nodded. "Have you considered feeding him ambrosia?"

Thanatos winced, but he wasn't going to lie, not to either of them. He nodded.

The look on Lach's face would have been priceless if it hadn't been so heartbreaking. "You have? Seriously? Me?"

Gaia nodded, half turning to Thanatos, to bring him into the conversation. Again, he was reassured for the continuance of Martina's personality, since such a thing would never have occurred to Gaia, who had been so long without a human body. "I can retrieve it if you wish."

"Sounds good to me," Lach agreed without a second's hesitation.

The sound Thanatos made was a touch embarrassing, a cross between a moan and something pained.

Lach looked concerned. "What? Are you okay?"

"This isn't a dinner invitation, Lach. This is eternity. At least pretend to think about it! Consider what you'll be giving up!" Thanatos hated to keep hammering on a single point, but it was important. It had been millennia since Lach had seen his family, and if he chose to eat ambrosia, to stay with Thanatos, he would never be allowed to stay with them.

"Eternity in Elysium, right. But you go there sometimes," Lach pointed out contrarily. He couldn't help himself, of course. Contrary was the core of his nature.

Thanatos wanted to throw his hands up and walk away, but he recognized that was because if he did, he would end up getting exactly what he wanted: a Lach with golden ichor running through his veins. "I think you should visit Elysium before making a choice."

"But wouldn't I be dead then?"

Thanatos finally had to roll his eyes. "God of death, love. If anyone can bend the rules a little, it's me."

Lach grinned like a kid at a carnival. "Let's go, then. A visit with Mom, Dad, and Philon, and home in time for a nice lunch of ambrosia." He turned to Gaia. "What does ambrosia even taste like?"

Gaia shrugged, and touched her fingers to her lips. "It has been long since I experienced such a thing. I have no need of it. We shall learn it together."

"But, um," Lach said, turning back to her. "Martina is okay, right? She wanted this? She doesn't want, um"—he coughed—"she doesn't want you to go back?"

Thanatos's heart melted even more. He was never going to have Lach's love of the archaeologist, but Lach's loyalty was a wonder.

"You are the best friend any being could wish for," Gaia whispered to him, in a voice slightly closer to Martina's. "And yes. The part of us that is Martina chose this. When the danger passed, we discussed the situation over 'fish and chips,' and decided to remain together. We have much to teach each other. Her mind has opened so much to Gaia that we never thought possible. We are going to change everything. No more reliance on Demeter, fear of Cronus, or need for the scythe. We will make our own fate."

"Whoa," Lach said, taking a deep breath and rubbing at his eyes. "Well, I'm glad you two like each other so much. I've always been a fan of you both." He threw his arms around them in a tight hug, and after a second of surprise, they returned the gesture.

The moment was so intimate Thanatos almost wanted to look away. Except that Lach looked so happy, he had to watch. He had to commit that expression to memory and make it return as often as possible, for as long as he had Lach.

Finally, they separated, and Lach pulled away. "Okay then. We're off to Elysium. What a trip. Be back in time for lunch, you two. Can't wait!"

Thanatos sighed but took his hand and inclined his head to Gaia before reaching out to the underworld and pulling.

ELYSIUM WAITS

To travel to the underworld, Thanatos didn't need any votives, prayers, or haplessly dead. He took Lach's hand, and in a shiver, they moved through the realms.

Hades—the place, not the god—was nothing like he was anticipating. Didn't matter that Thanatos had told him what to expect—there was still that animal sense in his gut that said that dying meant losing. For a long time, he hadn't had much to lose; now, he had everything.

As Lach looked around at the twilight—a diffused glow that touched everything but came from no discernible point above—he sucked in his cheeks. "Is this it? I dunno, Thanatos. Everything is kind of gray. Not a lot to recommend the place."

Thanatos rolled his eyes. And that was it—in this whole place, his eyes sparkled like amber, brighter than anything else.

"This isn't where I belong," Lach said.

"You're not getting out of this that easily, Lach," Thanatos chided. "I want you to see everything."

There wasn't time enough for *everything*, but Thanatos didn't mean it literally. Lach chewed the insides of his cheeks. As flippant as he could be about seeing his family again, it'd been millennia. He'd done his best to take care of his father and brother after his mother died. In some ways, he'd succeeded, but only if you allowed for cheating, stealing, pissing off gods, and running away. Count all that against him, and he must've been an enormous disappointment.

But that cow of Helios's that he'd killed, he'd killed because his family was starving. His family had been able to eat, but the titan had thrown him into the sea, and Lach had washed up on shore hours later. It was the first time he'd met Thanatos, who'd stood over him with a furrowed brow and said he should've died.

He didn't understand until later that Poseidon had saved him, not out of mercy, but because it amused the sea god to annoy Helios. Once Lach had won his favor, the fish around the island were plentiful. Rains came more often. They didn't go hungry again.

He also hadn't realized until later that he was immortal. A change like that should've registered, but immortality wasn't the kind of thing he could recognize without experiencing. It had taken years for him to understand. By the time he had, Philon was larger than he was. His little brother's face had born more wrinkles than his own, and the villagers had begun to whisper about witchcraft and demigods.

He'd fled then, leaving behind his village, his family, everything he'd ever known. And Thanatos.

He felt the smile on his face flinch as he plastered it in place. "Right. Obviously."

"If we're going to find them, you'll have to think about them," Thanatos said gently. "I'm not connected to Markos, Alexia, and Philon as you are."

Lach closed his eyes, gave his shoulders a little shake. When his breath jumped, Thanatos brushed his thumb across his knuckles. "You can stay with them," he offered.

"What, are you gonna murder me?" Lach asked, peeking one eye open.

Thanatos only looked distressed. Best to get this over with before he started getting the wrong idea about Lach's nerves.

He let himself think about the crinkles at the corners of his father's eyes, his gentle hands, the way Philon had clung to his hand when he was little and clapped his shoulder with the full force of Zeus's might when he'd started to tower over him. He thought about the last time he'd seen his mother. He'd been little when she died, and he didn't remember much, but he remembered her round belly when she'd been pregnant with Philon. Her soft laugh and the way her hand rested on the swell. He felt another pull. They moved, and he kept his eyes shut until he heard the crash of waves.

Underfoot, the sand was warm and loose. The water was bluer than Thrinacia's had been all those years ago, and as he stared into it, a small hand tapped his leg.

He turned around to see a girl no higher than his hip with bright blue eyes and hair dark as an oil slick. "Who are you?" she asked in Greek, the same as he'd heard it while he was her size.

"Lach—" He flinched. That name was no good here, to people who'd never heard it. "Glaukos," he corrected, leaning into the hard sounds he'd abandoned when Rome rose. "Who are you?"

"Glykera," she said, tipping up her chin like she was daring him to challenge her. "We haven't had anyone new come here in—in a long time."

"Really?" Lach asked. He let go of Thanatos's hand to crouch down in front of her. "How long?"

"Well, I had nieces and nephews. And their nieces and nephews. And almost ten generations after that. But they slow down. Less and less come. Grandpa says they always stop coming eventually."

Lach frowned. That sounded like a flaw in the mechanism, but when he looked up at Thanatos, the god seemed unconcerned. "Families are drawn to each other," he explained, "but as the world changes and the ties between them loosen, they disperse. End up other places."

Sure. Lach might remember his grandfather, but his great-grandfather? He hadn't even known him. If he wound up dead in the arms of a stranger, that'd hardly be a comfort.

"Ten generations in one place is rare," Thanatos clarified.

Glykera nodded. "We've got a big family."

"I'm looking for someone in particular. Do you know a man named Philon?"

Again, she nodded. A smile crept across her face—a tricky kind of smile that Lach liked immediately. "Come on."

She took his hand and tugged him up the dunes. Right where it should be, his village lit the dark night.

"Glykera!" A voice boomed that made a shiver run up Lach's back.

She let go of his hand and rushed into the arms of an enormous man with a full beard and merry eyes. He looked even more like their father than he had the last time Lach had seen him.

"My girl, what are you doing?" he asked, kissing her cheek. There were other people in the village—all cut of a merry mold. Hale and healthy. "Who's this?"

Philon finally looked at them, and all the blood rushed out of Lach's head. He was going to faint. This wasn't his place. He didn't have any right to be here.

And then Philon was on him. One broad arm wrapped around his back and jerked him in, crushing his daughter against Lach's side until she squirmed to be let down. Only then did he pull away.

"Glaukos," he said fondly, tears sparkling at the corners of his eyes. "I was beginning to think that you would never make it."

"I'm not staying," Lach said hastily. He'd always thought it best to lead with disappointment, but there wasn't a trace of it in Philon's smile as he held Lach's cheeks in both hands.

"Never mind that. Tell me how you are! Who've you brought with you?" Philon's gaze settled on Thanatos. His smile faded. "I've seen you before."

Slowly, Thanatos inclined his head. "When you were ill and young. I came for you, and your brother begged I spare you."

At once, Philon's smile returned. "You saved me!"

"Well, no—" Thanatos began.

"He did," Lach confirmed. "He called Hermes to save you."

Philon embraced Thanatos, who looked about as uncomfortable as any god would to be treated so casually by a mortal. Or maybe it was something else. Philon had grown up on the same stories Lach had. He knew who Thanatos was. Now, in Elysium, he didn't pause a beat to be afraid of him.

"I have a wonderful life to thank you for," Philon said, gripping Thanatos's shoulders as he leaned back. He looked between Lach and Thanatos. "Is that why you've been missing? Father never believed the gossip about Zeus and our mother—" Lach shuddered. Pretty much everyone who had Zeus for a father had been severely fucked up in a major way. He was lucky he didn't. "Are you lovers?"

Lach wiggled his eyebrows. "Sure are. But that's not why I'm not here. It's a long story."

"And I demand you tell it!" Philon's voice was loud enough to get the attention of a dozen people, and before Lach knew what had happened, he was sitting around a fire with his family, spinning tales of immortal cows, nefarious cults, and chariots that drove themselves—that had been a big hit. No one believed him when he tried to say how much the world had changed. Lach had seen it all happen, and it still seemed impossible.

"And you can talk to anyone anywhere?" his mother asked when Lach showed her his flip phone. When she smiled, there was a calculated glint in her eye. He hadn't gotten his shifty streak from his father.

"See?" Lach said, dangling the phone in front of Thanatos. "It's still damn impressive."

Lach turned back to his mother. "You can keep it," he said, passing it to her. "I doubt it'll work down here, but who knows?" When she hesitated, he offered, "I can always get another. They're everywhere now."

She touched his cheek. "If I didn't know better, I'd think you were a mage."

Lach laughed aloud. "No. Not a lick of magic in my blood, and you know it." His gaze slipped back to the god beside him. "But Thanatos has plenty for both of us."

His father offered him food that Philon's wife had begun to serve around the fire. He felt Thanatos tense at his side, but Lach held out a hand to refuse the plate. Everyone there knew what happened when Persephone had eaten those pomegranate seeds, and Lach had no intention of getting caught. "No, thank you."

Markos smiled softly and shook his head. "Of course not. Thanatos?"

Thanatos also refused, though he didn't have to. Lach thought he looked vaguely ill, which was impossible. Well, impossible outside of a boat.

Eventually, Lach extricated them with the promise that he would visit again. The only one who pressed for him to stay was Glykera, who only wanted more stories.

For once, their disinterest in keeping him there didn't make Lach feel unwanted. Philon and his father had accepted him without a pause. His mother had been overjoyed to see him grown. They hadn't asked for explanations for his behavior, because they didn't need them. If Lach had been selfish or disappointing, it hadn't seemed to quell their love for him.

And now, if they did not ask for more, Lach trusted it was because they understood he had what he needed already. In all this time, Elysium hadn't been a place for him. Even seeing them now, that did not change. He was happy to know that they had lived well, and would like to see them again, but he could not settle there.

By the time they stepped away, the light had faded. A facsimile of stars scattered overhead. Lach sighed as they stepped through the sand.

"There's a place for you here," Thanatos said softly. "If you want it."

Lach licked his lips. He knew he couldn't say no to Elysium just for Thanatos's sake; he'd never accept that. For once, he tried to measure his words before he spoke them.

"I love Philon. And I love our parents," Lach began. Already, Thanatos's face was beginning to fall. He tried to cover his disappointment, so Lach tugged on his hand and pulled him to a stop. "And yes, this place could be mine if I wanted ease and comfort. But when have I ever taken the easy way out of things?"

Thanatos scoffed then, rolling his eyes and ready to tell Lach he was being ridiculous.

Lach stepped into him, cupping his cheek firmly and dragging Thanatos around to look into his eyes. "There is no version of paradise for me without you. I couldn't be happy here."

Thanatos's eyes swam with concern and disbelief that Lach didn't know how to brush away.

"I don't want this," he insisted. "I don't want to live among the ghosts of my brother's family. All that evidence of a life well lived. I'm happy for him, but I want my own. You and Mis—people who chose me and my own family to grow with." Thanatos's lips had begun to tremble. Lach smoothed the pad of his thumb across them. "I spent so long wanting people of my own, thinking I'd spent my only shot on my fear and ego. Thanatos"—his voice choked—"you're it for me. I want forever with you. All the messes, all the mistakes, and all the make-up sex." That, finally, got the hint of a smile from Thanatos. Lach full-on grinned. "So, yeah, if you'll have me, that's what I want. No contest."

Thanatos nodded, his locks sliding against the back of Lach's hand. Lach drew him in and kissed him soundly and thought, for maybe the first time, that the world might have more blessings for him than he thought.

"Let's go home," Lach whispered. "I want to taste ambrosia, and maybe something sweeter."

EPILOGUE

Thanatos didn't frequent Dionysus's bar. Hysteria was lovely, he was sure, for a dark, loud club with flashing lights and drunken, dancing mortals, but none of that was Thanatos's speed. As Dionysus would probably tell him, his only speed was slow.

On this evening, a Tuesday in April, the place had been closed down for a private party, and it was perfect. The lights were on and the bartender was serving fruit punch. Okay, there was a version that had rum in it for Lach and the other scoundrels, but the fact that there was a fruit-only version was an improvement from the alcohol-heavy stuff that Thanatos didn't see the point of.

That wasn't actually the part that mattered. What mattered was that most of the people Thanatos loved were there, together, celebrating. Dionysus had called it a celebration of the return of spring.

Appropriately enough for that, Persephone and her children had come. The goddess was on her fifth or sixth glass of punch and telling everyone who would listen about how, sure, she was doing her job on the surface, but tonight, she was going to go home and sleep in her own bed, with her husband.

Her youngest, Lysandros, was following behind her, making sure she didn't tip anything over or drop her cup, which she'd tried to do at least twice. Also, cringing whenever she referred to his father's prowess in bed.

He was shooting dark looks at his fiancé, who looked amused, rather than horrified, at his future mother-in-law's antics.

The party was so far beyond a celebration of the true return of spring, though.

It was a party welcoming Lach to their number, now that he was truly a god, not simply a mortal who had made a questionable choice. Most of the gods seemed not simply accepting, but downright pleased to have him.

Hebe had offered the ambrosia without hesitation when Gaia and Thanatos had gone to her together. She'd given a crack of her bubblegum and rolled her eyes. "Oh please. You two never ask for anything. Have him. Have a dozen dirty pirates. Pirates are still in, anyway."

And with that, Lach was going to be a part of forever. Thanatos might have fantasized about such a future the first time they'd been involved, but he hadn't imagined it possible.

It was also a party welcoming Gaia back to the fold. It wasn't that she'd truly left, but she had spent the better part of many millennia slumbering.

"It's time," she had confided to him after they had retrieved the ambrosia. "We've been allowing others to control our destiny for too long. It's time for both of us to take it back and begin choosing our own future."

Somehow, he felt as though she didn't simply mean the newly formed duality of Gaia and Martina Paget, but both them and Thanatos. It was true—he'd been drifting for a long while, letting time pass. It was time to grab those moments and make them mean something.

He watched Lach across the room, drinking his rum punch and relating a story—something ridiculous and massively exaggerated, no doubt. The way he used his arms to punctuate the story made it entertaining without even knowing what he was talking about. A fish, Thanatos guessed by the way he held his hands a good two feet apart to indicate some kind of measurement.

"He talking about your dick?" Hermes asked, sidling up beside Thanatos.

Thanatos slowly turned his head, giving Hermes his most deadpan expression. "No. His."

Hermes almost spit his drink everywhere and proceeded to have a coughing fit. "You just made that joke. You really did."

"I'd say you should see it, but you probably already have," Thanatos said, but he found that where there might have been jealousy before, now there was only a warm feeling that even if it were true, it wouldn't be again. Lach was with him, and for good.

Hermes's gaze slid away as though he had something to feel guilty about, but Thanatos rested a gentle hand on his shoulder. "How are you doing, Hermes?"

That earned him a sigh. "Eh. I've got most of the cultists, but Dad is still . . . you know, he's Dad." He took a swig of his own drink, one that smelled heavily of rum. "Hey, I forgot to ask you, did you grab Chuckles?"

"Who?" Was he talking about a clown? That would be just like Hermes, to expect Thanatos to recognize some popular modern figure.

Hermes looked downright confused. "You know, Chuckles. Charlie. The dude who tried to eat your man with a side of fava beans and a nice chianti. Chianti would go crappy with humans, by the way. Sure, it's got the acid to handle all that fat, but a white would be better. Chardonnay, maybe."

Thanatos could only stare at him for a moment in astonishment.

"What?"

"You're recommending a wine I should drink while eating Lach." Thanatos waited a moment, and Hermes shrugged awkwardly, one side of his lips turned down in a "what can you do?" expression. As though cannibalism weren't one of the highest crimes according to Olympus—and little wonder, given how Cronus had eaten his own children. Thanatos shook off the thought and returned to the actual conversation. "And you want to know if I retrieved the soul of the man I last saw screaming because Cronus was trying to consume him and inhabit his body?"

"I guess it seems kind of unlikely he died merciful. Though in his case, death might have been a mercy by itself." Hermes shuddered and seemed to try to shake off the thought. "I was wondering, since I hadn't seen him. Maybe Cronus managed to eat him before Gaia broke the scythe. I wonder if that means they're together in Tartarus now, or if Chuckie's just, y'know, gone."

Thanatos considered the possibilities for a moment and found that, for once in his existence, he didn't care what had happened to a mortal soul. He didn't try to justify it to himself. He didn't need to.

Turning to the bar, Hermes made moon eyes at the bartender until she took pity on him and refilled his cup. She rolled her eyes at him, but her expression was tolerant. She knew him well, likely, if she'd been working for Dionysus for long. The brothers were as close as any of Zeus's children.

"You've done well gathering the cultists," Thanatos told him. He wasn't precisely certain it was true, but he assumed. Hermes did most things well. And Thanatos knew for a fact that no matter how well the kid did, Zeus wasn't going to give a damn.

Hermes perked up and shot Thanatos a smile. "Thanks! Some of them have been slippery little suckers."

"Things that ooze out of the sewer usually find it easiest to ooze back in when a light shines in their direction," Thanatos answered. It was unsurprising that they had run for the hills, but if there was one thing men who craved power could be counted on for, it was that they would come back when they saw an opportunity.

"Do I wanna know what you two are on about?" Lach asked, sauntering up to the bar, holding out his empty cup. He waved to the bartender when she came to take his glass. She gave him a wink and a little smirk along with his refill, and still, no burn of jealousy or possessiveness came to Thanatos.

"Your boyfriend was trying to decide whether to put you to work as his assistant, or to hire some hot new young thing to help out," Hermes said, and he sounded stunningly sincere. The god's ability to deceive was breathtaking.

Lach was less impressed. "Yeah, right. We both know if Thanatos hires somebody to help out, it's gonna be somebody's ninety-year-old grandma, and she's gonna mercifully reap souls while handing out cookies and hot cocoa."

While Lach had been joking, that sounded like an excellent idea. Someone who had been through a long existence and knew how important human life was, both to those who survived them and to those dying, seemed the perfect kind of person to help Thanatos out. Of course, that could also describe Lach, and it wouldn't require making anyone else immortal.

He shook his head and leaned over to kiss Lach on the cheek. "Doesn't matter. As long as I have you and Misericordia to come back to, I don't mind work."

"So forever, then," Lach said, his roguish grin firmly in place. "Sounds like a sweet deal for me and Mis."

Hermes made a disgusted sound and walked away, waving his arms as though abjuring them.

"It sounds like a pretty good deal for me too," Thanatos whispered to Lach, wrapping an arm around his waist. "For the record, are you wandering around Mis wearing nothing but those sweatpants when I get back?"

Lach's grin turned lascivious and promising. "Guess you'll have to keep coming back to find out, won't you?"

"It's a deal."

"Ooooh," Lach whispered, breath ghosting over the shell of Thanatos's ear. "I just made a deal with Death. That seems like the kind of thing that shouldn't have me suggesting you god-zap us back to our bedroom, doesn't it?"

"And yet here we are," Thanatos answered, trying to hold back a chuckle. That tiny bit of remaining tension, of wondering when Lach was going to point out that Thanatos was death itself again, started to unwind. He was Death. And Lach loved him.

Lach skimmed his hands down Thanatos's arms, taking both his hands. "Quick, while no one's looking, why don't you make us not here anymore?"

"Everyone is looking," Thanatos pointed out.

Lach turned to give the room at large a saucy wink before turning back to Thanatos. "Even better. Now they know I'm a lucky bastard. Let's go home and screw."

So Thanatos squeezed his hands and thought of that ridiculous bobble-headed shrine on Misericordia.

Home.

AFTERWORD

We hope you enjoyed Patron of Mercy! If you're into Greek mythology like we are, you probably know we've taken some liberties. Glaucus in the myth might've ended up more fishman than fisherman, but it was hard enough convincing Thanatos to get on a boat. You try coaxing him into the ocean depths! Anyway, we think they'd approve of our liberal interpretation.

Or possibly drown us in the Styx.

We'll keep you updated.

We hope to have you back for Sons of Olympus, a new series in the same universe that will follow Zeus's wayward sons as they find love and fight an ancient evil.

ALSO IN THE LORDS OF THE UNDERWORLD UNIVERSE

Prince of Death

Prisoner of Shadows

SONS OF OLYMPUS (COMING SOON)

Wildfire

Fireforged

Warfire

LORDS OF THE UNDERWORLD SHORT STORIES

Heart of the Sea by W.M. Fawkes

EXCERPT FROM WILDFIRE

Sons of Olympus Book One, Coming Soon

The new professor was chirpy.

It was the only word he could think of to describe the way she fluttered around the office like a lost bird, pacing and reading at the same time, letting out little noises of surprise or happiness at random intervals. He couldn't imagine what she found so fascinating in the term papers of freshman history of magic students, but lucky him, she occasionally decided they were worth sharing.

It wasn't like he was also busy grading papers.

"Oh, isn't this adorable?" she crooned, holding one up. "He wants to study the practical application of Spiritus magic in a medical setting. Isn't that clever?"

Wilder quirked a brow at her. "Is he going to tell the patients their fortunes?"

Okay, fine, he knew that Spiritus did more than that. A little more, anyway. Enough for Dean Woods to give a Spiritus mage the full-time teaching position Wilder had wanted.

It wasn't that Wilder disliked Theo Ward. He'd been a damn sight better as an office mate than chirpy Helen—that was for sure. They had mostly sat in silence, grading papers together. He hadn't realized how nice it was until Ward had moved into a huge private office and been replaced by the bird woman who wouldn't let him grade in peace.

Might as well go home and do his grading there. At least it was quiet at his place, since David had moved out. That was the benefit of one's long-term boyfriend leaving, saying they had "grown apart." Grown apart, meaning Wilder hadn't gotten the promotion they had expected, and David wasn't willing to date a failure.

Wilder didn't blame him too much. He *was* a failure. He was almost thirty years old, teaching classes part time, and sharing an office with a woman he was sure had been a sparrow in another life.

"Would you listen to this—"

He stood and dropped his pen onto his desk, and she startled, turning to stare at him. "I just remembered I have to feed my cat," he told her. "She gets annoyed if I'm late."

He shoved the papers into a loose pile and stuffed them into his satchel. It wasn't as though the students put much effort into them; he didn't see why he should either. Okay, fine, maybe one or two of them had actually put thought into their work.

What?

He would give them the grades they deserved.

Chirpy Helen was staring at him like he'd grown another head. "I didn't know you had a cat."

He blinked at her. "Oh?" He didn't know what difference that made to her. It was the kind of thing Ward hadn't bothered him about. The reason that, though he'd never admit it, he missed the tweedy stick-in-the-mud.

"What's her name?"

Was this some kind of test? Did she doubt that he had a cat? "Melisandre."

She tittered like a schoolchild. "That's an odd name for a cat."

First she didn't believe he had a cat, and now she was making fun of her name. Incredible. He took a deep breath, closed his eyes, and counted to three. His therapist said it was always a good idea to do that before saying what he was thinking, on the presumption it gave him time to consider whether he should say it at all.

His therapist was right. Nothing good would come of telling Helen that Melisandre had a better name than she did, so she should learn to shut up before insulting the beloved pets of her peers. He'd chosen that name, dammit, and he liked it.

He snapped the latch on his satchel closed and turned to the door.

Halfway there, he realized he'd left his jacket, but he didn't go back. It was late April—plenty warm—and he'd be fine.

Hell, the cherry trees in DC were finally blossoming, almost a month late though it was. It had been a strange kind of spring: cold and wet, nothing growing anywhere until, suddenly, it was, almost overnight.

That had been the day David left: the day things had started to grow. And it didn't even feel ironic, in the proper or improper usage of the term.

He felt a thousand times better out in the hall, away from Helen and her pacing and her constant chatter. He'd tried to ask her to stop once, when she'd first moved into the office. She'd given him a wounded look, like he'd questioned her cat's name, and he'd never tried again.

He turned the corner into the main hall, only to find two men directly in his way.

Not only that, but one of them looked quite pale, lying on the floor on his back and not . . . breathing. He was one of the seniors, Wilder thought, about to graduate and leave Banneker College of Magic once and for all.

But maybe he wasn't going to leave in the way anyone had expected.

The second man—a short, slight man with golden hair and features that could only be described as cute—was leaning over him, pulling one eyelid up and then the other. He shook his head sadly. "Doesn't make a damn bit of sense."

"Is . . . is he dead?" Wilder demanded, even though his breath was trying to freeze in his chest.

The man looked up at him. "What?" He glanced back down at the student and blinked like it was a surprise to find a corpse there. "Oh, you mean him. Wait, are you talking to me?" His eyes widened even more as he looked back up at Wilder, as if the body had been shock enough, but someone speaking to him was beyond comprehension.

Wilder glanced all around and back at the man, holding out his hands to indicate the empty hallway. "Who else would I be talking to?"

The guy gave a lazy shrug and grinned, far too casually to be keeping company with a dead body. "Dunno, you professorial types are always talking to yourselves, aren't you? I think all those books make you funny in the head."

"Maybe if you read a book of two, you would realize that 'dunno' isn't a word," Wilder pointed out. He didn't have a problem with the slang, really, but he was surprised and bothered and feeling wrong-footed, and when he felt uncomfortable, he tended to ignore his therapist's advice.

The man hopped up to his feet, grinning at Wilder like a man who belonged in a madhouse. "S'pose so, huh? Dunno what I'd do with all them fancy words, though. My head might explode if I filled it too full."

Wilder opened his mouth and closed it once, and then twice. "Matthew," he said, unintelligently.

"Huh?"

"His name is Matthew. I just remembered. One of his term papers is in my bag."

The man looked once again down at the body between them, then gave Matthew a little nudge with his toe. Matthew didn't rouse. "I guess you don't gotta worry about grading that one."

Even for Wilder, that was a little flippant. He looked at the man, expecting to find the same inappropriate grin in place, even as he joked about the death of a student. He was frowning, though, looking at the body like a puzzle, and one he wasn't enjoying.

"Disappointed?" Wilder asked.

He looked up at Wilder and shook his head. "No. Just can't figure it out. He's the second one like this. Can't see what killed him—he's just gone." He looked around the hallway. He seemed to think he'd find the young man standing somewhere else and no longer lying on the floor. Then he shook his head. "Gone."

He was right. There was no sign of what had killed Matthew. He was just pale and cold, eyes staring sightlessly at the ceiling.

"Dad's gonna be pissed," the guy muttered. "Nothing to be done now, though. I gotta get back to work. Later, Prof!"

"Hey! You can't just leave. We need to call—" Wilder's head snapped up to stare at the man, but he found himself alone in the hallway with his student's corpse.

ABOUT SAM BURNS

Sam is an author of LGBTQIA+ fiction, mostly light-hearted romances. Preferably ones that include werewolves, dragons, magic, or all of the above. Most of her books include a little violence, a fair amount of swearing, and maybe a sex scene or two.

    She is a full-time writer who lives in the Midwest with her husband and cat.

For more information:
www.burnswrites.com
Sam@burnswrites.com

ALSO BY SAM BURNS

THE ROWAN HARBOR CYCLE

Blackbird in the Reeds

Wolf and the Holly

Fox and Birch

Hawk in the Rowan

Stag and the Ash

Adder and Willow

Eagle in the Hawthorn

Salmon and the Hazel

Wren and Oak *(Coming Soon)*

WILDE LOVE

Straight from the Heart

Sins of the Father

Strike Up the Band

Saint and the Sinner

A Very Wilde Christmas

ABOUT W.M. FAWKES

W.M. Fawkes is an author of LGBTQ+ urban fantasy and paranormal romance. She lives with her partner in a house owned by three halloween-hued felines that dabble regularly in shadow walking.

For more information:
www.fawkeswrites.com
waverly@fawkeswrites.com

Made in the USA
Columbia, SC
26 December 2020